Praise for Veronica Henry

'It's a glamorous and absorbing read, a well-written romp with a cast of believable, empathetic characters whom you'll be fascinated by from the start'
Daily Mail

'A perfect summer delight'
Sun

'The book is first-class chick-lit and a great beach read'
Sunday Express

'Compulsive reading'
Woman & Home

'Beautifully written and dreamily descriptive, this delightful read will make you laugh, sob … and pack up the car for a trip to the Cornish coast'
Closer

'Warm and brilliantly written'
Heat

'A fast-paced gossipy read, set in glamorous locations, with sumptuous descriptions and lively dialogue'
Telegraph & Argus

'A great summer read. Veronica Henry's creation of a clever web of characters, each with their own story to tell, makes this a real page-turner'
Cornwall Today

'This sweet book would be a great beach companion'
Star

Veronica Henry worked as a scriptwriter for *The Archers*, *Heartbeat* and *Holby City*, amongst many others, before turning to fiction. She lives with her family on the coast in North Devon. Visit her website at www.veronicahenry.co.uk or follow her on Twitter @veronica_henry

By Veronica Henry

Wild Oats
An Eligible Bachelor
Love on the Rocks
Marriage and Other Games
The Beach Hut
The Birthday Party
The Long Weekend
A Night on the Orient Express
The Beach Hut Next Door
High Tide

THE HONEYCOTE NOVELS
Honeycote
Making Hay
Just a Family Affair

High Tide

Veronica Henry

An Orion paperback

First published in Great Britain in 2015
by Orion Books
This paperback edition published in 2015
by Orion Books,
an imprint of The Orion Publishing Group Ltd,
Carmelite House, 50 Victoria Embankment,
London EC4Y 0DZ

An Hachette UK Company

1 3 5 7 9 10 8 6 4 2

A CIP catalogue record for this book
is available from the British Library.

ISBN 978 1 4091 4685 8

Typeset at The Spartan Press Ltd,
Lymington, Hants

Printed and bound in Great Britain by Clays Ltd,
St Ives plc

The Orion Publishing Group's policy is to use papers that
are natural, renewable and recyclable products and
made from wood grown in sustainable forests. The logging
and manufacturing processes are expected to conform to
the environmental regulations of the country of origin.

www.orionbooks.co.uk

High Tide

I

Autumn has come to Pennfleet.

A small town on the mouth of the river from which it takes its name, its harbour is full at high tide, so full it looks as if it might burst. The tide is pushing the water out to the sea, valiantly. Sometimes it seems pointless, as the sea never seems grateful, but the tide carries on, day in, day out, providing the rhythm the town has always lived by.

The river's banks are covered in tangled woods hiding voles and otters, water-rats, kingfishers and herons. Further up, narrow creeks meander away from the main tributary, leading to tiny villages, some with only a cluster of houses, an ancient church and a post box.

The tide might be high, but the autumn sun is low, hovering in the sky over the harbour. It wraps the scene in a rich burnished glow, a syrupy marmalade lustre that heralds the falling of leaves and the shortening of days and the onset of winter. It is more subtle than the harsher summer sun. It is mellow, seductive, comforting. Everything looks more beautiful in its glaze.

And yet – yet – catch it at the wrong time and there is danger.

For the autumn sun is deceptive. You turn a corner

and the full force of its strength hits you. You are dazzled. You lose all sense of where you are. You blink, shield your eyes with your hand, but the light is relentless, burning your retina.

And then you turn another corner and the glare recedes. You can see again and the way forward is clear. It was just a moment of blindness. It is, nevertheless, dangerous, that moment when all is lost.

Season of mists and mellow fruitfulness, yes.

But beware the autumn sun.

2

Funerals in Pennfleet were rather like busses. There wasn't one for ages, then two came along at once.

As the sun began to glide down into the harbour that Thursday evening, the verger opened the door of St Mary's to check everything was in order. The little grey church nestled at the top of the high street, plonked in the middle of a small but immaculate graveyard, its steeple poking out over the top of the higgledy-piggledy slate roofs like an eager pupil with his arm up.

Inside, it was cool and quiet, the still air thick with ecclesiastical mustiness combined with the scent of roses and lilies. The ladies on the flower rota had done themselves proud. The last of the evening light slanted through the stained glass, sending the dust motes and the pollen spinning. The stage was set for the next day's performances.

Joy Jackson and Spencer Knight. Both well-known figures in the town. Both influential in their own way. But poles apart. About as different as you could get.

Unassuming, down-to-earth, get-on-with it Joy. Kind, caring, a pillar of the community. District nurse, stalwart of the parish council, the church hall committee, the choir, the WI . . .

And flashy, look-at-me, show-off Spencer. Who made his presence known whenever he was in town, with his prestige cars and wads of cash. Of course, the town had benefitted from his munificence. He spent a lot, he tipped well, and he had made generous donations to various causes – not least the local lifeboat and the yacht club, where a huge glittering trophy bore his name. Yet it was almost as if he used the town for his own pleasure as and when he wanted, showering gifts upon it as a man with a mistress might in order to keep her happy. And Pennfleet wasn't fooled. Somehow, he didn't quite belong in the town, even though he owned the biggest house. Not in the way that Joy had.

The verger knew the morning's funeral would be packed with locals, all coming to pay their respects to someone who had touched most of their lives at one time or another.

The afternoon's would be packed with out-of-towners dressed up to the nines, jostling for pole position in the front seats.

He slotted the hymn numbers for the first funeral into the wooden holder. *Fight the Good Fight. All Things Bright and Beautiful.* Jolly and uplifting. Just like Joy. She would be sorely missed.

Whether Spencer would was anyone's guess.

The executive saloon Kate had hired at Heathrow could barely squeeze down the winding hill. She found herself breathing in as she navigated her way past an ancient Mini on one side and a plumber's van on the other. She was never going to be able to park – parallel parking was her worst nightmare at the best of times, and the chances of a space long enough on Captain's Hill were slim. She never drove in New York. She took town cars. And if she ever rented a car, to head up to the coast at weekends with friends, it would always be automatic and the parking spaces would be generous.

Here, in Pennfleet, she was going to have to drive up to the car park at the other end of the high street and hope there was a space big enough. First, though, she pulled up outside a terraced cottage. It was painted deep blue and fronted straight onto the road. A small wooden sign read *Belle Vue*. And a fine view it had indeed, as Captain's Hill led straight down to the harbour at the mouth of the River Pennfleet.

Two weeks ago, Kate's mother had slipped at the top of the integral stone staircase that led up to the front door of the cottage. Her arms were full of recycling so she hadn't been able to break her fall. Kate imagined the familiar body tumbling, limbs flailing, bottles flying, the fragile skull cracking against the bottom step . . .

There had been no point in Kate rushing back from New York. The local hospital had notified her, breaking the news with a gentle sensitivity, reassuring her that everything was under control. She'd communicated with Toogood's the undertaker by email: they'd sent her brochures for coffins, advised on the order of service, all with a polite efficiency and lack of pushiness that reminded her what it was to be English. She appreciated their discretion. She didn't need any more stress. It was awful, being so far away, yet at the same time there had been no point in dropping everything to get on a plane, for it wouldn't have brought her mother back.

She was only going to be able to take a few days away

from work, so it had made most sense to get back in time for the funeral and then stay on afterwards to sort out the house and put it on the market. It wasn't like when her father had died, when her mum had needed her straight away. Then, Kate had jumped on the first flight out of JFK, driven by the need to hold Joy tightly in her arms.

They had both known that in some ways her father's death was a release from the dementia that had plagued him, but that didn't make their grief any less, for they were grieving the kind, gentle man he had been, not the empty shell he had become.

This time, though, there was no one to come back to.

She pulled the handbrake on hard. She was going to block the road for a few minutes while she unloaded her luggage, but it didn't matter – people round here were used to it. It was only out-of-towners who got impatient from time to time if the traffic backed up the hill, but they found themselves ignored. Kate ran round to the boot and took out her case, lugged it to the top of the steps and left it in the alcove by the front door. No one would steal it in the ten minutes it was going to take her to park and walk back. This was Pennfleet. Not Harlem.

Before she got back into the car, she breathed in, taking a gulp of the salty, brackish air. You could bring her here blindfolded and she would know where she was. She'd grown up on this sea breeze. She could feel it seep into her veins, bringing her strength. She looked down to the harbour, glimpsed between two buildings at the bottom of the hill, a seemingly endless blue where the water met the sky, sprinkled with boats swaying with the tide. Most of the boats would be coming out of the water for the winter before long.

Five minutes later, she had found a space in the car park down by the yacht club and set off back down the high street. Now she was on foot, she had a chance to take in everything that was new along this familiar route. The buildings were just the same: some local grey stone, some whitewashed, some daubed in bright seaside blues and pinks; some with large sash windows, others with tiny latticed ones, depending on when they had been built.

The Neptune was still there holding court at the end, its sign swinging, the unmistakable smell of sweat and booze and chip oil drifting out onto the street. She remembered endless nights pumping money into the juke-box; the motorbikes of the local bad boys parked up outside; the promise of danger. The pub was the last vestige of the old Pennfleet, a harking back to the time before the town had become a holiday hotspot for the upper middle classes, when it was still very much a working port. Only locals ventured into the Neptune. There was nothing to draw in the tourists, unless they wanted cheap beer and a menu offering a variety of deep-fried frozen foods.

Further along, the new incarnation of Pennfleet began. Art galleries jostled next to silversmiths and ceramicists displaying their wares, usually around a nautical theme: lighthouses, mermaids and lobsters abounded. The standard was high. The rates in Pennfleet now meant only the best could afford to set up shop here, and their prices were considerable accordingly.

A fishmonger and a wine merchant had also appeared, and a boutique hotel called the Townhouse by the Sea. Kate remembered the hotel as sombre and smelling of polish: now it was chic and plush with a parasol-studded deck overlooking the water. A sign outside advertised an extensive cocktail list, sharing plates and Bloody Mary brunches.

There were several new clothes shops selling the kind of clothes people who went to boutique hotels wore: casual but expensive, making you look as if you spent your down-time sailing or surfing, even if you didn't.

Scattered amongst this new crop of aspirational shops and eateries were the familiar mongers of her childhood that still had enough trade to give them staying power. The chandlery, its windows stuffed with rope and life jackets and torches. The electrical shop, displaying portable fans and digital radios and toasters. The old tea-room where she'd once had a Saturday job, serving cream teas and cucumber sandwiches and Victoria sponge on flowery china plates.

She passed the general store, where she'd been sent from the age of five for a block of ice-cream to go with Sunday lunch. She had stopped off in there on her way home from school to buy sweets – Opal Fruits and Curly Wurlys and Galaxys, then when she was older sneaky cigarettes (long given up) and bottles of orange-gold cider. It smelled just the same, of newsprint and stale chocolate, and the smell turned her stomach upside down with nostalgia.

At the top of the high street, before she turned up the hill that led to her family home, was a cluster of antique and second-hand book shops that didn't seem to have changed since she was here last: the window displays of Coronation china and Clarice Cliff and cellophane-wrapped first editions were identical to the ones she remembered. People's unwanted relics, which became the next generation of clutter as tourists convinced themselves that was just what they needed to take home with them.

Then she passed the church where her mother's funeral was to take place at eleven o'clock the next morning. She stopped for a moment to take in its comforting solidity. They hadn't been an overly religious family, but the church was such a vital part of the community it couldn't be avoided. Kate had attended countless weddings and christenings and carol services there over the years. She would know most of the people turning up tomorrow, yet she felt strangely disconnected, as if she'd had a bang on the head and woken up with partial amnesia, looking at things that seemed familiar yet couldn't be put into context.

Her mother had more friends than anyone she'd ever known. It was why Kate had felt confident that the funeral wouldn't really need her input. The community would pull together to make sure Joy Jackson got the send-off she deserved.

It was reassuring, but at the same time daunting, because Kate wasn't sure if she fitted in any more. Probably not. With her glossy New York patina, she was almost an outsider. Pennfleet had learned to tolerate outsiders. It had to: tourism accounted for more than half the jobs in the town these days. And knowing that she might be tolerated more than welcomed made Kate feel awkward.

And underlying that awkwardness, of course, was guilt.

It's your life, her mum and dad had told her repeatedly when she'd first been offered the job in Manhattan. They had insisted she should go without giving them a second thought. But it made it so very much worse, and harder to bear, that they had been so supportive and understanding and undemanding.

And now she felt profound guilt. Guilt that she should have been there, throughout the bleak years around her father's demise, even though Joy had insisted she could cope. Guilt that she should have been there for her mother, although she knew she could not have stopped her fall.

She sighed. The world would be a very different place if no one ever left home to forge their own way in the world. Her parents had never been in any doubt that she had loved them very much. She was sure of that. She had to be.

She walked on. Just after the church, before the turning that led back up the hill, she spotted what had once been the greasy spoon café where the fishermen used to have their bacon sandwiches and cups of dark-brown tea before they set off for the day.

It had been given a complete makeover. The woodwork was now painted in burnt orange and cream. Across the big picture-windows was etched, in a lower-case font, *sam's picnic emporium*. Inside she could see racks of stainless steel shelves holding baskets of mini tartlets, muffins, brownies and savoury croissants. Kate's mouth watered. She hadn't eaten anything since breakfast on the plane. She checked the church clock against the opening times: ten minutes until it closed, at six.

She opened the door. She was hit by the scent of freshly roasted coffee and the sound of Sly and the Family Stone, and it lifted her mood immediately. There was just one person serving. A grey linen apron with his name embroidered on the front told Kate this was Sam; presumably the eponymous Sam.

'Am I too late to be served?' asked Kate.

'Course not,' he said with a welcoming smile. 'As long as I'm here you can have whatever you like.'

He was, she guessed, a good few years older than she was, probably over forty, with the fashionably close-shaven head of the follicularly challenged. His face was open and smiling; his eyes a little too small and his nose a little too big for classic handsomeness, but his teeth were white and even and he wasn't carrying too much weight on his frame.

She would never have recognised the interior. Gone were the peeling lino and Artex. Now the walls were exposed brick; the floor was wide planks of distressed oak; the chairs and tables were bright orange metal. The overall look was industrial chic: rough but cosy.

She surveyed the blackboard.

'I'd love a smoked salmon and cream cheese bagel,' she said quickly, before she could think about the calories. 'And a flat white. And some freshly squeezed OJ.'

'Do you want that to go?'

She realised he was probably hoping she would say yes, so she nodded. 'Thank you.'

He set about preparing her food, half-dancing to the music as he moved about behind the counter.

She pulled out her phone, knowing the signal was sketchy in Pennfleet. New York would have woken up while she drove down the motorway. The working day would be well underway. She'd managed to resist checking her emails when she stopped at the service station, as she was eager to press on. But now, she couldn't resist.

'Do you have Wi-Fi? Is there a code?'

He pointed to a sign on the wall. *Hemingway*.

'Is that your last name?'

He laughed. 'No. I change it to a different author each week. My last name's Perry. Sam Hemingway, though – that would be cool.'

Kate laughed, then typed in the code and watched her emails swarm in while he grabbed a sesame bagel and sliced it neatly in half with a sharp knife.

She bit her lip as she searched through them anxiously, reading each one with a forensic scrutiny. She'd promised herself she wouldn't deal with anything until after the funeral, but it was impossible not to when you were a perfectionist. She trusted her team, of course she did, but she found it impossible to let go completely. She assessed each one, forwarding some, asking to be kept in the loop on others, until she was satisfied that nothing needed her immediate attention.

She put her phone back in her bag and smiled at Sam, who was juggling oranges to 'Papa Was a Rolling Stone' before lobbing them into the juicer and flicking the switch that would pulp them into oblivion.

'So – are you here on holiday?' He layered some plump coral salmon on top of the cream cheese.

Kate shook her head. 'No. I'm actually from Pennfleet.'

He looked at her with a slight frown.

'Oh. I haven't seen you around.'

'I don't live here now. I'm . . .'

She swallowed, suddenly unable to tell him the reason she was here. She realised this was the first proper conversation she'd had since leaving JFK, apart from murmured niceties to cabin crew or passport control.

To her horror, she made an unladylike choking sound as she tried to get the words out.

'God, are you all right?' Sam put down the cardboard cup he was about to fill with coffee and came round to her side of the counter.

Kate put her hands to her face, mortified.

'Sorry... It's just... I've come back for my mother's funeral. It's tomorrow. In St Mary's.'

She pointed vaguely back down the road to the church.

She'd had no idea she was going to react like this. Why now? She hadn't cried yet at all. And she wasn't going to now.

Sam could see she was upset, but he didn't seem unduly perturbed. He put an arm round her and led her to a table.

'Come on. Sit down and I'll bring you your coffee.'

She sat down, half laughing at herself. 'I feel such an idiot.'

'You're not an idiot.' He patted her shoulder. 'Go on, have a good howl. I don't mind.'

He was so solid, so kindly, so English. One of those people you immediately felt comfortable with, as if you had known them for ever.

'I'm fine. Honestly. It just suddenly hit me,' she told Sam. 'Jet lag, I suppose. And lack of food.'

'You don't need an excuse,' he said.

Moments later he put the bagel, bulging with salmon, in front of her, together with her drinks, and pulled up a chair opposite. He sat there with her while she ate and drank. As she licked the last of the cream cheese from her fingers, he stood up, lifted a chocolate brownie from underneath a glass dome, and put it on a plate.

'On the house,' he said.

She stared at it as if he'd handed her a pipe of crystal meth.

'It's a brownie,' he said helpfully. 'Not a gateway drug.'

'I never eat stuff like this usually.'

'Well, you should. There's nothing much that can't be sorted by a triple-chocolate brownie.'

Kate had a strict healthy eating/fitness regime. After all, you didn't fit into size four jeans by eating brownies. But it looked darkly delicious and comforting. And she felt that to reject it would be the worst kind of uptight and, above all, rude.

So she picked it up and bit into it. Sweet but salty, crumbly but moist, she could feel it giving her strength. She crammed the last bite in and washed it down with the remaining drops of coffee. While she ate, Sam moved around the café, wiping down tables and putting the chairs up on them.

'I'm not hassling you,' he told her. 'But I need to get home in time for supper...' He flicked the coffee machine off. 'It's the only chance I get to see my kids before they plug themselves in.' He mimed thumbs moving over a games console.

'Ah. The twenty-first-century epidemic has reached even Pennfleet.'

'There is no escape.'

Kate dug in her handbag for her purse, pulling out a twenty-pound note. She laid it on top of the counter.

'My name's Kate, by the way,' she told him. 'You'll probably be seeing a lot of me over the next few days. Cooking's not my strong point.'

'I'm Sam,' he confirmed as he handed over her change.

'And I do the best breakfast in Pennfleet. Home-cured bacon, free-range eggs, forest mushrooms and vine-ripened, slow-roasted tomatoes.'

Kate groaned with anticipatory pleasure. 'Sounds amazing.'

'Or we can rustle you up a super-food salad for lunch. Quinoa... whatever.' He made a face.

'To be honest,' said Kate, laughing, 'I wouldn't care if I never ate quinoa again.'

'Come and have one of my toasties, then. Equal measure of fat and carbohydrate.'

'Deal.'

He smiled at her. 'Good luck with everything.'

She gave a sigh, and nodded. 'Thanks. I guess it's going to be tough, but I'll get through it.'

She turned to go.

'Wait a minute.' He grabbed an empty cake tin and went over to the window display, filling it with a selection of things Kate would never usually eat.

He handed her the tin.

'Have these. I won't be able to sell them here as they're past their best now, but they might sustain you over the next few days, or if anyone calls in. They're not off or anything.'

She took the box. 'That's so kind. Thank you. Are you sure?'

He grinned. 'My kids are sick of them. It's you or the bin.'

'Thank you,' Kate repeated, slightly stunned by his generosity. It gave her a warm glow, which went a little towards offsetting the cold lump of dread in her gullet.

The one that had been sitting there since she'd had the call.

She left the café and began to make her way up the hill. No matter how fit you were, no matter how many times you climbed it, the steep gradient made your calves scream. Eventually she came to a halt outside the cottage and stopped to catch her breath – her chest was tight, despite the fact that she worked out four times a week.

She looked back down the hill. Below her she could see the harbour, shining silver in the last droplets of sun, the boats rocking as gently as a cradle at bedtime. As the soft evening breeze wrapped itself around her, it seemed to whisper: why did you ever leave?

3

Sam watched his last customer go up the hill as he turned off the sound system and picked up his jacket.

She'd seemed so alien, with her sleek exterior: designer jeans, suede jacket, not a hair out of place even after a transatlantic flight and a long drive. People in Pennfleet, by and large, didn't much bother with ironing or blow-dries or make-up, except some of the wealthier weekenders with their gin-palaces.

Yet despite Kate's polish she had been vulnerable. He was glad he'd been able to fortify her, if only with a brownie. As a vicar's son, Sam had been used to death – or at least its impact – from a young age. He had witnessed his father provide solace to so many parishioners over the years. And it had made him, if not comfortable with, then not daunted by, people's grief. He found it best not to say much, just to be, to listen. There was, after all, not much you *could* say. It was always time that healed in the end.

And he knew that better than anyone. Though actually, you never healed. You just got used to it. Somehow, at some point, the grief went from unbearable to bearable. From sharp to dull. But you never went back to being the old you, the you before it happened.

He took off his apron and tucked it into the laundry

bag along with the other aprons and tea towels he needed to take home and wash. Running a seaside café was never-ending toil, especially as it had been open seven days a week during the high season. And Sam wasn't confident enough of his profit margin yet to take on any more staff than the three he had helping him, or allow himself the luxury of sending his washing to the laundry. He had survived his first summer, but he had a long way to go before he was in the black. He had the winter to get through, and no way of gauging how busy he would be, or whether it was worth him opening at all: many places shut down in the quiet season. It was all to play for.

Now, it was time to go home. He prided himself on being home by half six for the children, no matter what. Even then, he still had to wash the aprons and tea towels, do the orders, fill in his spreadsheets, do the rest of the week's staff rota . . .

He flipped the sign on the door to Closed and slipped out into the street.

As he walked back the short distance from work to home, he thanked his lucky stars he'd had the courage to make the move to Pennfleet. How many people had a daily commute that involved wandering along the riverbank, breathing in the freshest air imaginable? How many people could glimpse their own boat, albeit an ancient and scruffy boat, bobbing in the water on their way home? And how many people had a view across an estuary and out to an infinite sea: a view that made you glad to be alive, despite everything, when you woke in the morning?

If he hadn't had the courage, he'd be stuck in the car in some snarl-up somewhere, inching along the outskirts of south-east London. Or he may have been on his way *to* work, rather than from, because being an A&E consultant meant working shifts, so he could have been doing that commute any time of the day or night.

It was the shifts that had crucified him in the end. Being a widower with two teenage children didn't sit easily with shift work. He'd always loved his job, and when Louise was alive it had worked perfectly, but . . . well, everything had changed, hadn't it, the day she died?

It was every A&E consultant's worst nightmare. A cinematic cliché, to have your loved one brought in and rushed to theatre. It was exactly like being in an episode of *Casualty* or *ER*. It could have been scripted down to the last letter. The recognition of the stripy scarf as the RTA was brought in, the realisation that it was Louise, the colleague pulling him away as he tried to rush to her side. Being shut in a room while Louise underwent surgery for a burst spleen, a crushed rib-cage, a punctured lung – courtesy of some motherfucker texting on the school run. Those familiar words 'massive internal injuries'. Followed by 'I'm so sorry'. A hand on his shoulder. Sympathy and anguish from his own staff, who were paralysed with the shock, even though they dealt with cases like this every hour of the day. But when it was close, when it happened to one of your own . . .

Her death turned everything upside down. People said 'life goes on', but life as he knew it didn't. Nothing fitted anymore. Nothing in his life had remained unchanged. Everything was affected. Every tiny little thing.

How did you throw away someone's toothbrush when it sat in the mug, expectant and upright? What did you do with the food in the fridge they had bought? Did you carry on eating the spreadable butter until it ran out? Even the radio in the kitchen had been a case in point. They'd had a never-ending battle between Radio 2 (her) and Radio 6 (him). Sometimes they agreed on Radio 4, but otherwise, each of them would retune the DAB radio to their preferred station. Only once Louise had gone, Sam hadn't the heart to move the dial, so now he was stuck forever more with Chris Evans in the morning.

Widower. It was such a hunched-up, grey sort of word. Nothing like widow, which had a hint of glamour, conjuring up images of swirling black capes and spider webs. A widow was a challenge, an intrigue. A widower was someone who was cast aside and forgotten. Someone to be avoided in case the state was catching.

Sam hated being a widower. Not just because it meant his wife, the woman he had loved, was dead. But because no one quite knew what to do with him, socially. Including himself.

Everyone had been amazing. Colleagues, friends, school staff: there was a seamless rota of people who checked up on him, helped him out, offered to have the kids, brought round casseroles, invited him for Sunday lunch.

He didn't want to be ungrateful, but he couldn't bear the concern and the sympathy. He wanted to be treated like a normal person again. Every time he bumped into someone he could see the concern in their eyes. 'Is he managing?' 'Poor Sam.' 'What else can we do to help?' And he could tell they couldn't work out when to *stop* asking how he was, or offering assistance. When did you stop being a widower? Never?

Anyway, he was fine. He was heartbroken, but he was functioning. He had to carry on. For Daisy and Jim. And actually, for himself. What had happened was cataclysmic, but Sam was not a giver-upper. Life without Louise was empty and difficult and frustrating and made him angry and sad and bewildered, but even the darkest days had glimmers. Moments when he forgot his grief, if only for a short while. Hopefully those moments would start joining up. He would never be the person he had once been, but he could be someone new. Strange though it would be without his wife, his lover, his soulmate.

He and Louise had always been a team, from the day they had met in the refectory at university during Freshers' Week, and started up a conversation over the rather revolting chicken biryani they had both chosen for lunch. Louise looked severe, her dark hair cut in a too-short bob, her clothes dull, and when he sat next to her he'd done it out of politeness rather than any hope that she might be intriguing. But he soon found out she had a dry bluntness that was refreshing.

'You're all right, you are,' she told him when he made her laugh by deconstructing the food they were eating as if it was a post-mortem. 'Not like some of the blokes on this course. You're posh,' she clarified. 'But you're not a knob.'

'Oh,' said Sam. 'I'm glad to hear it. Though actually, I'm not posh. My dad's a vicar and my mum's a swimming teacher.'

'Do you live in a vicarage?'

'It's *called* the vicarage, but it's probably not what you imagine: some rambling rectory with church fetes on the lawn. It's a modern box on the edge of the town.'

'Oh.' He could see her visualising what he'd described.

'Nevertheless, one up from a council estate on the out-skirts of Leicester.'

Was that her accent? He hadn't been able to place it.

'Nothing wrong with being brought up on a council estate.'

'*Some of my best friends live on council estates.*' Louise did an uncanny impersonation of a middle-class person pretending to be down with a working-class person.

Sam raised his eyebrows. 'Actually, our house was right on the edge of a council estate. So I spent most of my time hanging out there.'

'Trying to get everyone to go to church?'

'No.' Sam frowned. 'Just because my dad's a vicar doesn't make me a Jesus freak. On the contrary. I'm a hopeful agnostic.'

'Does he mind?'

'He's only too delighted to have someone to argue with.'

She put her fork down, unable to face any more of the luminous yellow gloop. 'I bet you went to a private school, though. Like the rest of them here.'

'Nope,' said Sam. 'Do you know how much vicars earn? Obviously not.'

She chewed the inside of her cheek. 'Sorry. I know I'm chippy.'

'Yeah. You need to get over that. Life's not fair, and so you have to make the most of it.'

She looked at him in surprise. He smiled. 'Would you like to go for a decent Indian one night?' he asked her. 'There're some great places round here that won't break the bank.'

They had a wonderful night. Her eyes had sparkled at

him over the top of her wine glass. And later he had been surprised to discover that she was not nearly as demure as she looked.

So here he was, trying to make sense of life and keep his little family afloat without the spirit of the woman who had been the centre of their world, the source of light and warmth and laughter. The thing about Louise was she had always been so *certain*. She wasn't ambivalent about anything. Which was sometimes infuriating, but at least you knew where you were with Louise. And now, Sam sometimes wasn't at all sure where he was.

And despite trying his best, every day all he could see was her absence. In his bed when he woke, in the kitchen as he made toast and tea and tried to remember vitamins and permission slips and cookery ingredients and rugby boots – all the things Louise had done while dancing to Blondie on the radio. Her absence was everywhere.

It was the arrival of the letter through the door one Saturday morning that provided the catalyst. It floated down onto the coir mat and lay there, self-important, a cream vellum envelope with thick italic writing on the front, saying 'To The Occupier'.

Sam picked it up and tried to second-guess its contents. Perhaps an invitation to a Safari Supper from an unknown neighbour? That sort of thing was becoming more commonplace. He slid a finger under the flap, eased it open and pulled out a letter typed on headed notepaper.

We are looking to relocate to this area. We have pinpointed your house as being of particular interest. We are cash buyers in a position to proceed, ideally completing in the next few months. Please get in

touch if you would consider selling. We are happy to
pay above the current market value. We attach a copy
of a solicitor's letter confirming available funds.

Sam was impressed. He admired the forthright tone of the letter, the fact that it was entirely unapologetic. He wasn't interested, though. The children didn't need another upheaval. The house was the one constant in their life.

He went to put the letter in the recycling. Halfway to the bin, he stopped.

Maybe this was an opportunity to change things? Maybe they needed to make their life different? Maybe trying to carry on as before but without Louise was never going to feel right? They were surviving, but they weren't thriving, any of them. It was early days, of course, but when he thought about it, he didn't have much time left with the children. In just over two years' time, Daisy would be off to uni; in four, Jim. He hated the thought that they would stumble through that time trying to grab happiness, clutching at anything that reminded them of the past, stumbling about in the remnants of their former life, trying to make sense of it all.

And in the meantime he was wearying of his work. Hospital politics were grinding him down. He knew what he was doing was for the greater good, but actually – what about the good of Sam? Was it selfish to want to do something different? He hadn't signed a contract that said he had to save lives for the rest of *his* life. Maybe this was a golden opportunity? A golden ticket out. Someone was offering to buy their house, at over the market value. There would be no agent's fees; no hassle. He and Louise had stretched themselves to buy it when they were young, taking out the biggest joint mortgage they could afford, and the area had improved dramatically in the meantime. The house was worth a small fortune, and it was too big for just the three of them, really. This offer was carte blanche to change the future. For all of them.

He mulled the prospect over. Where would they move, given the chance? Pennfleet, he thought, was the place they were happiest. They went there every summer for a fortnight, renting a cottage on the harbour front. There, time seemed to go more slowly and life was less complicated. The children had more freedom. He suspected it was naive to think that holiday feeling could extend to the rest of the year, but in fact – why not? They wouldn't spend their lives rushing, stuck in traffic jams, breathing in smog, fighting for a parking space.

He decided to research the possibilities. It started off as an experiment, but the further he looked into it, the more excited he became. He began by looking at houses for sale on the internet. There were several that would be suitable. One in particular that would be a dream come true, a stone cottage overlooking the river, in need of TLC but just waiting for someone to love it and bring it back to life.

And then he saw the lease on a small café near the harbour and a whole new possibility unfolded. He could see it in his mind's eye with a breathtaking clarity: a deli-cum-café stuffed with upmarket delicacies for holiday-makers to take on their picnics or boat trips or bike rides.

Sam had always been a foodie. He was much more interested in cooking than Louise. He always had a sourdough starter on the go, and baked fresh bread every weekend. He made pizza with the kids, spreading out the toppings so they could create their own, and taught them how to make chocolate-chip cookies and hand-roll sushi and grind spices for curry. It was always Sam who did the cooking for dinner parties: he'd spend days researching recipes and tracking down ingredients, dragging Louise to Borough Market to exclaim at the glorious selection of vegetables, with their rainbow colours and crazy shapes: romanesco broccoli and purple carrots and nobbly Jerusalem artichokes. He would inhale the musty stink of artisan cheeses as if they were a potent drug, and would spend hours buying new spices and herbs. Once he stared longingly for fifteen minutes at a glass jar holding a rare white truffle, and Louise laughed at him – but when she gave him his birthday present a few weeks later, he didn't need to open it to know what she had bought him. He could smell its rich, earthy, musky scent through the paper. She laughed at his reaction: his delight and his reverence as he unwrapped the tiny delicacy which was almost worth its own weight in gold.

Running a café or a restaurant had long been a secret ambition. Well, fantasy: Sam wasn't a fool. He knew it would be hard work, and that profit margins were slim. But he could see it so clearly in his mind's eye, and it gave him a fizzy sensation in his stomach, and he realised that this was the first thing that had made him feel hopeful since Louise had died. He worked out that if he got what these mystery buyers were offering, he would have enough to buy the riverside house and do it up, secure the lease on the café and reduce his mortgage by half.

How could it not make sense? He would have more time to spend with his children, precious time that was slipping away all too quickly. At the moment, they had a complicated rota that involved far too much latchkey for his liking. All too often the kids were fending for themselves. It was far from ideal, given that they were still both vulnerable, even if they were old enough to make beans on toast.

He spent a week talking himself in and out of the idea. One minute it was logic, the next it was madness. Friends' reactions varied wildly, from telling him he was insane to give up a secure job with a pension plan, to urging him to live the dream. He tried to imagine Louise's reaction and was distressed to find he couldn't gauge it, which made him realise how long she had been gone. He couldn't feel her influence any more.

In the end, he decided they needed a family conference.

He assembled a file. He printed out the house and café details, and drew out his plans for each of them. He sent off for the local school prospectus. He did comparative pie charts of the finances. He didn't believe children should be left out of financial affairs. How could they be expected to handle their own if they didn't understand borrowing and risk taking?

And then he sat down round the dining-room table with Daisy and Jim and painted as vivid a picture as he could of how life would be in Pennfleet, being sure to point out the pitfalls as well as the advantages.

'I'll have to work weekends – during the day – but you can both have jobs in the café, waiting or washing up. There won't be a big cinema or an ice rink or glittery shops. The winters are long. You'll be leaving your mates behind – though they can come and stay, obviously.'

'Can I do Art A-level?' asked Daisy. 'Instead of maths?' She was ever the negotiator.

'Can we have a boat?' asked Jim.

'Well,' said Sam. 'Yes to both, I suppose.'

Daisy and Jim looked at each other and grinned.

'Is that a yes?' he asked them, and they replied with a resounding cheer.

Sam felt his stomach flip slightly. He was scared. This was a massive decision. But he was also excited, and it was nice to have a feeling other than dull dread in his stomach.

And now, here they were. He'd bought the house from an elderly couple who were moving into sheltered accommodation, and it hadn't been touched for at least thirty years. And of course, despite a reasonable structural survey, once the builders started ripping things out and knocking walls down, all manner of hideousness revealed itself. Now, however, it was perfect.

It was three storeys high and right on the water, just downstream from the harbour, overlooking a wooded bank on the other side of the river. Sam worked hard with the builders to make it as bright and spacious as possible. They knocked down walls to make a ground-floor open-plan kitchen/living/dining area. Everything was painted dead-flat white; the kitchen units were white gloss; the big modular sofa and blinds were dark blue. Not a strikingly original colour scheme, perhaps, but perfect for a seaside family home. Practical and nautical.

At the far end of the room were bi-fold doors that opened out onto a narrow balcony. And from the balcony was the special bit: a trap door, from which dropped down a ladder. A ladder that plopped straight into the river when the tide was in. Here, they tied up the dinghy they used to row out to their boat. There was no garden, but who needed a garden when the river and the sea were theirs for the taking?

The first thing they all did when they moved in was to hang a canvas blow-up print of Louise. A black and white shot of her in a pixie bobble hat, laughing, looking ten years younger than the thirty-nine she had been when the picture was taken.

'Where do you think Mum would like to go?' Sam asked, holding the canvas in both hands and surveying the blank walls.

'She'd like to look at the sea, I think,' said Daisy.

Jim agreed. They hung her on the wall that looked out across the harbour over the Atlantic. Sam hoped the gesture wasn't mawkish or sentimental. It wasn't a shrine. It was a reminder. He was never going to pretend to anyone Louise hadn't existed. And he certainly didn't spend unnecessary amounts of time looking at the picture. It grounded him every now and again, that was all. Gave him reassurance and strength.

It was getting dark as Sam reached home. And it *was* home, even after just one summer there. The house welcomed him as he pushed open the front door. There were all their coats and wellies and skateboards and bicycles in the hall, their clothes drying on the rack in the utility room, the scent of Daisy's perfume (Daisy by Marc Jacobs, which Sam had given himself extra points for finding last Christmas) and the smell of microwaved popcorn the kids had made to keep them going until he got back and cooked them supper.

As he pushed open the door to the kitchen, he realised

Daisy was already cooking, while Jim sat at the island glued to his iPad.

'Hi, Dad!' Daisy greeted him, standing by the hob prodding at a pan of pasta. 'I'm doing us pesto penne. Jim and me are starving.'

'That's great, sweetheart. Thank you.' Sam gave his daughter a hug, kissed the top of her blonde head and ruffled Jim's hair.

'Hey, Dad,' Jim managed.

'How did you guys get on today?'

They'd been at their new school a month, and so far the signs were good. No teething problems. He was yet to attend a parents' evening, but they were both as conscientious as a father could hope for.

Jim sniggered. 'Daisy got on OK, didn't you, Daze?'

Daisy rolled her eyes and gave her brother one of her looks. He just grinned back at her, wide-eyed. Sam raised an eyebrow. There was something going on. He wasn't going to press, though. He would hear about it in good time. The way her cheeks were tinged with a pale-pink blush told him there was probably romance in the air. He'd been waiting for it with part dread, part curiosity.

Daisy wasn't going to give anything away, though.

'I got started on my art project – I'm doing Vivienne Westwood. Her influence on fashion. It's going to be cool.'

Daisy was fashion-mad, which was ironic given they were so far away from London now. But she didn't seem to mind. She still managed to maintain her own individual style. She customised all her clothes. At least she wasn't a sheep, thought Sam.

'Fantastic. Jim? Physics test?'

'Fine.'

'Fine in your opinion, or mine?'

'Sixty-seven per cent. Which was one of the highest.'

Kids did this, Sam had noticed. Presented their results in comparison with the rest of the class.

'That doesn't mean anything, does it? It could have been the highest out of a lot of not-very-good results.'

Jim just looked at him, and Sam smiled as he flipped open the fridge to get out a bottle of beer. 'OK. You know what you need to do. I'm not going to nag. I trust you.'

He never knew quite how much to breathe down their necks, or how much input to have on their homework. He settled on taking an active interest, but not interfering. He was there if they needed help, but he wasn't going to be a tiger father. Louise had always said it was up to them to motivate themselves. But he was very aware they had both started at a new school, and he wanted to be supportive.

Daisy served up the penne and they sat round the island, eating and chatting. Sam wondered if Daisy would let slip whatever Jim had been alluding to earlier. A boy, obviously. His stomach clenched a little at the thought. It would be a turning point, with its own set of worries. He hoped he was going to be able to handle it. Because, of course, no one would be good enough for his beautiful, elegant, funny, quirky daughter. He looked at her grating parmesan onto her pasta, her head wrapped up in a white and gold scarf like a turban, her eyebrows groomed and darkened into a shape that gave her face a definition it hadn't had before, and he realised she was a young woman, not a girl.

Jim, at the other end of the island, with his tufty hair

and geeky hipster glasses, was very much still a boy, gawky and spindly and able to recite the spiel of every alternative stand-up comedian seemingly after just one viewing. He was funny, which went a long way in this world.

Hold your nerve, Sam told himself. They are going to be fine.

Later, when they had both gone upstairs to their rooms to finish off their homework, Sam flopped down on the sofa and stared at the blank television screen mounted on the wall. This was the time he missed Louise the most. He just wanted someone to lean against while he finished his beer and watched the next box set. He'd done them all over the summer: *Game of Thrones*, *House of Cards*, *Breaking Bad*, *The Killing*... He was four episodes into a gritty French cop show at the moment. He sighed, flicked the telly on with the remote and pressed the buttons until he found the next episode. It would take him to Paris for an hour or so. Then he could go to bed.

Upstairs, Daisy and Jim were watching Stewart Lee re-runs in Jim's room instead of doing their homework. Jim was in his gaming chair and Daisy was sitting on the floor applying a silver crackle glaze to her nail varnish.

Jim looked at her. She'd already plucked her eyebrows – again. He didn't get it, really, the obsessive attention to things that didn't matter, like the shape of your eyebrows and the colour of your nails. But he was used to it with Daisy. Their mum had been a lipstick-if-it's-a-really-special-occasion sort of person, whereas Daisy had a different look for every minute of the day.

And, of course, now there was a bloke in the offing it was only going to get worse.

'You going to tell Dad about Oscar?'

'Yes,' said Daisy. 'When the time's right. So you can shut up.'

'I'm not going to say anything!' Jim protested.

'It's not as if there's anything going on. He asked me out, that's all. And I haven't even said yes yet.'

'He thinks he's God,' said Jim.

'No,' said Daisy. 'Everyone else thinks he's God. He's actually really nice. And quite shy.'

'What does he see in *you*?' asked Jim.

Daisy spread her arms out. She was in a panda onesie, her hair still wrapped up in a turban, her face plastered in a moisturising mask.

'Why do you even ask?'

The two of them rolled about on the floor, laughing. They were both used to Jim teasing her. It was just what they did. Underneath they were unbelievably close.

Daisy screwed the lid back on her nail varnish. She had been really surprised when Oscar had sat next to her on the bus that afternoon and asked what she was doing at the weekend.

'There's a band on at the Neptune, if you want to go. I don't know what they're like. But it could be a laugh.'

Oscar had been the first person Daisy really noticed when she arrived at her new school. He was very tall, and wore a greatcoat with silver buttons and the collar turned up, skinny jeans tucked into big boots with the laces undone, and a paisley scarf with long tassels. With his dark, messy hair and long eyelashes, he stood out a mile.

She supposed he'd asked her out because she was a novelty, a newcomer from London, which was where he was from, too. She hadn't said yes, because she wasn't sure if her dad would let her go to the Neptune. She was plucking up the nerve to ask him, because she wanted his approval. Daisy knew her own mind, but she wasn't a rebel, not really. And she respected her dad.

She could also sense the other girls at school would be a little jealous of her being asked out by Oscar. There was no doubt he was the coolest boy in the school. Daisy felt a bit funny inside when she thought about being alone with him.

She didn't want to talk about it with Jim, though, so she changed the subject to something she'd been thinking about for a while.

'You know what?' she asked. 'I think it's time Dad got a girlfriend.'

Jim gave her a pained expression. 'Are you serious?'

'Course I am.'

'What about ... you know. Mum?'

'In case you haven't noticed, she's not here any more.'

'No, but ...' Jim looked upset as he absorbed the notion.

'Seriously, you know what? Mum wouldn't mind. Dad needs company. He needs someone to hang out with. All he does is work. And watch TV. And look after us.'

'I can't imagine him with someone else.'

'He can't stay single for the rest of his life. And it has been four years.'

'Yeah, I know, but ...' Jim frowned and shrugged. 'It makes me feel weird, thinking about it.'

Daisy touched her nails to her cheek to make sure they were dry. 'Don't you think he must be lonely?'

'He's got us.'

Daisy gave her brother a level look.

'Oh God,' said Jim. 'You've got sex on the brain.'

'I'm not just talking about sex. I'm talking about . . . companionship.'

Jim looked baffled.

'I guess you wouldn't understand.' Daisy blew on her nails to accelerate the drying process.

'What can we do about it, anyway? Isn't it up to him?'

'I don't know,' said Daisy.

Jim looked down at the floor.

'No one would be like Mum.'

Daisy looked at her brother. Sometimes he drove her nuts, but he was still her little brother. And suddenly he seemed really young and not that annoying at all.

'Hey.' She sat down next to him and gave him a hug. 'Of course no one will ever be like Mum. But that doesn't mean Dad has to be on his own for the rest of his life.'

Jim didn't answer for a while. He just stared at the carpet. Daisy felt bad she'd even brought the subject up. Jim was much more protective of their mother's memory than she was. It wasn't that she didn't care. Or that she didn't miss her. She had to be robust about it in order to survive. She was about to squeeze him even tighter when he looked up. He was grinning, and there was a gleam in his eye behind his glasses that Daisy recognised.

'I've got an idea,' he said.

4

Kate had forgotten how minuscule Belle Vue was, even by cramped New York apartment standards.

The front door opened straight into the kitchen, with a row of dilapidated dark-brown units, a larder and a downstairs loo. The back door opened onto a courtyard, an open-tread staircase led upstairs to the two bedrooms, and a doorway hung with an orange curtain opened onto the living room. It seemed incredible to think that she and her parents had muddled along together in the tiny space for so many years.

The air smelled musty and dank and stale. Kate threw open the kitchen window to let in the evening breeze. It used to smell of home in here. Of fresh laundry drying on the overhead rack. Of recently baked cakes. Of the thick bar of Imperial Leather that always lay beside the kitchen sink, the familiar label clinging to the soap until it became so tiny it was stuck onto the new bar. And underlying all of that the rich fug of oil from the Aga.

The Aga her mum used to air her pyjamas on every night. And her uniform every morning. They would lie neatly folded on top of the hotplate, a gentle heat permeating through, so Kate would feel warm before she got into bed or set off for school. Inside the Aga there

36

would always be a pot of homemade soup, swarming with vegetables, or a casserole thick with pearl barley.

But tonight the Aga was stone cold. Someone had been in to turn it off, or it had turned itself off, as was its wont, which meant there would be no hot water. Kate opened the door that hid the mysterious workings, lit one of the long matches from the box on the side and held the flame against the wick.

She heard a *wump* as the flame took hold, breathing life into the house again. Soon the kitchen would be as warm as toast, the water piping hot, and the hotplate would be ready to receive the kettle. Its familiar whistle, increasingly persistent, had been part of the soundtrack of Kate's youth.

She pulled out a chair and sat down at the Formica-topped table, tracing the flowers with her finger. How many meals had she eaten here? How many times had she done her homework, spreading her books and papers all around her? Or sat with her hand curled around a cup of cocoa, munching flapjacks and talking to her mum?

The house might have been small, but it never seemed to matter. Her friends crowded into the kitchen of an evening, huddled round the radio. Her mum would bustle amongst them, chattering; her dad would just smile and nod benignly on his way to watch the news, his single nightly bottle of Newcastle Brown ale in his hand.

Those days were gone for ever. Kate shivered, knowing that she had to face the pain, that nothing would dull it, that it had to be experienced in its full ferocity, because you couldn't run away from grief. She wasn't ready to let it in just yet, though.

She humped her suitcase up the stairs, pausing on the

landing. The door to her mother's room – her parents' room – was shut. She didn't want to look inside. She was too tired and cold, fragile and uncertain. A lump came into her throat and she felt an overwhelming need for her mum. Joy had always been relentlessly reassuring. She had taken the fear out of every situation and boosted Kate at every opportunity. Whether it was exam nerves, or falling out with a friend, or being dumped by a boy, her mother had provided advice and comfort: a stout shoulder.

And now, when she needed her most, she wasn't here. Kate swallowed down the lump as best she could and pushed open the door of her own bedroom. It hadn't changed, yet it seemed to belong to someone she could barely remember. Someone from a lifetime ago. She remembered her dad doing up her room when she started her A-levels. Remembered the excitement of the pink and grey wallpaper she'd chosen. She had thought it the height of sophistication, but now it looked dreary and cheap, with brown patches where the damp had come through and then dried. They'd bought a white melamine wardrobe with gold trim, and a dressing table, and a mirror that lit up. She knew if she slid open the drawer it would still be crammed with make-up. Maybelline and Rimmel and Number 17. And the wardrobe would be bulging with teenage impulse purchases. Clothes that would hang loose on her now, because she was a good two dress sizes smaller than she had been. She'd never been fat, but far too sturdy for A-list New York. Her clients wouldn't take any notice of her if she wasn't the size she was. They wouldn't take the advice of anyone wider than a pencil.

She looked around, at the pink and grey striped curtains that matched the wallpaper. The lumpy single bed with the pink mirrored bedspread. Scarves, candles, paperbacks, CDs, strings of beads, ornate wooden boxes – all the detritus of her youth still there as if she had just popped out for the evening.

She pulled back the cover and checked the bedding. The sheets were cool to the touch. Kate shivered. The heating would take the chill off, and she could make a hot-water bottle.

She put her case on the floor and opened it, taking out her pyjamas and laying them on the bed. Then she opened her flight bag and searched for the Ziploc bag containing her travel bottles and her sleeping pills.

It wasn't there.

Heart hammering, she rummaged through the cashmere cardigans, iPad, flight-socks, pashmina, phone chargers, adapters... It still wasn't there.

The last time she had seen it was in the ladies' at Heathrow, when she'd applied a layer of moisturiser to her skin to rehydrate after the flight. She could picture it in her mind's eye, on the shelf next to the sink. She must have left it there. She felt hot panic. She was never going to sleep, not with everything going on in her mind, and the jet lag, and the time difference.

Calm down, she told herself. She could go to the doctor in the morning and get a prescription. There was absolutely nothing else she could do. Were she in New York she could pop out to the twenty-four-hour pharmacy and pick up something to help her, but she knew without looking there would be nowhere open in Pennfleet peddling pharmaceuticals at this time.

She went back down to the kitchen. By now the house

was warm, and started to sound a bit more like its old self, the pipes ticking and clunking.

The phone rang, making her jump. She picked up the receiver cautiously.

'Kate! Thank God. I keep trying your phone but it goes straight to voicemail.'

It was Carlos. Her boss. 'I told you there was no signal here.'

'How totally quaint! But you got there, right?'

'Obviously.'

Carlos never really got sarcasm. Mostly because he didn't really listen to what anyone else said, so it didn't register.

Kate regretted giving him her mother's number. She wasn't in the right frame of mind. His voice was too intrusive in the confines of her childhood home. But maybe he was just checking she was all right.

Wishful thinking.

'Honey, we have a big problem. Gloria Westerbrook got done for possession of cocaine last night.'

Kate was immediately on high alert.

'You're kidding?'

'I wish. She's out on bail. But the papers are going to be all over it.'

Everything else receded in the light of Carlos's announcement.

'Shit,' she said. 'That's a disaster.'

'I know, right?'

Gloria was guest of honour at the launch of a new charity for homeless kids that most of the trophy wives in Manhattan were falling over themselves to attend. Kate was organising the launch. Gloria was a hot young actress from New Orleans who had been homeless for two years in the wake of Hurricane Katrina, and had seemed the ideal face to front the campaign. But no one likes a known Class A drug user to represent their charity. Even though Kate had seen most of the committee members themselves snorting up lines of coke in the rest rooms. How else did they keep so thin?

She thought through the problem. There wasn't time to waste. Her mind raced through the implications. She came to a rapid conclusion.

'OK. We keep her on. We'll get more publicity that way, and kudos for supporting her. We'll exploit the story by highlighting the drug issues related to homelessness. If we ditch her, it makes us look bad; we'd have to find someone else and no one wants to play second fiddle to a coke head. '

'This is why I love you, Kate. This is why I need you.' Carlos paused. 'Can you do me a press release?'

Kate sighed. 'Carlos . . .'

'I know, honey, but I don't trust anyone else to do it. It will take you fifteen minutes max.'

This was the problem with New Yorkers. Career took precedence over everything. Even death.

'OK. But I don't have any internet.'

'No internet?'

She might as well have said no oxygen. She supposed she could take her laptop down into the town and find Wi-Fi somewhere, but she was too tired.

'I'll have to dictate it.'

'Huh?'

'It's this thing they used to do, back in the day. You've seen *Mad Men*, right? I read what I've written over the

41

phone, and you take it down. Or get someone else to take it down.'

She could only imagine Carlos's baffled expression.

'I'll get one of the girls to call you. And you are an angel. I'll make it up to you. Get this done and then you can get a good night's sleep.'

'I doubt it. I left my sleeping pills in the bathroom at Heathrow.'

'Oh my God!' It was as if she had admitted to forgetting some life-saving medication. 'Kate. That's insane.'

No, thought Kate. What was insane was the fact that both her and Carlos's reaction to losing her pills was so extreme. That it seemed inconceivable for her to function without them. When had she turned into someone who was reliant on prescription drugs to get her through life?

'It's fine. I have jet lag. I'm exhausted. And the sea air will knock me out.'

'Sweetie, you need to get to the doctor in the morning and get a repeat.'

'Sure. Look, let me get on with this press release. I'll speak to you anon.'

She put the phone down and went to plug in her laptop. She was surprised to find that despite everything, she could focus. Within ten minutes she had drafted a provisional statement from the charity, expressing their support for Gloria and twisting the situation to suit their message. As she saved the document, she supposed this was what Carlos paid such an astronomical wage for: her clarity and vision together with her organisational skills. Plus the fact that everyone in New York thought she knew Kate Middleton, because they were about the same age.

Before she went to bed, she made a cup of hot chocolate

and poured in a slug of cherry brandy from a dusty bottle on the side. Then she settled down in her childhood bed. It was hard and lumpy. She had never noticed when she was young. The duvet was thin and measly. The linen smelled slightly musty. The pillow might as well not have been there, it was so flat. She didn't want to use her mother's pillow, so she went down to the living room and lifted some cushions off the sofa. She put the pillow on top of them, but it was still unsatisfactory – too high and not soft enough.

In the end, she drifted off at about three, to wake with a start at six thirty, when the seagulls began a tap dance on the roof over her head – a sound that had once been so familiar, but took her a while to identify.

This was the first time ever she had woken in her own bedroom without her mother peeping round the door with a cup of steaming, deep-brown tea. She would set it down on Kate's bedside table and pull the curtains, letting in the morning light. Joy firmly believed lying in bed to be a waste of time, and it was one of the habits that Kate had kept, even now. She had never seen the point of a lie-in, much to the mystification of more than one boyfriend.

She stared at the door, willing her mother to open it, hoping that the last two weeks had been a terrible dream, that in fact she was just on a visit and any minute Joy would appear with her brew.

She could tell, though, that apart from her the house was empty. There were no tell-tale sounds of running water or flushing loos or Radio 2 weaving its way up the stairs or the clatter of cups and plates. She put her hands to her face. How was she going to manage? How was she going to get through today?

She was truly on her own, for the first time in her life. It seemed impossible that her mother wasn't there for a giggle or a gossip or a timely piece of advice. Joy was the least judgemental and most practical person Kate had ever known. It was why their relationship had worked so well – because Joy had never judged her for leaving, for beginning a new life so far away.

'I know where you are if I need you,' she had told Kate, 'and you know where I am. The apron strings can stretch that far.'

And they had. Even though her mother had never managed to embrace the wonders of Skype or Facetime, and telephoned Kate from her landline at vast and unnecessary expense, they spoke at least three times a week. She came out to visit twice a year, and although Joy looked like a fish out of water in New York, she embraced everything it had to offer – the galleries and restaurants and shops.

Kate managed to smile at the memory of her mum in her comfy shoes and elasticated trousers and anorak striding round Bergdorf's, talking away to the assistants at the jewellery counter, who found her utterly charming even though it was clear she wasn't a potential customer. The thing about Joy was she was comfortable in her own skin; she needed no embellishment. She genuinely didn't give a fig what she looked like or wore, and she was all the more beautiful for it.

Kate sometimes wished she had an ounce of her mother's confidence, for confidence it was. Even in the confines of the most glamorous and expensive sushi restaurant in town, Joy sported a navy-blue round-neck jumper, a denim A-line and flat lace-ups, with no adornment or make-up, yet she beguiled the waiters, who blossomed under her attention: within moments of arrival she had them eating out of her hand – or rather, the other way round, as they sneaked the tastiest morsels from the kitchen for her to try.

Kate was so proud of her funny little mother with her Cornish burr and her twinkling eyes and her ability to talk to anybody on the planet.

She wasn't here any more. She would never hear her voice again.

She opened the window and leaned out. The air was sharp and cold and delicious on her face. She looked down the street. From up here, she could see nearly all the town that had once been her world, and the road ribboning down to the harbour, dark blue with morning chill. She took in a deep breath as if to gather strength from the slight mist that was still clinging to the rooftops and chimneypots.

Run, shower, breakfast.

Call the doctor.

She should call the undertakers, too, to tell them she had arrived and make sure everything was in hand.

Then change.

Then…

She wasn't going to think that far ahead. She needed to focus on the now, if she was going to get through it. She pulled on her sweat pants and a T-shirt and laced up her running shoes. She was good to go.

5

At seven o'clock on the morning of her husband's funeral, Vanessa Knight sat on the cobbled terrace of her house and drank a pot of strong coffee. She loved being up before anyone else. Well, most people; you had to be up very early indeed to beat the Pennfleet fishermen.

She watched their fishing boats setting off for the day, the little white lines they left in their wake cutting through the blue.

She watched the gulls circling, beady eyes vigilant, never missing an opportunity to scavenge.

She watched the early-morning clouds drift away and make way for the sun.

But she didn't see any of them.

She pinched her arm, to make certain she was actually still there. She wasn't at all sure what it was she was supposed to be feeling, but she was fairly confident it shouldn't just be nothing.

Not grief. Not shock. Not distress, or anger, or bewilderment. Or fear.

She didn't even feel numb.

She felt normal. As if today was just another day, not the day she was burying her husband of seventeen years.

She shivered slightly in the morning freshness. It was

as if the weather knew the calendar had changed, for the moment September ended the sun seemed to have shed its warmth on rising, taking longer to heat up. The air smelled different: sharper and sweeter and smoky, and breathing it in brought a sense of change; of new horizons. Gone was the fevered heat of summer. The calmness of autumn was here.

Vanessa relished the quiet, because tonight the house would be bursting at the seams – twelve guests had been the last count reported to her by Mary Mac, who was in charge of the organisation. No one had bothered talking to Vanessa about arrangements, even though she was presumably the head of the house now. They all went through Mary, Spencer's housekeeper and right-hand woman since long before Vanessa had appeared on the scene. Not that Vanessa minded. She was used to it, and Mary Mac was her greatest ally. Vanessa thought she would have long gone mad if it wasn't for Mary's common sense and kindness. And she was the one who would get her through the next twenty-four hours. Since the day Vanessa had been swept down to Pennfleet House by Spencer all those years ago, Mary Mac had done everything to make her feel welcome and looked after from that day onwards.

Consequently, Vanessa had turned to Mary as soon as she heard about Spencer's massive stroke. They had hugged each other, chastened with shock, unable to believe that the forceful personality who had dominated their lives for so long was gone. The house already felt like a shell, as if it had lost its purpose, like a ship without a captain.

'Come on,' Mary said eventually. 'We can't fall apart. We've got things to do.'

It was Mary's emotional support Vanessa couldn't manage without. Never mind that she ran the house like clockwork – Vanessa didn't much care about gleaming surfaces and freshly ironed sheets and full freezers. She could do all that for herself – not as well, of course, but then Vanessa didn't have Spencer's exacting standards. Not that he had ever found that out, because she'd never had to lift a finger.

Lucky, some would say.

Vanessa refilled her coffee cup and stirred in some of the cream she had found in the fridge. It was probably for the pavlova which was going to follow the chicken casserole, also waiting in the fridge, ready to feed the hordes tonight. Spencer's ex-wife Karina and his children Daniella and Aiden, his brother, his two best friends and their wives. His business partner and his PA. His coterie. His entourage. None of whom ever paid Vanessa much attention. They viewed her as a mild irritation, someone who didn't quite fit into their picture of how things should be.

She imagined them all getting ready to set off on the journey down to Cornwall, donning crisp white shirts and sombre suits; demure dresses in black silk or linen. Most of the women would wear hats. It would be a fashion fest; a competition as to who could look the most chicly grief-stricken.

Vanessa knew she should make an effort. Three days earlier, she'd driven to a boutique in the next town to find a suitable outfit. She laughed at the memory of the assistant who had asked her, 'Is it for something special?'

'It's for my husband's funeral,' she'd said, and the girl had looked horrified, not at all sure what to say: she'd backed away behind the till and busied herself with some paperwork. Vanessa hadn't found anything in the end, because it was all summer stock: wafty whites and turquoises which didn't seem suitable. Spencer wasn't the sort of man who would want people to wear bright colours to his funeral. He would expect black.

Then she realised she didn't have to do what Spencer expected any more.

Yet she didn't want to draw attention to herself. She didn't want any of his family looking at her askance. Or Karina. She'd had enough of that over the years. Sometimes she felt like a curiosity he'd brought back from a zoo: something to be wondered over and petted then put back into its cage. The glorified shop girl, posh but poor, who'd caught his eye when she helped him choose a wedding present. He'd rushed into the shop en route to the church, in a blind panic because he was late. She'd picked out a stunning serving plate, wrapped it and bedecked it with ribbons and bows and found him a card. And a pen. And dictated a thoughtful message for him to write to the happy couple. He'd come back later, after the wedding, more than a few glasses of champagne in, and asked her out for dinner.

'I'm not leaving until you say yes,' he'd said, standing in the middle of the fine china she was in charge of. She'd been dazzled by his insistence. And he took her to Quaglino's, where she'd always longed to go . . .

And that night, as now, she had worried about what to wear. She put down her coffee cup and wasn't sure why she was so anxious. She had millions of black dresses. Dresses Spencer had chosen and sent to her by courier, arriving on padded hangers in linen clothes carriers from a designer website, for the nights when she escorted him to the social functions that kept his business afloat. So what if she wore one she'd been seen in before? Karina would know – Karina would give the tiniest flicker of her perfectly threaded brow – but Vanessa didn't care.

She didn't really understand why a funeral required such formality. Surely it was better to turn up as yourself? Which in her case would mean faded jeans, a flowery tunic and flip-flops. She hated dressing up these days, though once she had dressed up to the nines for him.

In the beginning, all his friends and family had thought she was a gold-digger, a shop girl who had lured him into a honey trap, because Spencer had made a fortune in the garment industry and his fortune showed no signs of shrinking, unlike the cheap clothes he peddled. She was never going to persuade them otherwise, so she stopped trying, even though it was miles from the truth. She had fallen for him because he wouldn't take no for an answer. She was young and very pretty and extremely impression-able and naive and he'd swept her off her feet. And what wasn't to like about being spoiled and doted on and put on a pedestal?

She'd done trophy wife for ten years, sparkled and radiated and networked on his behalf. But after the baby thing, after the ectopic pregnancy that nearly cost her her own life and meant she could never have children, she couldn't face it any more. Spencer had brought her down to their weekend house in Pennfleet to convalesce, and she had never found the strength to leave. She found peace by the seaside. She never wanted to go back to their St Johns Wood mansion block. Their marriage became one of convenience.

It had been a funny old relationship. Maybe it had been perfect? She had no idea. It was the only one she had ever known. She spent the week in Pennfleet making the house ready for Spencer and his friends at the weekends so they could relax after a hard week doing deals and making money. And as Mary Mac did most of the work, all she really had to do was decide menus, book tables and make sure his latest fad was readily available – whether it was wagyu beef or artisanal gin, Spencer liked to be up to date with everything, as long as it involved a hefty price tag.

She looked out across the water to *Poseidon*, Spencer's pride and joy, crouched on the water, predatory and powerful, arguably the most expensive boat in the harbour. He'd loved that boat. What on earth was she supposed to do with it now? It shouldn't even be in the water still, but Spencer had wanted to squeeze the last few weeks of fine weather out of it. She supposed she would go out on it to scatter his ashes, though she didn't have a clue how to drive it. Someone in Pennfleet would help her out. They'd probably jump at the chance to have a go. It was worth more than most of the fishermen's cottages that lined the banks, even though they were going up in price.

She sighed. The sun was warming up and it was going to be the most glorious day. A day for walking into town and buying a crab sandwich and sitting with your legs hanging over the harbour wall while you ate it, and trying to stop the seagulls pinching the crusts out of your hands.

A feeling settled on her but she couldn't identify it. She shut her eyes to analyse it, and finally put her finger on her emotion. She did feel sad, but not sad because Spencer was dead. Sad because she didn't feel sadder. Had she loved him? She couldn't be sure. They had rubbed along together well enough, in benign disinterest. They never argued. They simply didn't have anything in common. They barely spent any time alone together. They'd resorted to separate bedrooms years ago. Vanessa knew this was partly her fault. She had frozen up after the ectopic pregnancy. Spencer certainly hadn't forced her into anything. Separate rooms had stopped sex being the elephant in the room. And if Spencer found other women to keep him entertained, he was very discreet about it.

She had never embarked on any sort of clandestine relationship herself. She wasn't sure how Spencer would have reacted if she had and he had found out. She hadn't the confidence or the inclination or the opportunity. In the meantime, she had buried herself in her shop.

Spencer had bought Adrift for her, as a sort of consolation prize for not being able to have a baby. A clumsy but well-meaning gesture that she hadn't the heart to object to. The sort of gesture that wealthy men made when they felt guilty and weren't sure what to do with their wives.

She was surprised as anyone to have subsequently fallen in love with it. Maybe Spencer knew her better than she knew herself? And she made a success of it, too. She had learned a lot about retail in the shop where they had met, and she used those skills to open a gallery selling artwork and jewellery inspired by the sea, using strictly local artists, of which there were plenty. And of course she had Spencer to learn from, although her motives were entirely different from his when it came to business. She wasn't out to make massive profits. For Vanessa, it was about discovering and nurturing new talent, giving artists their first break and watching them flourish. And if she happened to make money (which she did, because she had a good eye for what tourists wanted) she invested in new talent. Profit gave her the luxury of being able to take risks.

Adrift was her baby and her lover. It gave her a sense of identity and purpose. It was shut today, out of respect, and the two girls who worked there would be at the funeral. No doubt they would be wondering what would happen now, whether Vanessa would keep the shop on. Of course she would. Too many livelihoods depended on it: artists and craftspeople who already had limited outlets. She couldn't just cut off their source of income. And the approaching winter was when she would have time to discover new talent. The summer had been hectic. Now it was time to take stock, literally, and discover new possibilities.

She poured the last inch of coffee out of the pot but it was too cold by now. She wasn't sure what to do while she waited for the funeral to start. She thought about phoning Squirrel and then thought – no. She needed to get today out of the way first. Squirrel could wait until tomorrow.

Kate called the surgery on the dot of half past eight and managed to wangle herself an emergency appointment with Dr Webster at nine. She decided to walk to the medical centre. It was up yet another steep hill on the outskirts of the town, but it was quicker to walk than going to fetch the car.

As she left the house and stepped out into the street, her mother's next-door neighbour shot out of her side gate. Sunny had the longest plait of anyone Kate had ever met, and dressed in the colours of the rainbow. She ran the health-food shop in the high street and sold crystals and talismans and incense. She had a heart of gold, and had been in and out of Belle Vue all through Kate's child-hood, offering various cures and remedies and dietary advice. Kate remembered the crumbly blocks of halva Sunny sometimes gave her, and the little biscuits made of sesame seeds that gave a snap when you bit into them.

'Angel!' Sunny had a list of endearments she varied. She threw her arms around Kate's neck. Kate breathed in some sort of exotic essential oil that took her back. 'You poor baby. Your poor mother. She didn't suffer, though. You do know that?'

'They said it was instant.'

'Anything I can do, you know that.'

'Of course.'

'How are you?' Sunny held her at arm's length and surveyed her, a deep crease between her eyes.

'Honestly? I'm not sure.' This was true. Kate still felt as detached from the news as she had when she first heard it. Nothing had happened so far to make it seem true.

'If you don't want to stay in the house on your own, you can come and stay with me.' Sunny lived in a yellow cottage that was full of cats and dream-catchers and the smell of curried lentils.

'I'm fine – honestly. I'm quite happy. Anyway, listen – I've got to get to the doctor's.'

'Are you OK?'

'Yes – I forgot my sleeping tablets, that's all.'

Sunny frowned. 'You shouldn't be taking those.'

Kate shrugged. 'I can't sleep without them.'

'I'll bring you some Rescue Remedy from the shop.'

Kate smiled. She didn't want to say that if Rescue Remedy worked on her, she'd be using it. Sunny meant well.

'I must go or I'll miss my appointment. I'll see you at the church later.'

Sunny wrapped her in another hug. 'Take care, lovely.'

Kate hurried on, up around the back of the town and along the road that led to Shoredown, where the warren of lanes containing the less salubrious houses of Pennfleet spilled out, with their jacked-up cars and overflowing bins and drawn curtains. It wasn't always a picnic, living at the seaside. People forgot that behind the picturesque harbour and the bobbing boats and sense that life was one long holiday there were people struggling to make a living in a town that had little industry but for the tourists. And the winters were long for those who made their money from those tourists. If the permanent inhabitants of Pennfleet knew anything, it was how to make hay while the sun shone. And that sun would be dwindling even more in the next month or so, along with the number of visitors, until the long dark winter finally arrived.

Kate could remember only too clearly the hardship of some of her friends at school – the debt and the poverty. It was surprising there wasn't more hostility towards the second-homers. They were seen as a necessary evil, propping up the economy, but also inflating the house prices.

'Kate!' A voice was calling after her. 'Kate! It's me.'

She turned to see a woman running down the hill carrying a small girl, waving at her with her spare arm. She recognised the voice rather than the slight figure with the long black hair, dressed in skinny jeans and a pink vest with silver glitter.

Debbie. Her best friend from school. Her partner in crime since they'd first set eyes on each other on arrival at Pennfleet High. It was probably ten years since they had last spoken.

'Oh my God! Debbie!' Kate beamed with pleasure.

'I thought it was you!' Debbie panted as she came to a stop. The child on her hip gazed solemnly at Kate while they spoke, her fine blonde hair tied up in a Pebbles ponytail on top of her head.

'I'm so sorry about your mum.' Debbie's face was screwed up in anxiety. She was fully made up, even at this hour in the morning, heavy eyebrows and full lips drawn in and ridiculously long lashes.

'Thank you.'

'She was amazing, you know. She was brilliant to me just after I had Leanne.' Debbie indicated her daughter, who was casually kicking her mum with a leopardskin baseball boot. 'I broke my leg. I couldn't do a thing. She was so helpful. She got me back on track. I was right depressed.' Debbie tickled Leanne under the chin. The little girl giggled. 'I'm going to try and get to the funeral later if I can get someone to pick up Leanne.'

'That's really kind of you. But you don't have to.' Kate was touched.

'No. I want to! She was a very special woman.'

'Yes. I know.'

'Shout if you want anything. I'm usually about. Got my hands full with this lot – she's number four.'

'Goodness.' Kate couldn't imagine having four children. 'They must keep you busy.'

'Just a bit. I work down the Neptune weekends to keep

56

body and soul together – Scott has the kids. Gives me some of me own money and gets me out of the house.'

Debbie shook back her long black hair with the thick blunt fringe and smiled. She was as thin as a rake with tattoos on her shoulders; her arms muscular from lifting her children. Kate supposed she didn't need an expensive gym subscription to keep her figure: running around after four kids probably did it.

She thought about the nights she and Debbie had spent in the Neptune, eyeing up the boys they fancied, getting drunk on cheap vodka cocktails. They'd had so much in common then. Homework stress, clothes stress, boy stress. The boredom of living in Pennfleet stress. Debbie had pierced Kate's ears with a bottle of hydrogen peroxide and a needle in her bedroom. They'd painted each other's toenails and dreamed about getting away. Kate had managed it. Debbie hadn't.

What was the difference between them, she wondered? And who was the happier?

'You got any?'

'Any?'

'Kids.' Debbie looked her up and down and decided that gave her the answer. 'Nah. You look way too together.'

Kate managed a laugh. 'I live in New York. I've got this crazy job. No way could I fit kids in. I can't even fit a boyfriend in.'

'It sounds perfect.' Debbie laughed, crooked her spare arm round Kate's neck and hugged her, swamping her in a cloud of cheap perfume and hairspray and cigarettes. 'I'll see you later, sweetheart. I've got to get this one to nursery.'

She ran off down the hill.

Kate watched after her. It had been strange but lovely to see her. She had often wondered where her mates were now, what they were doing, and she always felt a tiny needle of guilt that she hadn't kept up with any of them. When she'd left for New York social media hadn't been established in the way it was now, making it easy for people to keep in touch. She didn't have time to trawl through Facebook looking for old schoolfriends – and none of them had ever tracked her down. Re-connecting with Debbie had given her an unexpected lift. Debbie had been so kind, so genuine. Their friendship, it seemed, had survived the intervening years.

As she climbed further up to the crest of the hill, Kate reached the point where she could see right over the top of the town and out to sea. She had forgotten quite how spectacular it was, and stopped for a moment to drink in the infinite shades of turquoise and ice blue and slate and silver and steel and glittery deep green. The slightest change in light could change the colour of the water, depending on where the sun and the clouds were hovering.

Summer had long slipped away on the tide, disappearing over the horizon to the other side of the world, and in its place was autumn, demure and subtle and in many ways more alluring, with her softer, more mellow light and her wispy, misty mornings.

Her mother loved this time of year. Kate remembered Joy's hands snagged by blackberry tangles, and the ritual making of bramble jelly and sloe gin. There would, she knew, be ranks of jars lined up in the larder, all labelled in her mother's comforting handwriting. What was she to do with them? She couldn't take them back in her luggage. She couldn't imagine them lined up on the stainless steel shelf in her apartment, which only had room for exotic coffee beans and expensive olives. Would she just throw them away? It seemed a waste. Or give them to her mother's friends? Did people want jam and pickle made by a dead person? Was it ghoulish, or the perfect memento?

By now she'd arrived at the medical centre, an ugly flat-roofed building which had caused great excitement when it was built twenty years ago. Kate could remember her mother's glee at the brand-spanking-new facilities. It was now looking pretty tired, with grey carpet, yellow walls and hundreds of out-of-date magazines.

She only had to wait five minutes before she was called through to Doctor Webster, who had been their family GP since Kate was small, and was now in her early sixties, a slight woman with cropped grey hair and a perspicacious gaze. Kate remembered going to her over the years for ringworm, a lingering chest infection, a persistent sty – and, as a teenager, asking to be put on the pill and praying Dr Webster wouldn't mention it to her mother…

'My dear, I wondered if it was you when I saw your name. I'm so sorry.' The doctor clasped Kate's hand in both of hers. Her touch was cool and reassuring. 'You know how very much we valued your mother here at the surgery. I'm hoping to be able to come to the funeral and pay my respects.' Dr Webster smiled. 'I learned a lot from her over the years. She was a very wise and special woman.'

'I know,' said Kate. 'She's a very hard act to follow. But thank you. It's lovely to hear how much she meant to people.'

'And what can I do for you?'

Kate tried not to grip the handles of her bag too tightly. Now she came to vocalise it, she was embarrassed.

'I've just realised I left all my medication in the bathroom at the airport.'

'What medication was it?'

Kate looked down. It was hard to explain without sounding desperate.

'Well, my sleeping tablets. I can't sleep without them. I'm worried about how I'm going to get through the next few days, especially with the jet lag and the time difference...'

She could see Dr Webster processing the information. She steeled herself for a grilling.

'How long have you been prescribed sleeping tablets?'

'Um... I don't know.' Kate tried to remember the first time she'd asked the swanky Upper East Side doctor for some help to get her to sleep. 'Maybe... two years?'

'Two years? Without a break?'

Dr Webster's gaze bored into her. Kate knew she wouldn't get away with a lie. She was the kind of woman there was no point in lying to.

'I've got a stressful job. I work anti-social hours.'

'What is it you do, again? I know from your mother it was something very high powered...'

Kate looked away. She couldn't, just couldn't, tell this intelligent, hardworking, conscientious woman that, when it came down to it, no matter what fancy title you gave it, she was a party planner.

'I'm an... executive... events... executive. I have to be on call twenty-four seven.'

In case some princessy party thrower got arsey about her guest list or her goodie bags.

Dr Webster didn't comment. She just smiled.

'It's a tough job,' said Kate weakly, 'but someone's got to do it.'

'When are you going back?'

'Only about a week. I'm expected back at work as soon as possible.'

Compassionate leave wasn't really in Carlos's lexicon. She had an open ticket but she'd sworn not to leave him too long unattended.

Dr Webster consulted her computer.

'I'm not keen on prescribing sleeping pills long term without a detailed history and some sort of sleep management plan, but under the circumstances... Your body clock is going to be all over the place anyway, and it's a tough time. I don't think throwing you into cold turkey is going to help matters.' She started to type. 'I'll give you enough to tide you over until you get home. If you need more, come back and see me.'

'Thank you.' It was worrying, thought Kate, how relieved she was. Maybe that was a sign of dependence?

Who was she kidding? Of course she was dependent. She couldn't remember her last night's sleep without them. She took them as a matter of course.

Dr Webster looked at her, stern but concerned.

'I really recommend you find some way of coming to terms with your sleep problems without resorting to medication. Lifestyle, diet, exercise – these can all be a cause but they can also help. Relaxation. Yoga—'

Kate's phone chirruped in her bag. There must be a stronger signal here at the surgery, and all her messages were getting through at once. She resisted the urge to burrow in her bag and check them immediately.

'Sorry,' she apologised.

Dr Webster smiled.

'Being a slave to your phone doesn't help. I give myself a rule not to check mine after six p.m. I shut it in a drawer when I get home.'

Kate tried not to laugh at the suggestion. She might as well have said don't breathe after six p.m. That was when the really important messages started to come through. From drunken clients or bolshy chefs or flaky performers.

'Try to find a doctor who will help you with your dependence. Rather than enabling it.'

Easier said than done, thought Kate. She felt sorry that she wasn't going to be here longer. She knew Dr Webster wouldn't indulge her dependence for any longer than was necessary.

'I'll deal with it as soon as I get back.'

Doctor Webster handed over the prescription. 'I hope the next few days go as well as can be expected.'

Kate almost snatched it out of her hand. She'd have just enough time to go and fill it at the chemist before getting home, changing and making it to the church.

Kate filled her prescription at the chemist halfway down the high street, the same one where she had bought her first lipstick, countless Alka-Seltzers after a heavy night at the Neptune, and the pregnancy test for Debbie when she'd had a scare. A chemist, she thought, held so many secrets, as her tablets were handed to her in a white paper bag.

She hated herself for the relief she felt.

Then she hurried home.

She'd hung her funeral outfit up the night before to get rid of the creases. A black Prada dress and courts. A pair of sheer black tights. A three-strand pearl necklace – fake, but expensive. She sighed as she looked at the clothes on the hanger. She would look ridiculous. Totally overdressed. It wasn't as if she needed to impress anyone. This wasn't Manhattan, where to be anything other than immaculate was a hanging offence. This outfit was totally inappropriate. She would look as if she thought she was better than everyone else. Her mum's friends would be turning up in whatever they happened to be wearing that day. Pennfleet didn't stand on ceremony.

Nothing else she'd brought with her seemed suitable.

And so she opened her wardrobe. It smelled of the lavender-stuffed hangers her mum had given her one Christmas. And the Dewberry Body Shop scent Kate used to wear. She breathed in her youth: so sweet. It was comforting.

She pawed through the remaining clothes: baggy jumpers, bright cotton skirts, a denim jacket, a chunky Arran cardigan with a hood that she used to wear all winter. At the back was her favourite dress, the one she had worn to death since she'd bought it with the money her parents had given her for her eighteenth, on a shopping trip to Exeter. It was dark-green velvet, with tight sleeves and covered buttons all down the front and a fishtail skirt. She'd thought she was the bee's knees in it.

The dress still fitted. Like a dream. She slipped on a pair of flat black suede pumps with it. With her hair down, and a pair of earrings she found in her dressing-table drawer, she looked more like the girl who had left Pennfleet all those years ago.

This was the girl her mother would want her to be. At least for today. Joy had been proud of everything Kate had achieved, of course she had, yet Kate felt a little like a stranger whenever her mum had come to New York. As if she was playing or pretending to be someone she wasn't.

Which was the real Kate? This one, natural and unmade-up, or the pimped-up version who had swept into town. Both of them, maybe. You could be more than one person, couldn't you?

Either way, the Kate in the mirror was the one she wanted to be today. The one who had come home to say goodbye.

There was a discreet knock on the front door. She shut her eyes. It would be the undertaker. She knew if she looked out of her window, the hearse would be pulled up outside Belle Vue, her mother's wicker coffin inside. People would gather outside the shops and houses and bow their heads. Pennfleet still respected tradition. Was she ready? She felt tears well up. She prayed she wouldn't break down as soon as she opened the front door.

'Buck up, love,' she imagined her mother saying. 'Crying won't bring me back.'

She pressed her fingertips underneath her eyes, as if to push the tears back in. She took in a deep breath. She shook out her hair and pushed back her shoulders, walked down the stairs and opened the front door with the bravest smile she could muster.

'Miss Jackson,' said Malcolm Toogood, the undertaker, holding out his hand, and she took it, and felt strong. Strong enough, at least.

*

In the end, the funeral was rather wonderful. Or 'Joy-full', as the vicar had joked. It truly was a celebration of her mother's life, and Kate felt uplifted rather than sad as she came out into the churchyard afterwards, to shake hands with mourners and read the heartfelt messages on the bouquets of flowers.

'Kate.' The voice of the next person in line was familiar. She looked up into a pair of light-green eyes. 'I'm so sorry. Your mother was a legend.'

Rupert Malahide. She was startled to see him. She hadn't given him a thought for years. She took his prof-fered hand. What on earth was he doing at her mother's funeral? Surely he lived in London? The Malahides only came down in the summer, to Southcliffe, the mad ram-bling tumbledown house they had further downriver.

'I brought Granny. She wanted to pay her respects.' Rupert was the sort of man who somehow managed to get away with saying 'Granny' without sounding ridiculous. 'She thought the world of your mother.'

Rupert's grandmother Irene was the most redoubtable of matriarchs – his father's mother, who ruled a roost of her unruly grandchildren over the summer while their parents did goodness knows what. The Malahide brood had mixed in with the locals when it suited them, for sport and entertainment, but they were a law unto themselves. Rich and beautiful and wild. Rupert, espe-cially, had considered the local girls to belong in his own personal toy box.

Including her. Kate shut out the memory for the time being. There were enough emotions swirling round inside her; she didn't need another one. It was hard, though, for here he was, looking like a pillar of society in a dark-grey suit, the hair that had once been matted and bleached with salt now swept back. But still those fine features that could only come from the most patrician gene pool. And those devil's eyes that could undo a button at fifty paces.

'It's very good of you to bring her,' she said. She could see Irene, standing in the church doorway. She was wearing dark glasses and carrying a stick – Kate remembered Joy telling her Irene was losing her sight. 'How is she?'

'You can imagine. Absolutely refuses to believe there is anything wrong or that she needs to change her lifestyle one iota. She drives me nuts.'

His smile contradicted him with its fondness.

'It must be awful for her,' said Kate.

'I promise you, it doesn't stop her doing anything she wants.'

Kate watched Irene head down the steps. She could sense her determination. A woman who wasn't going to let anything get her down. Rather like her own mother. They were poles apart on the social scale, but Irene and Joy were made from the same mould. Kate hoped she'd inherited her mother's doughtiness.

'Are you here for long?' Rupert's question broke her reverie.

'I need to get back to New York as quickly as I can.' Kate felt a surge of pride at being able to tell him this. She felt so much stronger and more colourful than the girl she had once been. 'But obviously there's a mountain of things to sort out. Probate. The house . . .'

'Let me know if there's anything I can do to help.' She was taken aback by his solicitousness. 'I've got an office at

Southcliffe if you need any photocopying done, or a fax machine. Probate in this country is still out of the ark.'

'That's very kind.'

'Honestly. Just give me a ring.' He handed her a card, and she put it into her bag without looking at it. 'And if you're at a loose end, maybe we could have dinner?'

Now Kate really was startled.

'I thought you were married?' The words came out before she could stop herself. She didn't think, she *knew*, because her mother had told her. Hadn't she? She tried to remember the details.

He gave a wry grin. '*Were* being the operative word.'

'Oh. I'm sorry.'

'Don't be. It's fine. We were both too young. And we're still the best of friends.' He grinned. 'The Townhouse by the Sea has a great restaurant. Maybe not by New York standards, but if you've had enough of Cornish pasties . . .'

Kate hated herself for wanting to say yes on the spot. She felt so much more comfortable in his presence than she had done when she was young. She was a successful businesswoman now, socially confident and self-aware, not a naive, unsophisticated ingénue. Yet he still had the power to make her stomach swirl. He was standing inches from her, and she could feel his body heat, smell the sandalwood undertones of his cologne and she felt her blood warm. No one had done that to her for years. She'd had boyfriends, dates, flings, but none of them made her feel this primal—

Dear God, what was she thinking? This was her mother's funeral, not a speed date. How inappropriate

67

could you get? She wasn't going to miss the chance, though.

'I'd love that,' she said impulsively. It was true. She was a match for him now, and she wanted the opportunity to spar with him. She wanted him to know exactly what he'd missed out on.

'Great.' If he was surprised by her response, he didn't show it. 'Shall we say Tuesday? Eight o'clock?'

'Tuesday at eight,' she said, and turned to greet his mother. 'Oh, Mrs Malahide. I do appreciate you coming.'

Irene reached out with the hand that wasn't holding her stick and squeezed Kate's. 'My dear, your grandmother was an example to us all.'

'I know. I'll never live up to her.'

'Well, she was very proud of you. You should know that.'

'Thank you.' Again, Kate felt overwhelmed by the goodwill towards her mother. She felt proud. And sad. So many emotions... She faltered for a moment.

She felt a hand on her shoulder. She turned to find it was Rupert's. He had a look of compassion on his face that surprised her. She could feel the heat of his fingers burn through her dress.

'Excuse me... I must... There are so many people...' She moved away from the Malahides. She could still feel his touch. For a moment, she wanted to laugh, pull Debbie to one side, have a whispered exchange just as they had done as teenagers. 'Oh my God, he's asked me for dinner...' But now was neither the time nor the place. The churchyard was emptying, as people headed to the hall for tea. She should head there herself, make sure everything was in order.

As she left, she saw another hearse heading up the high street, a fleet of cars behind it. She wasn't the only person in the world mourning, it seemed. She wasn't sure whether that was a comfort or not.

6

The last time Vanessa had walked up the aisle to the front of St Mary's was the day she had married Spencer. The little church had been as full then as it was today. A lot of the people were the same, too. There was just one notable difference. None of her family was here.

Her father wasn't, of course, because she hadn't seen him since she was four years old. Nor was her mother. She and Squirrel had agreed to differ on Spencer a long time ago.

'I'll come if you want me to, of course, darling,' said Squirrel.

But Vanessa couldn't face the extra tension. Even though Spencer was dead, it would still be there. Far better to have a stress-free send-off and spend some time with Squirrel afterwards.

So here she was, outnumbered by Spencer's family. She slid her way into the front pew that had been reserved for her. Mary Mac was already there, the only other person she wanted with her. She was in a smart navy jacket and skirt with lipstick on. Vanessa didn't think she'd ever seen Mary in anything but a sweatshirt and jeans, make-up free.

Mary took her hand. Her warm sausagey fingers were a

reassurance. Vanessa smiled her thanks. She knew everyone was looking at her but trying to pretend they weren't.

Karina, Daniella and Aiden were in the right-hand pew: Karina in a sleek black suit which she would have spent hours on Net A Porter choosing; Daniella pale and red-eyed in a too-tight, too-short dress and Aiden awkward in a suit, looking as if he would rather be anywhere else in the world. Vanessa thought he was probably wondering where his next spliff would come from. She'd caught him smoking more than a few times when he'd been to stay. Her silence hadn't bought Aiden's respect or affection, though – he still treated her with utter indifference, although she had never blown the whistle on him. Daniella was equally hostile, as if it was somehow Vanessa's fault that their mother had left their father, three years before she'd even appeared on the scene. They had bought into the gold-digging myth perpetuated by their mother.

Vanessa had been as kind as she possibly could to them – why wouldn't she be? – but they still treated her with suspicion and disdain. In the end, she came to the conclusion that they were so spoiled they treated everyone like that. She never heard Spencer reprimand them for their manners or discuss their schoolwork or give them any guidance whatsoever. He just gave them whatever they asked for. At best this was guilt; at worst, indifference and laziness.

If they'd had children, she thought...

The vicar came to the front and looked out over the congregation with a benign smile. Vanessa looked down at her order of service, at the picture of Spencer at the helm of *Poseidon*. Mary squeezed her fingers again. A

7

Joy's funeral tea was held in the church hall, a draughty old building round the back of the graveyard. Courtesy of the fundraising committee, it had recently been painted a rather jolly yellow inside, and so felt more welcoming than it had last time Kate had ventured in. Probably, she thought, for the Christmas bazaar her mother had run for years: endless trestle tables filled with festive crafts that nobody really wanted but bought anyway, because it was all in a good cause and that's what you were supposed to do.

Today, those same trestle tables had been laid out with a spread that on any other occasion Kate would have forced herself to resist. Almost every single item was off her list. An array of fresh sandwiches cut into triangles: cucumber, roast beef, salmon. Tiny bridge rolls filled with egg mayonnaise. Next to them, sausage rolls and mushroom vol au vents. And on the next table, fruit loaf and Victoria sponge and flapjacks. All the sorts of things her mother used to make.

It made her feel nostalgic and homesick and above all moved by the generosity of her mother's friends, who had all pitched in and brought something.

Someone was pouring tea from the urn.

The cup that cheers but does not inebriate, thought Kate, accepting a cup and saucer gratefully. It was just what she needed. That time-honoured cure for all ills. There was no worry that her mother couldn't chase away with a cup of tea.

Kate never drank tea in New York.

She helped herself to a cucumber sandwich and was immediately transported back to the summer of her childhood. It was amazing how taste could hold so many memories. If she shut her eyes, she would be there on the beach, sheltered from the wind by a gaily coloured wind-break, her hair whipping round her head.

A woman touched her on the arm.

'You won't know me,' she said, 'but your mother was so kind to me. When I lost my husband, she forced me out of the house and made me join the choir. It was the best thing I ever did.'

Kate smiled. Her mother had taken the choir very seriously, even though she wasn't religious.

'Were you singing today?' she asked.

The woman nodded. 'I like to think Joy would have appreciated it.'

'The singing was beautiful. And she absolutely would have.'

'I was so grateful to her. She was very special.'

Kate ventured another smile, but she could feel her chin wobble slightly. She lifted the cup to her lips to hide her lack of composure and turned away. She stood for a moment, but she could feel the tears coming. She put her cup down and walked into the kitchen, hoping no one would notice.

The kitchen hadn't changed an iota. It even smelled the

same, of bleach and beef consommé. How many times had she helped her mum with functions in here, plating up ploughmans for the harvest supper, or scooping out mulled wine into plastic cups for the Christmas bazaar? She could remember her sixteenth birthday party, serving up hot dogs at nine o'clock because her mum (quite rightly) said everyone's stomach needed lining. Even now she could see the disco lights swirling round the ceiling, yellow and red and green, faster and faster because someone had tipped a half-bottle of rum into the punch.

She stood in the corner of the kitchen, behind the door of the cupboard that held the mops and buckets, and wept. She didn't think she was ever going to stop.

'Hey.' It was Debbie. Debbie, who unlike most of Pennfleet had done herself up to the nines in a shiny tight black dress and four-inch heels and her hair pulled back in a bun high on her head. 'Come here.'

She pulled Kate into her and held her tight, rocking her back and forth and shushing her, as she would her own children. 'You cry, my lovely. You cry.'

Gradually Kate's sobs died down. 'Sorry,' she said. 'This place brings so many memories of her, that's all.'

Debbie ignored her apology.

'I remember when I threw up all over your parents' couch after your party,' she said. 'We'd been drinking that punch all night and it was lethal. Your mum made me clear it up. But then she put me to bed and she was really kind.'

'Yeah – put you into *my* bed,' remembered Kate. 'I had to sleep on the floor.'

'You always had a better head for drink than me.'

'Not now,' said Kate. 'I'm a real lightweight.'

'Me too. With four kids. I fall over after one glass of wine.'

The two of them laughed. For a moment it was as if they were back in the school canteen, planning their next escapade.

'What are you doing tonight?' asked Debbie.

'I don't know. Just going home, I suppose.'

'You don't want to be on your own, surely?'

Kate didn't know what she wanted. She didn't want to go back to her parents' empty house, but at the same time she didn't want to be with people, putting on a brave face. Or worse, a not very brave face. Home seemed the easiest option.

'I don't mind. I need an early night. I've got to start clearing the house out tomorrow. I've got to get back to work as soon as I can.'

'I can give you a hand if you want.'

'I might need advice on where to get rid of some of the stuff.'

'No problem. And if you want to come over to mine tonight, I can do you some dinner. It won't be anything fancy. And it's mayhem. But it might take your mind off things.'

'That's really sweet of you. But I'll probably just go to bed.'

'Course.' Debbie put a hand on her arm. 'But the offer's there.'

Kate looked at the woman she'd spent so many crazy days and nights with all those years ago. They'd been best mates then, but they were worlds apart now. Their lives could not be more different. Yet there was still a strong connection. She felt genuine warmth and concern coming from Debbie, and she was grateful for it.

'You're really kind,' she said, and her voice broke a little bit.

Debbie looked at her in surprise. 'You'd do it for me.'

Would I, though? thought Kate. Would I even have the time to stop and worry about someone else? In theory, yes, of course. But would she take the time out to invest in someone just because they had once been friends, long ago?

'Just come and bang on the door if you want company,' said Debbie. 'Number four. Carlyon Terrace.' She grinned ruefully. Carlyon Terrace was where all the tearaways used to live. The problem families. 'It's not as rough as it was in our day.'

'Thanks again.' As she watched Debbie go, Kate gathered herself together. She really should get back out there and not stay snivelling in the broom cupboard. She wiped her eyes and made her way back into the hall.

People were starting to clear away cups and plates. Someone was putting cling film over the few remaining sandwiches. As the last of the mourners drifted away, Kate felt a gloom descend. She had felt so supported and uplifted by everyone's kindness, but now she realised she was on her own. She expected to see her mother any moment, wielding a broom.

She pulled on her coat and left. She couldn't bear to say goodbye to anyone, for she knew she would cry again, even though she wanted to thank them all. She felt bone-tired and lightheaded. She thought they would probably understand.

8

Spencer's funeral service finally ground to a halt.

Everyone waited, and Vanessa realised that, as the widow, she was expected to leave first. Mrs Mac took her arm, escorted her out of the pew and back up the aisle. She kept a gracious look on her face but avoided eye contact with anyone. She still didn't trust herself. She'd always had a terrible reputation for corpsing at school, in exams and assemblies and at moments of great solemnity. She was a giggler. It was nerves, really. Of course she didn't find her husband's funeral funny, but she knew at the slightest provocation she might dissolve. Thereby undoing any chance she had of Spencer's entourage taking her seriously. You couldn't control these things.

She made it out into the fresh air, into the churchyard, and breathed in. Beyond the lych gate, real life continued, with the occasional passer-by glancing to see what was taking place: the black clothing soon told them it was a funeral rather than a wedding or a christening, and they hurried on. There but for the grace of God.

The crematorium was small and bland, with none of the comforting grace of the old church – just grey and municipal and lacking in atmosphere, as if to confirm the harsh reality of what was about to happen. The process was mercifully swift. No one wanted to be there: shoulders were hunched and expressions set.

As the coffin disappeared behind the curtains, an awful sound came from the right-hand side of the congregation: a low moaning that grew to a wail. Vanessa knew without looking that it was Karina. She tried not to look irritated as a swarm of sympathetic mourners flew to her side. She'd heard that sound before. It was Karina's default setting. The noise she made when something hadn't gone her way.

Now Spencer had finally departed, Karina wasn't going to be able to emotionally blackmail him for cash any more. She wasn't going to be able to twist him round her little finger, piling on the guilt, which he always assuaged by giving her a handout. Vanessa hated the fact that everyone seemed to be taken in by Karina's act, oozing sympathy for the bereaved ex-wife who had been usurped by a much younger model.

Vanessa clasped her hands in front of her and looked down at the floor. Mary Mac, too, remained impassive, but Vanessa knew she wasn't fooled either. She didn't want to catch her eye, though, just in case the expressions on their faces made their feelings apparent. It really didn't do to look askance at someone else's grief, and they could hardly accuse Karina of being a charlatan mid-cremation. It was a tricky social situation, and Vanessa didn't want to be the one who made things kick off. This was the last time she would have to see any of these people again. She wanted to emerge from the whole thing intact.

Eventually the wailing subsided, drowned out by some interminable piece of prog rock. Spencer had always joked about it being played at his funeral and Vanessa had seen no reason not to obey his wishes. An endless guitar solo meandered on as everyone came to terms with the fact that Spencer was gone. The silence when it finally came to a finish was solemn, as the music had given the impression of heralding an arrival rather than a departure. It felt like a huge anticlimax.

Vanessa led the way out. Behind her Karina staggered, face streaked with make-up, supported by a stressed Daniella and a mortified Aiden. Part of Vanessa wanted to scoop the two children up and whisk them away to comfort them, but it wasn't her place and neither of them would thank her. She felt sorry for them, though. Spencer had been their dad, after all. They had every right to genuinely mourn his passing, unlike Karina who, Vanessa knew, had done everything in her power to make her ex-husband's life as difficult as possible, right up until the very end.

Karina's behaviour had always upset Vanessa during their marriage. Not because she found Karina a threat, but because her endless haranguing phone calls, her demands for money, her *cris de coeur* every time something went wrong took up so much of Spencer's time and energy.

'She's your ex! She's had her settlement. You don't owe her anything,' Vanessa told him repeatedly, because Spencer always seemed to drop everything to help her. She didn't resent it; she was simply bewildered by it.

'She's the mother of my children,' would be his answer, and with that Vanessa couldn't argue. But did that mean he had to jump to her aid every time Karina had a minor domestic crisis, or a major financial one? It was such manipulative behaviour, and she didn't understand why Spencer had fallen for it every time, because he was nothing if not shrewd. Guilt, she supposed, just like with the children.

She turned to Mary Mac as Spencer's friends and relations streamed out of the crematorium, car keys at the ready, conferring with each other as to who should follow whom.

'I can't do it,' Vanessa told Mary. 'I can't go home and face all the disapproving glances and the recrimination. Everyone knows I had nothing to do with Spencer and Karina splitting up, but somehow I'm still getting the blame.'

Mary hesitated, but only for a moment. 'It's OK, love. I can take charge. It's only a question of serving up the casserole. And one of the men will do drinks.'

'Am I being oversensitive? I mean, none of them can stand me, so they'd be better off without me.'

'No.' Mary understood. 'You come back when you want. I'll keep you some food.'

Vanessa reached out and hugged her. 'You're a star.'

'Will you be all right?'

'I'll be fine. Just make sure everyone has plenty to eat and not too much to drink.'

She could feel everyone's eyes boring into her back as the undertaker led her down the path to the waiting cars. Why she was still the enemy she would never know, but she supposed she wasn't the only one. It was an occupational hazard, being the second wife of an extremely wealthy man. And Vanessa had a feeling being his widow would bring even more trouble.

Nathan Fisher sat at the wheel of the lead funeral car, a sleek black Mercedes with cream leather seats. He was in a dark suit and black tie with a black cap, his blonde shoulder-length hair swept back and tied in a ponytail.

He'd fought with his boss for ages about the length, and Malcolm had eventually capitulated, because Nathan was reliable, a good driver, empathetic and honest. Never mind that when he was dressed in his uniform he looked like something out of a Madonna video. There had, so far, been no complaints. And he'd even been to the chemist to buy proper black hair ties, not just elastic bands.

He watched the widow being led along the path. Vanessa Knight. She looked calm and dignified. No tears. No companion. No children. No hat. Nathan had long learned never to judge or make assumptions about mourners. She turned to Malcolm, his boss, and indicated that she didn't want to be escorted any further. She would be fine on her own. Nathan could see Malcolm wasn't happy – he hated anything that didn't fit into his vision of how a funeral should be – but he stood back and let her make her own way to the lead car.

She opened the door and fell into the front seat with a sigh, as if Nathan was her dad picking her up from a party earlier than all her friends. She was wearing a black silk jersey dress, wraparound, expensively forgiving. The skirt slithered off her legs as she crossed them, revealing sheer black hold-up stockings. She didn't seem to notice.

'Are you sure you wouldn't rather go in the back?' he asked.

She turned her head to look at him. Huge, cornflower-blue eyes with too much kohl and mascara and rather old-fashioned pale-pink lipstick. Her almost white-blonde pageboy had two inches of darker root. Her nails were short, painted dark-cherry red. Her stilettoes were sky high but down at heel, the suede rubbed bare in places. They had definitely seen better days.

She was a curious mixture of chic and unkempt, thought Nathan, as if she'd been caught unawares by the event and hadn't had time to get her hair done. Or maybe she just wasn't bothered. She smelled heavenly, though. The funeral car was filled with the scent of something sharp and dark and exotic that unsettled him and made him grip the leather of the steering wheel more tightly.

'Just get me out of here.' Her voice was low and husky, but that could be the grief – crying made people sound different.

Nathan checked his rear-view mirror to see if the other mourners had got into their cars. It was usual to drive off in an orderly cavalcade, at a sedate pace.

'Don't wait for that lot,' she told him. 'I'm not going back with them. Take me to the nearest pub.' She wrung her hands, the fingers twisting in and out of each other. 'The Neptune. You can park there.'

The Neptune was the roughest pub in town.

'Are you sure?'

'I have never,' she told him, 'been more sure about anything. I'm not going home to stand around being polite to his wretched relatives and all those brown-nosing friends of his. None of them ever gave me the time of day when he was alive so why should they start now?' She tipped her head back against the headrest and shut her eyes. 'Sorry,' she said. 'I just want to go and get horribly drunk.'

'Right,' said Nathan, nodding, but not really sure how to deal with the brief. 'Um – I should tell my boss first.'

'Why?'

'I'm supposed to take you straight to Pennfleet House.'

'I'm paying the bill, aren't I?' She looked at him, one

eyebrow raised. Yet she wasn't being grand. Her eyes were teasing.

Nathan nodded. 'Fair enough.'

'It's been a long day. I've been up since five. I couldn't sleep.' She pulled down the sun visor and peered at herself in the mirror. 'I look like death.'

'No you don't,' said Nathan.

She flashed him a sudden grin. It transformed her face; made her look impish and mischievous and about ten years younger. 'You're sweet,' she said, 'but I do.' She wiped the surfeit of make-up from under her eyes. 'I haven't been crying, by the way. My make-up always runs.'

'You're allowed to cry. It's a funeral.'

She stared at herself. 'Why couldn't I cry?' she asked her reflection. 'I always cry at funerals. And weddings. Even of people I don't know.'

Nathan didn't know what to answer, so he started up the engine and the Merc purred into life. He'd take her to the pub and phone Malcolm when he got there; explain the situation. She had a fair point, after all. The funeral was going to set her back the best part of ten grand, so if she wanted to go to the pub, who was he to argue?

Five minutes later, Nathan pulled into the Neptune car park. He felt awkward about letting his charge go into the pub unescorted. She might be putting on a brave face, but he knew funerals did strange things to people. And the Neptune wasn't really the place to be vulnerable.

'Let me buy you a drink,' he said. 'I don't think you should be on your own.'

'I'm tougher than I look.'

He shrugged, feeling foolish for asking. Then she touched him on the arm. 'Actually, that would be really nice. And I need something to eat. I couldn't face breakfast and now I could eat a horse between two mattresses.'

He grinned. 'Well, I don't know if you'll be able to get one of them. But they'll probably run to a steak sandwich.'

He felt his phone vibrating in his pocket. It would be Malcolm. He imagined he would be apoplectic. It was totally out of order, him driving off with the widow like that. Was it a sacking offence, he wondered? Suddenly, he didn't much care. He was tired of death, and all its ramifications. Eventually, he thought, he would have driven everyone in Pennfleet to the graveyard. It was a sobering thought.

He got out and went to open the door for her. She smiled up at him as she stood, and he saw a flash of something in her eyes. Was it defiance, or vulnerability, or was she grateful for his attention? He couldn't be sure.

At four thirty on a weekday afternoon, the Neptune wasn't bursting at the seams. The pub was tucked away at the end of the town: it had a courtyard garden overlooking the harbour that was littered with cigarette ends and dried-up pots of geraniums. Nathan led Vanessa into the lounge bar, and found them a window seat. She picked up the laminated menu.

'Actually,' she said, 'scampi and chips. I could kill for scampi and chips. I can't remember the last time I had them. Would you have some with me? Or whatever you like. My treat...'

This was crazy, thought Nathan. A beautiful widow buying him lunch in the middle of the afternoon.

'Go on then,' he said. 'I'll have the burger. And what would you like to drink?'

'A glass of white wine,' she replied. 'Large,' she said with emphasis.

He went to the bar and ordered their food and drinks. The barman gave him a quizzical expression.

'Trading up, aren't you?'

Nathan frowned. 'What do you mean?'

'She's got to be worth a few quid. Specially now. That boat alone's got to be worth three hundred grand.'

'I'm just buying her a drink. She's upset. It's what any decent person would do.'

'Course it is.' The barman handed him his change, and Nathan felt uncomfortable. That was one of the problems with Pennfleet. Everyone knew everyone's business, and knew about things before they'd even happened. Word would be out already, he imagined.

Yes, he found Vanessa intriguing. But not because of her money. Besides, she'd just buried her husband. He'd have to be pretty sick to hit on her. He just felt . . . What was it? He burrowed about in his mind, trying to define it, based on the fact they had only spent fifteen minutes together.

Protective. That was it. He felt she needed protecting. From speculation and gossip, at the very least.

He slid her glass across the table and sat down opposite her.

'OK?' he asked.

'I don't know,' she said. 'I feel OK, but I can't be. Can I?' She took a big gulp of wine.

'Maybe you just feel numb,' he suggested. 'Funerals can

86

do that. It's like you go onto automatic pilot. And it hits you a few days after.'

She looked down into her glass.

'The thing is,' she said, 'I'm not sure who I'm supposed to be now.'

'Just be yourself.' It was obvious to Nathan.

'We didn't have a conventional marriage, but I think I might miss him. In a funny sort of way.'

'Of course you will. He was your husband.'

'I'm a widow,' said Vanessa. 'A widow . . .' She wrinkled her nose. 'I don't feel old enough to be a widow.'

Nathan fought back the urge to tell her she was the sexiest widow he'd seen for a long time, and he'd seen a few.

'I've never lost anyone that close,' he told her. 'Only my nan.'

She put a hand on his. It was all he could do not to jump as a tingle ran through him. 'Nans are important,' she told him.

'Yeah, but you kind of expect them to die.'

'I suppose so.'

She took her hand away to lift her glass and he wanted her to put it back. He looked at the faint freckles under her face powder, and the ivory skin of her throat, and the blonde hair tucked behind her ears.

He could only imagine his grandfather's voice. 'Don't be a fool, boy.'

9

It was gone six when Kate got home. She sat in the kitchen while the kettle boiled on the Aga. Yet more tea. How had she managed to get through the last few years without it?

Apart from the hiss of the kettle as it came to the boil, the kitchen was balefully silent. She thought she might scream with the quiet. No sirens, no cars driving past with booming bass. She turned on the radio but it sounded all wrong. It jangled her thoughts.

As she poured boiling water into the pot, the phone rang, its bell echoing in the emptiness, making her jump. She wondered if it was Carlos again. She couldn't ignore it, because he would just keep trying until she picked up. So she did.

'Hello?'

'Joy?' said a man's voice. Cultured, but uncertain.

'No.' Should she qualify the statement? 'This is Kate. Her daughter.'

There was no reply. Kate frowned. 'Hello?'

The line went dead.

She shrugged and put the receiver back, wondering who it could have been. Whoever it was obviously didn't know about her mum. It unsettled her. The man's tone had been quite familiar, as if he were used to phoning. And why hang up just because she'd answered? Kate hoped it wasn't someone who'd been harassing her mother. Joy wouldn't have brooked any nonsense, very probably, but she was a woman on her own.

She wasn't going to find out, thought Kate. She shivered. The wind was getting up outside, a blustery gale coming in from the sea hurling itself against the windows. She imagined white-tipped waves frolicking in the harbour, the clanking of the buoys beating out a rhythm for them to dance to.

She looked at the time. It was way too early to go up to bed. By her body clock, it wasn't even afternoon. She would never sleep, and she didn't want to take a pill yet. She had to stay up until at least half past nine if she was going to acclimatise to local time.

She grabbed her coat and her handbag decisively, took the key, locked the door and made her way up the hill out of town – the same route she had taken that morning.

Ten minutes later she was standing outside a house. The front garden was littered with glittery pink bicycles and a neon-green scooter. She rang the doorbell but it wasn't working. They wouldn't hear her knock through the porch, so she picked her way over an empty flowerbed and rapped on the kitchen window.

Debbie opened the door and peered out. She was back in her jeans, but her hair was still up. She beamed when she saw Kate.

'Sweetheart!' she said. 'Perfect timing. I've just put a load of pizzas in. Come on in.'

Kate was ushered into the front room, where four kids of varying ages were lined up on a leather sofa the size of a small cruise liner watching telly. A man sat at a tiny table at the back of the room glued to a computer.

'I'm just about to put my final bid on,' he told Debbie.

'Fishing gear,' Debbie explained to Kate. 'On eBay. You remember Scott from school, don't you?'

Scott waved over at her without taking his eyes off the screen.

'Get in!' he shouted, pumping his fist. 'I got it.' He stood up from his chair and came over to Kate with his hand outstretched. 'Sorry about that, darling. I couldn't miss that bargain. I'm sorry about your mum.' He clasped her hand in his. He was as stocky and handsome as he had been at school – the fifth-form heart-throb. 'Let me get you a drink. What do you fancy?'

'Just some water would be lovely.'

'Water?' Scott looked at her.

'Honestly. I don't want a *drink* drink, and I can't face another cup of tea.'

She noticed four pairs of eyes watching her rather than the telly, round with amazement at the stranger in their midst.

'We don't have visitors very often,' explained Debbie. 'Kali, Kyle, Tyrone and you've met Leanne.' She patted the appropriate child on the head as she said their name. 'Say hello to Kate.'

'Hello!' they chorused.

'Was it your mum who died?' asked Kali.

'Kali!' Debbie looked mortified.

'Yes, it was,' said Kate, holding a hand up to indicate she was fine with Kali's interrogation.

'So are you sad?'

'Very.'

'You don't look it. If my mum died, I wouldn't stop crying.'

'I'm crying inside,' said Kate.

'Are you sure you won't have a *drink* drink?' asked Scott, proffering a bottle of red wine.

Kate looked at it. 'Go on then. Just the one.'

Armed with a glass of red, Kate stood in Debbie's kitchen while her friend pulled out an array of pizzas from the oven and sliced them up with a pizza wheel.

'Hey,' said Debbie. 'I saw you talking to Rupert Malahide. Outside the church.'

'I know. I was amazed to see him.'

'He's living back down here. Got his feet right under the table at his gran's.'

'He seems genuinely fond of her.'

'Oh, I'm sure he's fond of her. And her massive mansion.'

'Debs, you're such a cynic.' Kate laughed, but she wondered if Debbie spoke the truth. She took a sip of her wine. 'He's asked me out to dinner.'

Debbie piled up the pizza slices onto a plate. 'Tell me you told him to take a running jump.'

'No...'

'After what he did to you?'

'That was years ago.'

'Kate. Leopards don't change their spots. You know that.'

'I'm intrigued.'

Debbie rolled her eyes. 'Don't trust him.'

'What's he going to do?'

'He'll charm the knickers off you.'

'No, he won't. I'm not a silly little teenager any more.'

Debbie picked up the pizza plate and looked at her. 'You're back here two minutes and you've fallen straight into the trap.'

'It's not a trap. It's dinner. I'm in total control. I promise you.'

'You do know he's got a business? With his brother. They're buying up all the cottages in Pennfleet. Renting them out as holiday homes over the summer. Making a bloody packet.'

'No. I didn't know.'

'Yeah, well. That'll explain the dinner invitation.'

'You think he's after Belle Vue?'

'He'll get a grand a week, renting that out over the summer.'

'No way. That's silly money.'

'Kate, you wouldn't believe this place nowadays. There's all these posh people falling over themselves to spend the summer here. It's crazy.'

Kate knew Pennfleet had changed. She could see that from the shops and cafés, and from a few things her mum had said. But she hadn't appreciated quite how much it had altered.

Rupert wanted Belle Vue. He wasn't interested in her at all. He was going to butter her up so he could get what he wanted out of her. He hadn't changed at all. He was still a snake. A user. A chancer.

It was too late. She'd already agreed to dinner. How stupid of her. Of course, she could cancel.

Yet she knew perfectly well she wouldn't.

'Don't worry,' she said to Debbie. 'Forewarned is forearmed. I can handle Rupert Malahide.'

Vanessa smiled as Nathan brought her yet another glass of wine. She was losing count and her head felt slightly swimmy.

'Should have got a bottle, really,' she said. 'Though this had better be my last one. I don't want to go all maudlin on you.'

'I don't mind,' said Nathan. 'I'm only missing darts at the Town Arms.'

'I hope Mary Mac's coping.' Vanessa imagined the scene back at Pennfleet House. Mary running round after everyone. Karina behaving like Lady Muck. And nobody giving a toss that she wasn't there.

'Tell me about you,' said Vanessa, leaning forward. 'Have you always lived in Pennfleet?'

'Yep,' said Nathan. 'Born and bred. I wouldn't want to be anywhere else. I live with my grandad, just up the end of this road.'

'And you work for Toogood's?'

'Yeah. I'm one of their drivers. It's just a casual job. My main job's on the *Moonbeam*, in the summer anyway.'

'The *Moonbeam*?'

'My grandfather's boat. She's an old motor launch. She'd been stored away since my nan died, but we restored her a few years back. I take people up the river in her. For picnics and that.'

'I think I've seen her,' said Vanessa. 'From my terrace. She's beautiful.'

'She is.'

'How lovely, to do a job that brings people such pleasure.'

93

'Well,' said Nathan. 'I suppose it balances out the funeral work.'

The two of them laughed.

Then Vanessa stared at him and he looked down. There was an awkward silence.

He was adorable, thought Vanessa. A little bit shy and very polite and considerate but quietly confident. He hadn't really batted an eyelid when she'd insisted on him taking her to the pub. And he was very attentive. And funny. He made her feel sparkly. Which was unexpected but very nice. And a million miles better than what she would have been feeling if she'd gone back to the house.

She looked at her watch. She should probably go back, if only to make sure Mary was all right. They'd have her running round after them. And that wasn't fair. She sighed.

'I ought to go home, but I don't want to,' she told Nathan.

'Do you have to?'

'Well, yes, I do. Really. Where else am I going to go?'

He opened his mouth then thought better of it, and shut it again.

'Oh God,' she said. 'That wasn't a hint. '

'You'd be welcome,' he said. 'I'd sleep on the sofa and you could have my bed. Like I said, I only live up the road. You'd be very welcome. If you really don't want to go home.' He grinned. 'Though my grandad might get a shock if he found you.'

The two of them laughed and for a moment, Vanessa thought – why not? She wasn't answerable to anyone now

Spencer was dead. If she wanted to crash at someone else's place, who was to stop her?

'Thank you,' she said. 'But it's probably not a good idea. I've got a cat that needs feeding and Mary Mac will worry and anyway, I don't want them crawling all over my house, poking about. Which they will do.' She sighed. 'I need to sober up. I can't go back there half-cut. They'll have me for breakfast.'

'Who is "they"?'

'Oh. Spencer's entourage. Not that it really matters. But it does, in a way. I don't want to upset anyone.' She put down her empty glass. She'd drunk it far too quickly. 'I some need fresh air to clear my head. Let's go into the garden.'

Nathan could feel the barman staring as he led her out of the French doors onto the terrace. Outside, they looked up at the moon, bursting with self-importance, like a big fat pearl on a bed of black velvet. Vanessa shivered, and Nathan put his arm around her, more to keep her warm than anything. She snuggled into him. He put his other arm round her, to pull her in tighter. She let out a little sigh and rested her head on his shoulder.

'That feels so nice,' she whispered.

'I know,' he replied.

'You're really sweet,' she said. 'You've been so kind.'

She looked up at him.

He wondered, for a moment, if this was some sort of trap. If she was playing a game with him. If she wasn't the innocent she looked, but was daring him to overstep the mark. He lifted a hand to stroke her white-blonde hair out of her eyes, sweeping it back and then cradling the

95

back of her head. She bit her lip, her eyes wide, startled by the gesture. Yet she wasn't objecting.

And then she smiled, a slow, devilishly angelic smile.

'Kiss me,' she whispered.

He would have to be inhuman to resist.

He kissed away the last of her pale-pink lip-gloss. He put his other hand to the back of her head, running his fingers through her hair, caressing her neck. Her eyes were shut now, and he moved his lips up to kiss each of her eyelids, then over her cheeks, down to her jaw-line, then her collarbone. He moved his hands down to hold her rib-cage, his thumbs very tentatively stroking her breasts. She gave a tiny moan and pushed herself towards him, eager for his touch.

Her hands were inside his jacket, pulling his shirt up, sliding them underneath to touch his warm skin. They kissed again, and this time it was more frenzied. He felt her bite his lip, her breath getting more rapid. Every primal urge in him kicked in. He should stop, before it got out of hand, before he lost control. She'd just buried her husband, he reminded himself. And she'd had several glasses of wine.

He drew his mouth away from hers, reluctant. They stood, foreheads touching, steadying their breathing.

She eased herself away from him. She looked a bit shocked.

'I'm so sorry,' she said. 'I don't know what came over me.'

'Oh my God,' he said. 'Don't apologise.'

She gave a shaky laugh. 'I shouldn't be allowed out.'

She smoothed her hair, put her hands up to her face, looking up at the sky.

'I think I need another drink,' she said.

He stroked her arm. It was gentle. Reassuring. 'What would you like?'

'Cointreau. Cointreau on ice. I've got some money—'

She grabbed for her bag, but he waved it away.

'You're all right. I'll get it. I'll be back in a minute.'

Vanessa watched after him. Watched him with his broad shoulders, striding back into the pub, and wondered what on earth he was thinking. He was how old? Twenty-three or four, max? She began to laugh, horrified and thrilled at the same time. Her legs felt weak and she sat down on a bench. She looked down at the cigarette butts, trying to make sense of what she had done.

She couldn't remember the last time she had kissed someone. And she was shocked by the impact it had on her. Not just physically, but emotionally and spiritually. It had taken her to another place. As if after years of dry bread she had been fed a plateful of the sweetest macarons, or fallen into a feather bed after a lifetime on a hard mattress.

She supposed it wasn't surprising. She had lived in an emotional desert for so long, deprived of affection or another man's touch. Spencer was never cruel or unkind, but there had been no tenderness between them. A polite kiss on the cheek on greeting or departing, but no hugs. She had got used to going without. She supposed she had switched that side of her off. After all, it was far easier to do that than to seek what she was missing elsewhere. That would have brought far too many complications.

And that was why she had to walk away now. Spencer might be gone, but really – what she had just done was indecently premature. She'd just attended her husband's funeral, for heaven's sake. And she was drunk. Well, not drunk, but her inhibitions had flown out of the window. She didn't want gossip. Or a reputation. She'd kept her head down for so long in this town. People would be watching, because they always did. One false move and it would spread like wildfire.

If it wasn't spreading already. Nathan was probably inside texting his mates. 'Help. I've been attacked by a cougar.' She'd be a laughing stock. She felt her stomach roil in horror as she thought about it. She didn't want an embarrassing farewell scenario, with him feeling he had to give her his number. He'd done his duty and he'd been very kind and he was the most fabulous kisser, but she didn't want him to feel he owed her anything more. She couldn't bear to think he was working out how to make a swift exit.

She picked up her bag, made for the gate and let herself out of the pub garden as quickly as she could.

Kate sat on the sofa with Leanne on her lap and chewed her way through three slices of ham and pineapple pizza, relishing every forbidden mouthful. She couldn't hear anything on the television over the chatter and demands of the kids, but it didn't matter. It was comfortable and cosy and friendly.

The warmth and the red wine and the unfamiliar carbs soon made her eyelids heavy, and she drifted off.

Sometime later, she felt Leanne being lifted off her lap.

'Sorry,' said Debbie. 'I didn't mean to wake you, but I need to get this one into bed.'

Kate sat up. 'I should get to bed myself. It's been a long day.'

'Scott'll walk you home.'

'Don't be silly. I'll be fine.'

'I'll walk you,' said Scott, and Kate knew there was no arguing.

They walked in silence back down the hill. The lights of the town were twinkling beneath them, and the blustery gale of earlier had blown itself out so the air was now still. A large moon hung over them, milky white.

'If there's anything you want doing while you're here,' said Scott, 'you only have to say. Deb thought the world of your mum.'

'Thank you,' said Kate, especially as she knew his offer was genuine, and that if she called him at three in the morning and asked him to toast her slippers and bring them to her on a silver tray, he probably would. She wanted to hug him but she wasn't quite sure if it was proper.

'You'll be OK, then?' he asked as they got to Belle Vue, and she wanted to say no, she wouldn't, not at all, but if she did that then she would howl and it wouldn't be fair on Scott, to have a woman he hadn't seen since he left school bawling all over him.

So she said, 'Absolutely fine, honestly,' and when the door shut behind him she stared at it with her fists clenched and felt desperately alone.

She hurried up the stairs, scrambled into her night-dress, brushed her teeth and got out the prescription she'd picked up that morning. She didn't want to risk waking up in a few hours' time, her mind on overdrive. She swallowed the tablet before she could change her mind, and crawled into bed.

Vanessa wove her way back up the high street. The lamplights were still on but there was no one around, the shops all in darkness. Her shoes were killing her so she took them off. The pavement was cold beneath her stockinged feet. She'd never seen Pennfleet like this: still and quiet and empty. It was like a stage set for the perfect seaside town, waiting for the actors to turn up and begin their performance.

She came to a halt outside her shop, nestled between a wine merchant and a boutique selling autumnal knitwear. 'ADRIFT' read the turquoise and silver letters above the door. She felt a burst of pride as she looked at it. There were two bay windows, backlit, glowing gently in the dark. One held a display of delicate silver jewellery with a nautical theme: tiny silver crabs and oyster shells and starfish hung from charm bracelets and necklaces. The other side housed a collection of blue and white crockery glazed with a high shine, so fine you could almost see through it, decorated with a tiny lighthouse motif.

Whatever else anyone said about her, thought Vanessa, they couldn't take the success of Adrift away. She might have had a soulless marriage, and no children, but the shop was an achievement, something to be proud of. And it *did* make a difference. She always got a warm glow from seeing her customers' faces when they chose something they really loved, whether it was a painting or a pair of earrings. And she thrived on discovering new talent, nurturing and encouraging her suppliers, urging them to try something different. She had a meeting this week with a new painter: she couldn't wait to sit down with her and talk about what she might do. Vanessa was no artist herself but she had a strong feeling for what people liked without making her product range too commercial or saccharine. She liked an edge and for her artists to take risks. And she inevitably sold what they produced when they took those risks. It was exciting and rewarding. For her, for her suppliers, and for her customers.

She smiled at her reflection in the window. What was she like? Standing there all tousled and bedraggled, shoes in hand, her lipstick all kissed off? Mrs Knight, paragon of virtue, her reputation unblemished. Until tonight. She had to see the funny side.

She walked on, then turned left at the end of the high street towards the harbour, and the night air hit her with its full force. The weather was so fickle at this time of year, lulling you into a false sense of security: warm one minute, the wind biting the next. She walked right along the river until she came to the entrance of Pennfleet House, where she put her shoes back on. Lights were blazing, and she could hear loud music. She slid her key into the lock, pushed open the door, walked through the hall and into the kitchen.

Mary Mac was surrounded by dirty plates and glasses, looking disapproving.

'I'm glad you're here,' she told Vanessa. 'It's chaos. Karina's gone to bed; all the men are in the billiard room. I think Daniella's being sick upstairs. I've no idea where Aiden's gone.'

Vanessa sighed. 'I'm so sorry. I should never have left you. You're an angel, you know that?'

'If I were you I'd stay away till they've all gone. They

seem to think it's their house.' Mrs Mac flipped open the dishwasher and a cloud of steam came out. She started unpacking the crockery ready for the next load.

'Go home, for goodness sake. I'll do this,' said Vanessa.

'No – you're fine. You'd better go and see if Daniella is all right. She didn't look too clever.'

Vanessa glanced in the drawing room but shut the door quickly. The men had all taken off their jackets and were lolling about on the furniture in various states of inebriation with Spencer's sound system on full blast, singing their way through his favourite songs. The air was thick with cigar smoke.

She found Daniella in one of the upstairs bathrooms, her arms around the toilet. She'd stopped being sick but looked terrible, her face streaked with tears.

'Oh dear,' said Vanessa. 'You poor love.' She'd been there often enough in her youth. 'Let me run you a bath.'

Half an hour later Daniella was bathed and wrapped up in a cosy dressing gown, sitting cross-legged on her bed, hugging a hot-water bottle. The two children had their own rooms for when they came to stay.

Vanessa sat on the bed next to her and stroked her damp curls. She looked so much younger and prettier without all the make-up and her hair straightened.

'Feeling better?'

Daniella looked at her thoughtfully.

'You know, Mum hates you,' she said. 'But I think you're all right.'

'Thanks,' said Vanessa. As backhanded compliments went, it was a good one.

'Can we still come down here? In the holidays? Me and Aid?'

What could she say? She couldn't say no. She'd be a monster if she said no. She had to be careful, though. Daniella was perfectly capable of turning from vulnerable and self-pitying to quite nasty. She'd done it often enough in the past. Vanessa fell into the trap every time. It was as if she never learned.

'I don't know quite what's going to happen yet.' That was noncommittal.

'What do you mean?' Daniella sat up straight. 'You're not selling the house?'

She was on high alert. Vanessa suspected her mother might have charged her with finding out what she was going to do.

'I mean just that. I don't know what's going to happen. What I'm going to do.' Shut up, Vanessa, she thought. Leave it at that.

'But we come here every summer.'

As well as going on a Caribbean jaunt paid for by Spencer. And skiing every winter.

Vanessa suddenly felt terribly tired.

'Listen, I need to go to bed. And you should, too. It's been a long and sad day.'

Daniella frowned. '*Are* you sad?'

'Of course.'

Daniella surveyed her doubtfully.

'Daddy isn't very good at making people happy, you know. Only bank managers.' She thought for a moment. 'Wasn't, I mean.' Then she began to cry.

'Come here,' said Vanessa, and hugged her. It wasn't

Daniella's fault that she was spoiled. And she didn't have a very good role model in Karina.

Eventually Daniella cried herself out.

'Sorry,' she hiccupped.

'Oh, sweetheart,' said Vanessa. 'You don't have to apologise.'

She tucked Daniella into bed, then went back into her bedroom and threw off her funeral dress. She couldn't even be bothered to change into her nightie. By the time she climbed under the covers in her underwear, she had all but forgotten her evening of passion. She had a fleeting memory of Nathan, and his embrace, and she smiled, then fell asleep. Their encounter seemed like something that had happened to someone else a very long time ago.

Kissing the widow of the richest man in town probably wasn't one of his best ideas, Nathan thought.

He should have taken her straight home, not poured a bottle of Pinot Grigio down her.

But the tricky bit – the really tricky bit – the thing that had thrown him even more than the fact that he'd undoubtedly angered his boss, was . . . he liked her.

Liked her a lot. He couldn't get her out of his head. And it wasn't just because she was incredibly pretty, even though she must be nearly forty. Not that forty was old these days.

He knew, of course, that it was wrong to like a woman just for her looks, yet very often he didn't get beyond that. Not because he was shallow. But because, ironically, women often judged him on *his* looks. Inevitably they were drawn to his jeans-perfect arse and sculpted arms and laughing eyes, and didn't look for anything else. And once you had decided that's all you were worth, it was hard to believe there was more to you, so you tended to judge people on the same basis.

But there was something else about Vanessa Knight. She had a warmth that drew you in, and it had enveloped him and left him reeling. He'd been gutted to find that while he'd gone to get their drinks she had disappeared into the inky night, leaving the wooden gate ajar.

He knew where she lived, of course. Everyone did. Pennfleet House was perched on the edge of the river, long and low, softly white with powder-blue window frames that matched the sky and a terrace that overlooked the harbour. But he wasn't going to chase after her. He just stood there, with his pint of cider in one hand and her Cointreau on ice in the other, feeling bereft, shivering in the chill autumn air.

Now, Nathan lay on his bed staring at the ceiling with its skylight that revealed a sprinkling of stars and thought about the sweetness of her mouth on his. And realised that she had made him feel different.

He'd had older women before. Pennfleet had no shortage of them – they prowled its narrow winding streets during the summer, many of them left alone by wealthy husbands who only tipped up at weekends. Sunshine and Pimm's and loneliness made them easy prey.

Not that Nathan was predatory. Far from it. He didn't need to be. Women fell into his lap. Quite literally, sometimes. His life was a simple equation that he was in charge of. Work, pub, occasional flings. Not answerable to anyone but himself. It wasn't a bad life. Pleasingly uncomplicated.

So his encounter with Vanessa Knight threw him entirely. He felt as if she had run off with a piece of his heart. The full moon glowed down on him, intense with silver light, and he knew sleep was going to elude him. Which was good, as he was dreading the morning. Morning would bring reality. And consequences.

The consequences of doing something you really shouldn't have in a small town.

10

There were four of them. Tiny, squirming, chocolate-brown bundles with black teddy-bear noses. Six weeks old and delightfully determined, shoving each other out of the way, batting each other with their too-large paws, rolling around and wrestling while their long-suffering mum looked on.

Nathan picked up each of them carefully in one hand, checking them over for injury, examining their eyes and ears before plopping them back down in the pen. Then he inspected Monkey, checking her teats for blockages, making sure she wasn't too thin.

He still couldn't tell what breed the father might have been. Monkey was a border terrier, with a rough, dun-coloured coat, while the puppies were shinier and darker. She had certainly lived up to her name.

He'd named her when he went to choose her, two years earlier, from a farm right out on the moors. He'd picked her out of the litter and held her to him. She had put her paws either side of his neck, staring at him with bright-brown eyes. 'Hello, monkey,' he had said, and somehow the name had stuck.

And she *was* a monkey, squirming her way out of the back door when no one was looking while she was in season. And coming back looking as if butter wouldn't melt, two hours later.

And butter clearly had melted, if these four scraps of fur were anything to go by. Nathan had set them up a nest in one of the sheds in his grandfather's back yard, and made sure there was no chance of escape. They were warm and dry and cosy in here, and he cleaned them out three times a day.

This morning they took his mind off his hangover and the murky memory he had of last night. It was a mixed memory: part delight, part horror. He wished he could just recall the wonderful warmth he had felt without the cringing embarrassment.

He filled up the water bowls and added fresh bedding. The puppies were getting bigger and stronger every day. They'd be ready to leave their mum before long. He and his grandfather might keep one, but the others would have to go. If only he knew what the father was he could advertise them as some sort of exotic crossbreed of the type people seemed to go in for: a Borderpoo or a Jack-border. But they had no idea who the sire was.

Happy the puppies and their mum were all content, Nathan crossed the yard and went in through the back door. His grandfather was at the kitchen table, a pot of tea in front of him. He was studying the day's form in the *Racing Post*, chewing on a piece of toast spread thick with butter and marmalade.

He indicated the pot.

'Cup of tea in there for you.'

'Cheers. I need it.'

His grandfather gave him a sly grin. 'Yup. Happen you do.'

Nathan sighed. The Pennfleet tom toms were out already. It wasn't even nine o'clock.

'Mick in the paper shop?'

'Yup.' Daniel Fisher took another bite of toast and spoke through the crumbs. 'You want to watch them posh maids. Mark my words she'll look right through you next time you see her.'

'You speaking from experience?'

'Yup.' He grinned again. 'They think they like a bit of rough, but when it comes down to it . . .' He shook his head.

Nathan poured his tea, thick and brown. His eyebrows, which were dark compared with his sun-bleached hair, were knitted in consternation. 'I don't see myself as a bit of rough.'

Daniel chuckled. 'Course you don't.'

Nathan felt aggrieved. 'I treated her with the greatest respect. I looked after her. I bought her drinks. What's rough about that?'

'Don't get your hopes up, lad. That's all I'm saying.'

'I haven't got any hopes.'

His grandfather looked at him askance. 'You've got that look. You've got the look of a lad who's been love-struck.'

'To be honest, Grandad – I think it's more to do with one pint too many.'

Nathan didn't want to pursue the conversation. He wasn't sure how he felt himself, and he didn't want his grandad theorising and confusing him even further. There was nothing you could tell Daniel Fisher about the world and how it worked. He knew everything. Or thought he did.

Despite that, Nathan adored his grandad. When his

parents had moved up country, to Gloucester, to a shiny new house on a shiny new estate, Nathan couldn't bear the thought of leaving Pennfleet, so he'd stayed with his grandad, in the cottage Daniel and his wife had lived in since their marriage over fifty years ago. Rosie had gone, ten years ago now, but they muddled along, the two of them. The cottage was pretty much as it had been when Daniel and Rosie first moved in. No central heating, the windows rattled in their frames, the kitchen was prehistoric, the bath took half an hour to fill. But a variety of wood-burning stoves kept it as warm as toast, and the one thing Nathan had insisted on was fitting a shower into what had been the utility room, which he used twice a day and Daniel used never.

And outside was Daniel's yard, a ramshackle collection of stables and sheds and workshops containing a myriad projects-in-progress and things-for-men-to-mess-about-with. And, in the far corner, an aviary filled with Daniel's collection of prize-winning finches. In the biggest shed was stored every tool known to man, the wooden handles smooth with wear, the blades kept sharp, all in fine fettle and stored neatly until the day when they would be needed. For everything came in handy eventually. It was Daniel's mantra. He never threw anything away.

It was here that Nathan and Daniel had restored the *Moonbeam*, a painstaking project that had taken them all winter. She'd been stored in the barn for years, and was in a sorry state. They spent six months sanding down the wood and re-varnishing it. Taking apart the engine and replacing the parts where necessary – nine times out of ten Daniel could fashion the necessary item himself, but sometimes they had to send off for something, incurring cost that Daniel moaned about, but Nathan wanted it all ship-shape.

The final task was for Daniel to paint on the name of the boat, which he did freehand in rich royal blue. They launched her that spring, the *Moonbeam*, standing on the riverbank and guiding her into the water, listening with pleasure as the engine started up, as sweet as a nut, laughing, the pair of them, as they drove her down the river for her maiden voyage, restored to her former glory. There was nothing, nothing more satisfying then seeing the fruits of your joint labour, after months spent tinkering and fettling, even if there had been moments of frustration when the engine wouldn't start up, for no apparent reason, or another section of rotten wood had been discovered.

He'd got a booking on her this afternoon, an anniversary trip for a couple from up country. Things were winding down now autumn was setting in, but he'd had a fantastic summer. A couple of articles in Sunday magazines had resulted in more bookings than he could squeeze in sometimes, as he was restricted by the tide. People couldn't resist the romance of a picnic on a boat and men, it seemed, liked the idea as much as women, so there were lots of surprise bookings. It was the perfect job for someone who liked messing about on the river, preferred being outside to inside, and was good with people, for Nathan was affable if not extrovert.

The next few months were going to be tough, though. He'd put money aside to see him through, but it was a long time until spring.

He finished his tea, pulled on a thick fleecy jumper over his T-shirt and pulled on his woollen hat. The puppies would supplement his income – he'd get a hundred quid each for them, probably. He picked up the sheaf of adverts he'd made:

4 adorable chocolate-brown Bitzer puppies
3 boys one girl
Ready soon. £100 each. Can be seen with Mum.
Reserve yours now.

'See you, Grandad,' he said, and headed out of the door.

Daniel Fisher watched after him. His face was inscrutable but his fists were clenched. No one took advantage of his grandson and got away with it. No one.

Sam loved arriving at the café early in the morning and setting it up for the day, putting on the first grind of fresh coffee beans, the oily scent filling the air. It was the best advert possible, luring in passers-by seduced by the aroma. He put on Radio 6 at full blast, losing himself in the music as he moved amongst the tables, folding the day's newspapers into the rack, waiting for the first trickle of customers. In the height of summer the café would be crammed by this time, but autumn brought a gentler routine. Occasional regulars came in to read the Saturday papers over breakfast, then there might be a swell of locals around coffee time, a peak at lunchtime with any daytrippers, then a gentle downturn towards teatime. Daisy would be coming in at midday, to help with any lunchtime bustle. It was good for her to earn her own money and have some responsibility. And Jim would come in a bit later, to do the washing and drying.

It pleased Sam, that he could get the children involved, and it had helped integrate them into the town.

Mind you, if he had thought this career move was going to be easier than being an A and E consultant, he was mistaken. Of course, the chances of someone dying on your watch were less – though he did live in fear of salmonella – but the hours and the stress weren't any less, and customers could be as testing as patients at times. So he was looking forward to a lull in business and being able to take stock. To work out how he could make the café more enticing and draw in more custom. Wood-fired pizza? Breakfast burritos?

The door tinged, and Nathan walked in.

'Blimey,' said Sam. 'You look rough.'

'I'm hanging,' said Nathan to Sam, who laughed at him.

'No kidding. Bacon sandwich? Builder's tea? Coffee?'

Nathan hesitated. 'I've already had breakfast. I've just come to order a picnic for this afternoon.'

'Well, I'm going to have a bacon sandwich, so you might as well.'

Sam liked Nathan. He'd been really useful to Sam during the renovation, telling him which local handymen to use and who to avoid. And now Sam supplied the picnics for Nathan's river trips: little pies and pasties and cardboard boxes of exotic salads and plates of antipasti; gorgeous cakes and cheeses, all packed up in vintage hampers with striped linen napkins.

'You've twisted my arm. And I'll have a latte.' Nathan sat down and tried to count up how many pints he'd had after Vanessa had left. He calculated that he still wasn't safe to drive the Mercedes yet. It wasn't worth the risk.

Sam flung some oak-cured bacon onto a griddle and ground up some coffee beans, grinning as Nathan winced at the noise. A few minutes later Sam brought their sandwiches and drinks over.

'What's going on? You look terrible.'

Nathan usually looked as if he'd stepped out of an advert for some rugged all-terrain vehicle, or a watch with seventeen different dials that would still work on the moon. He was what back in the day would have been called a hunk: all shoulders and five o'clock shadow and work-boots. But today his blonde hair was all over the place and his eyes were bloodshot.

Nathan poured a stream of sugar into his cup. 'I'm in trouble,' he said. 'Deep trouble.'

'Good work,' said Sam.

'Not really,' said Nathan. 'I got hammered and left the work motor at the pub last night.'

'The Merc? Shit.'

'Malcolm is going to kill me. '

'I imagine so.'

'And . . .' Nathan put his head in his hands. 'I can't even say the next bit. It's too awful.'

'You can't say that and not tell me.' Sam had a salacious desire for gossip that he'd caught from the nurses in A and E. It had kept them going during the late shifts in hospital. Now, it was one of the pleasures of living in a small town. People came in and told him stuff. He was like some sort of priest. But like a priest, he never repeated what he was told. He could keep a secret.

He picked up the remote for the sound system. 'Spill,' he said. 'Or the Ramones go on full blast.'

Nathan looked up with a wry smile

'I kissed the widow. After the funeral yesterday. The *actual* widow.' He groaned and put his head in his arms. Speaking it out loud brought home just how inappropriate he had been.

Sam digested Nathan's confession.

'You mean Vanessa Knight?' Sam's eyes were wide with delighted outrage.

'Mmm hmm.'

Sam knew Vanessa. She bought a lot of deli stuff from him when her husband came down for the weekend. He didn't know her well; she was quite self-contained, but charming. Her husband less so. Not actually horrible, but one of those men who knew what they wanted and didn't much care how they got it. The kind who looked through staff.

'When you say kiss, you don't just mean a peck on the cheek, do you?'

'No.' Nathan shook his head.

'She must be...' Sam was doing calculations in his head. 'Almost my age. Forty odd.'

'Yep.'

'That would be like me kissing...' Sam shook his head as he estimated. 'Nope. I don't want to think about it. How? I mean – *how*?'

'She didn't want to go back to the funeral tea. We went to the Neptune. We had a few drinks and... you know how it goes.'

'Wow!' said Sam, impressed. 'Respect! Although actually – maybe not that respectful. On second thoughts.'

'No, I know.'

'Well, at least you're not going to have her husband after you.' Sam snickered.

Nathan looked at him.

'Sorry. It's not funny, I know.'

'Do you think I should go and apologise?'

'Good God, no.'

'Do you think she'll think I took advantage of her?'

'No. I shouldn't think so. It was pretty mutual, wasn't it?'

Nathan thought back. 'Yes. Yes! Totally. It was really intense.' He remembered the passion; her hands on his skin; her mouth on his; her body pressed against him – there had been nothing lukewarm about it. 'But then she ran off while I went to get more drinks.'

'She was probably embarrassed. She might have been having a bit of a mad moment. Grief does weird things to people. They don't always behave as they should.' He grinned. 'Look, you took her mind off things. Just forget it.'

Nathan took a bite out of his bacon sandwich.

'I'm not sure if I can.' He gave Sam a meaningful look.

'You've fallen for her.'

'It was pretty amazing.' He swallowed. 'She was amazing.'

'Nate. Mate. I think you might just have been a rebound snog. Sorry if that sounds harsh. Just chalk it up. Move on.' Nathan wiped away the crumbs from his mouth. Sam took away his plate. 'I know you're not going to listen to me. But I don't want to see you get hurt.'

Sam thought a lot of Nathan. He was a good bloke. But he wasn't very worldly wise, for all his good looks and the way he had women falling at his feet.

Nathan drained his cup. 'I've got to go and see Malcolm anyway, before I do anything.'

'I'll get your picnic sorted. It'll be ready about midday. In the meantime, keep your head down. In a few days' time it'll all blow over and you'll have forgotten about her. You can look back and laugh.'

Nathan put his cup down and stood up, digging in his pocket for a tenner. Today was going to be a long one, what with his hangover.

Sam waved his money away.

'It's on me, mate.'

'Don't be daft. You'll go bust if you start going down that road. First rule of surviving in Pennfleet: no mates' rates.'

Sam took the tenner.

'Oh, and can I stick one of these up?' Nathan handed him a piece of A4 paper.

Sam looked at it. 'Of course. Though I better not let Daisy see this. I'm being pestered to death for a dog.'

'Man's best friend,' said Nathan. 'I'll do you one for fifty.'

'I thought you said no mates' rates?'

Nathan just grinned and walked out of the door.

Sam watched after him then went and stuck the sign up on the notice board. It was next to an advert for Turn Back Time, the festival being held on the quay to mark the day the clocks went back. Live music, a hog roast – Sam was supplying the food and hot buttered cider – and fireworks at midnight.

He smiled at the thought. He loved living in Pennfleet. He really did.

He stood back and looked at Nathan's advert. There was a photo of the bundle of puppies, unbearably cute. Would it be mad? He thought it might be a good investment.

Something to hold his little family together. The puppy could come with him to the café – he allowed dogs; he would be cutting his potential custom by half if he didn't. Everyone seemed to have a dog these days.

A dog had been a non-starter in London, with the two of them working full time. But now . . .

And, he thought, it would be something to keep him company when the kids left. The empty nest wasn't so very far away. And much as he didn't like to think about it, maybe a dog would help fill the hole . . .

Back at the house, Daisy and Jim were sitting at the island in the kitchen in their pyjamas, staring at Jim's iPad.

'Right,' said Jim. 'I've set up an email address. And opened a profile for him. I looked through millions of sites and this seemed to be the best. Not too many sad-does or desperate cases. So.' He paused for a moment. 'What do we write? We need a profile name, for a start.'

'Are you really sure this is a good idea?' asked Daisy. 'Is it even legal?'

'What – like he's going to sue us? Dad just needs a nudge. He doesn't have to marry any of them.'

'OK,' said Daisy, still not sure but swept along by her younger brother's enthusiasm for the project. 'How about Telegram Sam? From that T-Rex song he likes?'

'Perfect.' Jim typed it in, then went through the next few questions. 'Height – five foot ten. Build – medium. Hair . . .'

'None,' laughed Daisy. 'Well, shaved. I guess.'

'Eyes – grey. Status – widower? Or should we just put single?'

Daisy made a face as she considered. 'Single dad? Widower might freak them out.'

Jim nodded. ' Children – two living with, fourteen and sixteen. OK, now the big one. Wants...? There's a suggested list here. What do you think?' He looked at his sister for assistance. '"Fun" just sounds dodgy.'

Daisy shrugged. '"Let's see what happens"?'

Jim nodded. 'We can always change it later. OK – now we need to describe him in more detail. "I was an A and E consultant and now I run a café/deli by the sea."'

'"I'm a great cook. Great singer. But a terrible dancer."' Daisy giggled. '"I do a great rendition of 'Moves Like Jagger'. In my underpants."'

'I don't think we'll mention that.'

'Likes photography. Fishing. Inventing cocktails.'

'Scandi crime thrillers. Joni Mitchell.'

'Mexican. He does the best Mexican.'

'*Dr Who*. He loves *Dr Who*.'

'Actually, I don't think he does. I think he pretends to because you do.'

Jim frowned. 'But I pretend to still like it because he wants to watch it.'

It used to be a ritual, their *Dr Who* sessions. Sam would make nachos with homemade salsa and melted cheese, and the three of them would snuggle up on the big sofa, even Daisy. It was times like that they felt as if Louise was still there with them, because they were a family and it was her spirit bonding them.

'Well – put "I love watching Dr Who with my kids."'

'That might scare them off.'

Daisy screwed up her face.

'Pigs. He loves pigs.' They always got him something

pig-related for his birthday. Piggy banks, pig aprons, pig garden ornaments, pig slippers, even piglet fairy lights.

'Do you think that's a selling point?' Jim looked at what they had done. 'He's not coming over very well on paper so far.'

'Oh, I don't know. At least he seems real. We're not bigging him up. We don't want to attract the wrong sort of women.'

'I suppose so. He just doesn't seem . . . special. And he is.'

'Cuddly. Kind. Funny?'

'Can you say those things about yourself?'

The two of them stared at their dad's profile for a minute. It was hard, summing someone up, when the things that were special about them weren't really definable.

In the end, Jim sighed.

'Let's just put this up and see what happens. We can tweak it as we go along.'

'OK . . .'

Jim put the finishing touches to the profile, and added a photo they agreed on – Sam in front of the deli, smiling proudly on opening day.

'Right – now I'm going to need your debit card. It's sixty pounds to join for three months.'

'What? You mean I've got to pay?'

'We don't get access to the profiles otherwise. And he won't get any "likes" if he doesn't subscribe. And no one will be able to message him.'

'Rip off,' said Daisy, but she went and got her purse. She had quite a lot of money saved from working over the summer.

She crossed her fingers as Jim entered the details and uploaded the profile.

'OK. Now we just have to wait. It's Saturday, so there'll be hordes of single women sitting with their laptops looking for the man of their dreams.'

'How do you even think this stuff?'

Daisy was always intrigued by the workings of her brother's mind. She looked up at the picture of her mum. Louise would be cheering them on, she was certain. Whether they'd find someone as lovely as Mum for their dad was another question, but they'd give it a go.

'I better get to work,' she said.

'Don't say anything to Dad,' Jim warned her.

'Well duuuh.' She grabbed her hoodie and put it on. 'See you later. Text me if anyone messages him.'

II

At ten o'clock Pennfleet House was still dead to the world, in a post-funeral slump. The only sign of life was Frank Cooper, the marmalade cat, who sat in the middle of the island in the kitchen looking round in consternation – and no little indignation – that no one had been to refill his bowl of milk. Around him were scattered empty glasses and bottles and ashtrays bearing the nubs of Cohiba cigars. The drinkers and smokers had at least managed to bring their detritus through to the kitchen, but they were the kind of people who didn't expect to do any more than that. They were all used to having someone pick up after them.

The back door opened and Mary Mac bustled in, slipping off her fleece jacket (she was starting to need that in the mornings now). She ruffled Frank Cooper's head roughly.

'Off there now, or you'll have those glasses over.'

She scooped him off the island and deposited him on the floor, then began to run a sink full of hot soapy water. Mary always did things properly – she wasn't going to shove the glassware in the dishwasher. It would all be washed by hand, rinsed and dried with a proper linen glass cloth.

She filled the kettle, too. She needed a cup of tea. She'd had a bad night's sleep, waking at four and worrying, worrying, worrying. Frank Cooper was not quite enough to give her a distraction or consolation.

And she was still smarting from the exchange with her mother-in-law earlier that morning.

'What you going in to work for on a Saturday?' asked Ruthie. 'When you don't know if you still have a job? It's not like a dead person can pay you.'

Mary didn't answer at first. There was no arguing with Ruthie. She knew that from bitter experience. And she couldn't rely on Kenny to stand up for her.

'It's the least I can do for Vanessa,' she replied, eventually.

Ruthie scoffed.

'Yeah. Cos she'd be right round here if Kenny died, helping you clear up.'

'She probably would, actually.' Mary didn't see why she should have to defend Vanessa, but she felt protective.

'She'll sell that house and be off without as much as a thank you,' predicted Ruthie. 'You'll be out of a job. And then where will we be? You need to go down there and ask what your situation is. Not waste your time helping out. You need to be businesslike.' Ruthie jabbed a finger at her.

'Leave her be, Mum.' Mary was surprised to hear Kenny intervene. He barely offered an opinion on anything these days, unlike his mother.

For the first year after Kenny lost his job at the boatyard, he had been resigned to the situation. And optimistic, despite having had his livelihood snatched away: something he had thought would be with him for ever, the thing that provided his security and the rhythm of his life and his companions. But eventually the optimism had faded, as Kenny's workmates all managed to find re-employment yet he didn't have so much as an interview. There seemed to be no reason for it. He had no less experience than any of them. Gradually, the fight went out of him. He had, quite simply, given up. He had retreated further and further into himself. He barely spoke or did anything. It was all he could do to get dressed.

Mary tried to be encouraging and keep his spirits up, but it was very difficult to galvanise someone who didn't want to be galvanised. She couldn't find the key to unlock him. She accepted that the burden of bringing money into the house lay with her, a burden made easier by the fact she liked working for Spencer, and he paid her well. She assured Kenny that she didn't mind being the breadwinner for the time being, but her reassurance only seem to compound his depression, not alleviate it.

Mary couldn't understand how their lives had changed quite so drastically. When Kenny was in work, they'd had a lovely life. Nothing spectacular, but easy. They had their house, their two boys, enough money to get by and have the odd treat. No flash cars or exotic holidays – but when you lived in Pennfleet you didn't need either.

But in one fell swoop, their boys had gone to live in Australia (a plumber and an electrician, both doing well), the boatyard had closed down, and Ruthie had arrived on the doorstep.

Ruthie had been a dancer on the cruise ships. She'd stayed on them even after she had Kenny, leaving him with her own mother. That was the real irony, that she'd been no mother to Kenny, yet now he felt a responsibility to her, even though she had effectively abandoned him for months on end as a child. And not, Mary knew, because she had to earn a living, but because she loved the life. The glitter, the glamour, the men.

Now, five stone heavier than she had been in her heyday, Ruthie held court in her pink velvet Parker Knoll in their front lounge, puffing away endlessly on her Richmond Superkings, her once dainty feet spilling out over the sides of her slippers. Her face was caked in make-up: her eyelids green, her lips sugar pink, and Mary wasn't convinced she ever took it off fully. She watched endless daytime telly and sent Kenny out for scratchcards – the floor around her chair was littered with silver scrapings. Mary prayed she would win the big one and bugger off, but she never did, only the occasional tenner which covered her fags. Mary certainly never saw any of it.

Ruthie was Mary's cross, and she had to bear her, because she didn't have the heart to throw her out. She just didn't. Her friends said she was too soft, but what was she supposed to do? Ruthie had been living with a man, in his house, and when they split she had found herself homeless. Mary couldn't throw her out onto the street.

Pennfleet House was Mary's respite. There, she could create order. She had the utmost respect for Spencer and adored Vanessa, and if theirs wasn't the most conventional of marriages, they had found a way to rub along together. And they were good to Mary, both of them. She was paid handsomely, and in return she was at their beck and call and ran the house like clockwork.

It was her duty to keep things running smoothly at Pennfleet House, even if her future was uncertain. She filled up the large glass teapot – she hated it; hated seeing the bags floating about inside, but Spencer had preferred it over a traditional pot – and got herself a mug. She should have time to sit and drink it before the mourners surfaced. None of them had been early risers on previous visits, and there was no reason why they should start now.

And so, for the first time since she had discovered it, she was alone to ponder her problem. Her heart hammered as she turned it over in her mind. It made her feel sick, and she felt powerless. Petrified. It could change everything. Everything. And what was she to do?

Upstairs, Vanessa gradually came to as the sun crept up and slipped through the window, between the undrawn curtains, and cast a beam of light on her face. She didn't want to open her eyes, not because of the light, but because she would have to face the day. And she wasn't really sure about it yet. Spencer was dead, she knew that. The house was full of his entourage, none of them her fan-base. She'd bunked off the funeral tea – no doubt some of them would have something to say about that.

And all she could really remember – all she wanted to remember – was a strong pair of arms and a warm pair of lips, kissing it all away. She remembered feeling safe and looked after. And then running away, because it was too good to be true. It was an illusion. It had to be, because fairy tales didn't happen in real life. Besides, she hadn't left behind a glass slipper for him to track her down. Though to be fair, he didn't need to be Sherlock Holmes...

She could still taste the cheap white wine she had drunk. She could feel the remnants of its chemical sweetness in her brain, leaving behind sketchy memories and a dull thud and a heaviness in her heart that only making a fool of yourself can bring. What a crazy thing to do, throwing herself at someone nearly half her age. Thank God no one had seen her. She cringed slightly as she thought about it, her cheeks pink and her underarms prickling.

Then she sat up. She couldn't go under. It was her life. She could behave how she liked and no one could judge her. She should get up, jump in the shower, put on some clothes that made her feel strong and in control, then sweep down to the kitchen and meet her detractors face on, with no conscience. So she'd lost control for a minute there. So what?

She threw back the covers and leapt into a steaming hot shower that drove away the pounding of her head and her misgivings. She pulled on a pair of leather trousers, a big slouchy cream cable-knit sweater, dried her hair and put on foundation and mascara – just enough to disguise the ravages of time and a hangover.

In the kitchen she was met by a sea of faces, all sitting round the island while Mary Mac served coffee and tended a pan full of scrambled egg.

'I hope you all slept well,' Vanessa said, scooping up Frank Cooper and lugging him over to the fridge, where she pulled out the full cream milk that was his.

'Where did you go?' asked Karina, her voice loaded with accusation. She was power-dressed and in full make-up.

'I wanted to be by myself.' Vanessa put the cat down and filled his bowl, then stood up with the sweetest of smiles. 'You all seemed to be making yourself at home well enough when I got back.'

The kitchen was immaculate. Last night it had looked as if a bomb had gone off. There wasn't a glass or a plate or a crumb to be seen. Vanessa knew none of this lot would have lifted a finger. She felt a needle of guilt that she hadn't either, but she would make it up.

She went over to the stove. 'You sit down, Mary. I can do this. You've done enough.'

'You're all right,' said Mary. 'I'm at the crucial stage with the eggs.' She whisked vigorously.

Vanessa poured herself a coffee.

It was odd, being here in the kitchen with all these people who had been such a big part of Spencer's life. She could feel his absence. It left a huge vacuum. There was no momentum. Were Spencer here, the room would be filled with his restless energy. He would be showing off his latest piece of kitchen apparatus, making sure the eggs were not just free-range but that the chickens had been scampering about somewhere deeply fashionable and bucolic. And he would be making plans – probably involving *Poseidon* and a trip up the river to his favourite pub. He would have phoned ahead and given the pub rigorous instructions as to what they should be served. The pub didn't mind, because he tipped heavily.

Today, however, the atmosphere was stolid and slack. Time hung heavy, in loops of torpor. There seemed to be no purpose. She missed him, Vanessa thought, and she was surprised to realise just how much. She still hadn't addressed how she felt. Her feelings were suspended for the time being. She would unpack them when she was ready – spread them about and analyse them.

'So, what time are you all off?' she asked, in a light, cheery tone that said now wouldn't be soon enough.

Karina sniffed. 'It depends what time Daniella and Aiden get up. I don't want to put them under pressure. They're very cut up.'

'Of course,' said Vanessa, thinking that she would take Daniella up a cup of tea with lots of sugar in and see how she was.

With a bit of luck, they would all be gone by midday.

12

Nathan had thought Malcolm Toogood would be annoyed, but that he'd understand once he'd explained.

He didn't understand at all.

'You are totally irresponsible,' he raged, pacing up and down in his office. The funeral directors' was at the far end of town, on the edge of a small industrial estate. They'd moved there when it became clear that the old Victorian building they'd inhabited was ripe for conversion into profitable flats. There was a garage for the hearses and the funeral cars, the mortuary and private remembrance rooms, a memorial showroom, and the office. 'I didn't know where you were. Where she was. Or where the car was. Nothing like this has ever happened to me before, in over thirty years of undertaking. Where *is* the car?'

'At the Neptune.'

'Covered in seagull shit, I suppose. And you'll be lucky if someone hasn't scratched their keys down the side.' Malcolm came to a halt by his desk, scattered with catalogues for coffins and headstones. 'What if we'd had a funeral today?'

'But we haven't. I knew we hadn't.'

Nathan felt as if his whole life was spiralling out of

control. Malcolm's fury seemed disproportionate. Nothing made sense this morning. Was he losing his mind?

'You get the car back. You wash it. And then you go. That's it. We're finished.'

'You're sacking me?' Nathan hadn't believed Malcolm really would.

Malcolm glared at him. 'Of course I am. I can't have a driver who pisses off to the pub with a client. I can't ever trust you again. You've let me down. And I might remind you there are plenty of people round here who'll be happy to take your job. It's not as if they are two a penny.'

Nathan knew that only too well. Bugger. That was going to dent a massive hole in his finances. It wasn't big money, but it was regular and it was cash and it was handy. And it was a small town so it didn't look good to get the sack. But he couldn't argue with Malcolm. He *had* been irresponsible.

Although he liked to think he'd done some good. That he'd done the right thing. Followed his heart. Why did he have to follow the rulebook when it came to funerals? If taking Vanessa to the pub made her feel better about her grief, then surely it wasn't wrong? The funeral industry was so hidebound. Everything had to be done to the letter.

Nathan knew there was no point in stating any of this to Malcolm, who was firmly against innovation or spontaneity; the closer he could stick to a Dickensian-style funeral the better, not least because anything out of the ordinary was difficult to price. Also, he knew that Malcolm would find it difficult to replace him. Apart from this one indiscretion, Nathan was discreet, reliable, an exemplary driver, he knew the area like the back of his hand (Malcolm had lost a hearse on more than one occasion due to a dodgy satnav) and he had just the right tone with mourners – he wasn't intimidated by their grief. Plus he looked good. Say what you like, no one wanted an extra from the Addams Family driving their funeral car.

'Fine,' he said, and he tossed the keys on the desk. 'If that's how it's going to be, you know where the Neptune is.'

And he walked out of the office. It was probably the most rebellious thing he had done in his life.

13

When she woke up late on Saturday – it was nearly midday; the tablets had done the trick – Kate wasn't sure which emotion was uppermost: relief or dread.

Relief that the funeral was over and had passed off with no histrionics. Not that it had been likely to attract drama – her mother hadn't been that sort of person. And actually, it had been perfect: Joy would have approved of everything, from the flowers down to the food. And Kate had felt uplifted by everyone's kindness and generosity. A life well lived, that was what her mother had had, and Kate felt she lived on in everyone's hearts.

Now she faced the task she had been dreading. She had to clear out the house and arrange for its sale. There was no one else to share the responsibility. She had to make the decision about whether to keep or throw every item in the house.

It was going to bring back so many memories. Of both her mother and her father. She was going to need all her strength. She and Joy had gone through her father's things after his funeral, and had each other's shoulders to weep on if they came across something that brought back a particularly poignant memory. It was always the things you least expected: the prosaic rather than the sentimental.

The things that summed up a person. They hadn't been ruthless, though, her mother being of the mindset that most items 'might come in useful'. So they had really only thrown away his clothes, and even then not his boots or his jacket, which were still by the back door.

So this was going to be a purge. Kate was going to have to be very selective about what she kept, for she would have to take whatever it was back to New York. She had nowhere else, and no one to leave anything with.

It was daunting. On both a practical and an emotional level. It was going to be dusty, grubby work, so she put on track pants and a T-shirt. She decided she would go down to the café and get herself some food. Emotions always ran higher on an empty stomach, and she remembered Sam's description of his breakfast. Hopefully it wasn't too late.

'Hey!' Sam gave her a friendly smile. 'How did it go?'

'You know what?' said Kate. 'It was beautiful. The best goodbye.'

'I'm glad.'

'Now I need one of your breakfasts to stoke me up for the day. I have to clear the house.'

Sam made a face. 'Tough work. You definitely need fuel for that one.'

'And caffeine.'

'Take a seat. I'll bring it right over.'

Kate sat down by the window and picked up her phone to scroll through her inbox. It was habit rather than duty.

Carlos had sent three emails with alert flags. *Call me. Please call. Call!!!!*

Kate felt a flicker of fury. Carlos *knew* it was her mother's funeral the day before. What kind of a monster was he? All he wanted was for her to discuss the Gloria Westerbrook fiasco, she knew it. She supposed she should be flattered that he was so reliant on her, but she wasn't.

OK. If he wanted her to phone him so much, then she would. It would be early morning in New York.

The thought of it gave her a little satisfaction. She had two bars of signal, just enough, so she dialled his cell.

He answered almost immediately. Did the guy never sleep?

'Kate. Baby doll. I'm so glad you called. I have news. I have news.'

She gave a small sigh.

'Really.'

'We got the gig.'

There was so much pride in Carlos's tone. He waited for a response. Kate could imagine the expression of anticipation on his face. He really was nothing but a child.

The gig was the contract to arrange one of the biggest charity balls on the New York social scene. Almost as grand as the Met Ball. It was a huge deal, to be fair, worth a lot of money to the company, as well as meaning their profile would shoot up. They would be inundated with work as a result.

But right now, she really didn't care.

'Carlos, that's fantastic. I'm thrilled. Honestly.' She knew she sounded uptight and English in her response. But then, she was uptight and English, right at this moment.

'Honey, I don't mind saying. It's down to you. It was your proposal that swung it. Your pitch.'

It had taken her weeks. And she'd been proud of the

presentation she had given to the committee. She had everything covered; she fired back at their barrage of questions. She was much better at pitching than Carlos, who got too emotional, and froze if someone thought of something he hadn't, then took it personally if they quibbled. Kate was word perfect and great at improvising. It was nice to have that recognised.

'Well, thank you.'

'So – when are you back? We need to get a meeting scheduled in pronto. With the chairman of the committee. And the sponsors.' Carlos paused for breath.

Kate couldn't even bring herself to reply.

Even Carlos could detect the stone in her silence.

'Oh – and – uh – how did the funeral go?'

As an afterthought, it was spectacular.

'Oh, we were dancing in the aisles.'

Carlos didn't get the sarcasm. 'Honey, I'm so glad. It's important to celebrate a person's life. Now, when do you get in? I'll send a car. You can come straight to the office. I'll get some food ordered up. You won't have to think about a thing. But we need to get brainstorming.'

Kate couldn't summon up a response. She just hung up. She could blame the bad signal. Let Carlos sweat. He couldn't organise the ball without her. He didn't have an imaginative brain cell in his body. His lack of empathy to her situation was proof enough of that.

Sam put a plate in front of her. Her mouth watered. It had been a long time since Debbie's pizza.

'Perfect,' she told him. She picked up her knife and fork as her phone rang. Carlos again. She glared at the phone as it rang out and pressed 'ignore'.

The door tinged and a young girl came in with all the

bounce and verve of youth, her ponytail swinging. 'Hey, Dad!'

The two of them hugged, and Kate smiled. She started to eat her breakfast again and began to make a list. She would need black bin liners. Some decent laundry detergent and fabric softener. Some labels – or maybe some coloured string to tie up the bags. She was going to need several piles. Trash. Charity. Recycling. Keep. Oh God...

14

Spencer's funeral entourage hadn't gone by midday, but they had gone by two.

There had been a very awkward half hour, when Karina had broken down and begged to be allowed to take some of Spencer's artwork to remember him by.

'I never stopped loving him,' she sobbed. 'I don't know what happened. One moment I was the centre of his world and the next I wasn't good enough for him.'

'I don't think I'm supposed to give you anything until the will has been read.' Vanessa was cautious. 'I'm seeing the solicitor on Monday.'

'Just the painting over the fireplace,' begged Karina. 'We chose it together. We got it from a gallery after lunch at Le Caprice.'

After seventeen glasses of wine at Le Caprice, thought Vanessa, who'd heard Spencer's side of the story about his marriage to Karina and had no reason to disbelieve his version of events. She was histrionic and manipulative.

'He said the colours reminded him of my free spirit.'

The painting was a garish swirl of pinks and purples. Vanessa didn't care for it one jot. She had a feeling it was worth a lot, however, and she might get into trouble for passing it over. She didn't care, though.

'Take it,' she said. 'Will it fit in the car?'

'Oh yes,' said Karina, brightening. 'Maybe one of the men would put it in the boot for me.'

'I'll get some bubble wrap.' Anything to see the back of her.

Daniella appeared, pale and wan. Vanessa hugged her tight, and for a moment she felt genuine fondness for the girl. She'd lost a strong, pivotal person in her life in Spencer; Vanessa didn't think Karina was much of a guiding force.

'Come and stay, anytime,' said Vanessa, kicking herself.

'Can I?' asked Daniella.

Aiden was sullen and graceless and gave off a rank smell of weed. Vanessa wondered if Karina knew about his habit, but decided not to interfere. No one would thank her.

And then everyone was off, and the house was nearly empty, except for Mary, who insisted on vacuuming before she left, and lighting a raft of scented candles to get rid of the lingering pall of cigar smoke.

'It's so rude,' she said, 'when they know you don't smoke.'

'It's OK,' said Vanessa. 'We don't have to see any of them ever again.'

'Good.' Mary gave a curt nod that expressed her disapproval.

Mary didn't seem herself today, thought Vanessa. She seemed distracted and anxious. Several times she had seemed to want to ask Vanessa something, but checked herself. She must be worried about what was going to happen now Spencer was gone.

'Mary,' said Vanessa. 'I just want you to know that,

whatever happens, whatever I decide, I'll keep you on. For as long as you want to work here. I'm seeing Spencer's solicitor on Monday, so I'll have a better idea of where I stand, but as far as I'm concerned you are part of the furniture, and I value what you do. Hugely.' Mary was looking embarrassed and flapping her hand as if to stop Vanessa's eulogy. 'No, honestly. Your support has meant the world to me. And just because Spencer's gone, I don't want you to worry. I know how tough things are down here, and it's not easy to find work.'

'Well, I can't pretend I haven't been a little bit worried,' said Mary. 'So I appreciate it.'

'You're a star,' said Vanessa.

She sent Mary home with one of the pavlovas left from the wake, because she couldn't plough her way through all that sugar and cream on her own.

And when the house was finally quiet, she went and sat back on the terrace. The afternoon light danced on the water, and she could see the leaves across the river were starting to turn. Before long, they would be a fiery bank of orange.

Alone at last with her thoughts, she allowed herself to dwell on the one thing she had been keeping at bay for the past few days. She hadn't been able to face it before now, because it was going to be an ordeal in itself. It could go either way, and she had to be prepared. Now everyone had gone, she was.

It was time to call Squirrel.

The redoubtable Squirrel. Vanessa's mother. So named because she had kept her tuck squirrelled away under her bed at boarding school, and then sold off her remaining sweets when everyone else had run out. She had a keen eye for the main chance and a ruthless streak, did Squirrel.

'Making money,' she was fond of saying, 'is all about timing.'

Vanessa had had a tempestuous relationship with her mother, whom she found adorable and infuriating in equal measure. Vanessa's father had drunk himself into penury and disappeared off to rural France when she was four, leaving Squirrel to bring up Vanessa and her sister on her own. She had managed to buy a small house near the river in Hammersmith by doing ... Vanessa was never quite sure what. Something to do with releasing equity for people who had run up massive debts – short-term loans at huge interest rates. Vanessa had once suggested it was immoral. Squirrel had scoffed.

'Darling, no one forced that cocaine up their noses, or made them buy a BMW they couldn't afford. We aren't talking about starving people on council estates here – we're talking about wilful squandering. And part of my job is making sure they learn to manage their money. I'm practically a social worker.'

Vanessa suspected that 'managing their money' meant redirecting their funds to the company's advantage, but Squirrel was right. Her customers weren't victims. They were fools.

And whatever Squirrel's methods, she brought up her girls in comfort and sent them to the best school she could afford. Vanessa always felt as if she was the dunce. She found school bewildering and the future opaque and terrifying. All her friends, and her sister, were galloping

141

off to university and she'd had no idea what she wanted to do.

'It's fine,' said Squirrel. 'You'll be all right. You don't have to go to university to get on in life. You'll find your thing eventually. But you can't sit around moping about it. You have to get a job.'

Vanessa had eventually found a job as an assistant in a luxury homeware shop in Fulham, where the prices were inversely proportionate to the usefulness of the items. She came to love it. She learned that she had an eye for the aesthetic, and how to display things, and was quickly made head of her department. That was when Spencer had come along. And when the rift had begun. Squirrel had loathed Spencer on sight.

'He wants you as a trophy wife,' she told Vanessa.

'You're just saying that because he's older than me.'

'Older and richer. You want to be on equal terms with whoever you marry. You're not supposed to be a bauble.'

'I won't be just a bauble.'

'You'll be at his beck and call. He'll expect you at all his tedious dinners and parties and openings all glammed up, and he won't let you be yourself.'

Admittedly, Vanessa had been on her uppers when she met Spencer. She loved the shop, but she was only on shop girl's wages. She couldn't see how she was ever going to make enough money to change her life, or move out of the room in the scruffy flat in Parson's Green she shared with three other girls, or be able to afford any nice clothes. Not that she was superficial, and not that the flat wasn't brilliant fun, but she couldn't imagine how her life would ever change. And everybody else seemed to move on but her: get big promotions and opportunities and pay rises and make their way up in the world. The other rooms in the flat had changed inmate several times, but she remained the constant.

So being swept off her feet by Spencer had seemed timely. He was attentive and adoring, putting her on a pedestal. She had been in awe of his energy and ingenuity. If her friends and family seemed lukewarm, she didn't notice. Lukewarm except for Squirrel, who was glacial.

'I know his type,' she said. 'I work with them all the time. It's all front. Superficial charm. He's using you.'

Vanessa didn't listen. She felt safe and secure with Spencer. She didn't have to wake up wondering what on earth she was supposed to do with her life. He was clever. She was not. He made her grow up, dress and eat properly, drink decent wine instead of cheap pink plonk. He took her to places: restaurants, hotels, parties...

'And what do you do in return?' asked Squirrel. 'Just sit there and look nice?'

Vanessa didn't know what to say, but she found it upsetting Squirrel found their relationship so distasteful. They got on well, she and Spencer. They never argued. Even though she had been very young, she still recalled the arguments between her mother and father: volatile and vicious.

Spencer had comforted her. 'Perhaps your mum is jealous?' he suggested, and Vanessa agreed. It was what she had been thinking privately. Squirrel had never met anyone else since Vanessa's father. And maybe her nose was out of joint because Vanessa had bagged a wealthy man and now didn't have to work. Not that she'd set out to trap him. Far from it.

Right up to the night before the wedding, Squirrel tried to talk her out of marrying him.

'Why can't you see what kind of man he is?'

Vanessa took a deep breath in. She was going to say it.

'Well, at least he's not a useless drunk who abandoned his family.'

Squirrel stood up very straight. Vanessa never knew what her mother felt about her father. For someone who was very voluble about most people, Squirrel kept quiet on the matter. She looked more upset than Vanessa thought she would be.

'Did you really say that?'

'You take any opportunity you can to attack Spencer. You never give him the benefit of the doubt.'

Squirrel turned away from her daughter. She walked over to her fireplace, and fiddled with the few ornaments on the mantelpiece while she thought. When she turned, her face was grave.

'I'm sorry, but as long as you're with him, I can't have anything to do with you both. It's him or me.'

Vanessa put up her hands. 'Mum. It has to be him. What would I do without him?'

Squirrel gave her a disapproving glare. 'I didn't bring you up to be dependent on a man.'

'I'm not dependent. He's my husband.'

'I don't like seeing you controlled.'

'Maybe that's what I'm used to?'

That was a cruel barb and Vanessa knew it. Squirrel

had always been bossy and organising, but she always had other people's interests at heart.

Squirrel shook her head sadly.

'Let me know when you come to your senses. You will eventually.'

Once she was married, Vanessa did her best to keep her relationship with her mother going, but it was easiest to keep Squirrel and Spencer apart. They had lunch once a month but, whenever they met, Spencer's spectre hung between them and stopped any real conversation. Vanessa missed her mother, for all her infuriating and interfering ways, but their relationship could never be as it had once been for as long as she was married to Spencer.

Now it was time to bury the hatchet. She hadn't called her before, because she needed a clear head. She'd had to deal with the funeral, and Karina, before getting Squirrel involved. Too many strong personalities at an emotional time could be disastrous.

Her mother answered the phone. 'Squirrel Brown.'

Only her mother could get away with that name sounding authoritative.

'Mum?'

'Darling.' There was warmth in her voice. 'Are you all right?'

Vanessa stood by the garden wall and gazed out at the harbour beyond. Her head felt empty, but she knew it was because she was trying to keep all her thoughts at bay. How she felt about being a widow, how she felt about the future.

And how she felt about last night...

The only thought she allowed in was how much she wanted her mother with her. Not to have a shoulder to cry on, but just to have someone there who loved her unconditionally, and who would help to build some momentum in her life, because more than anything Vanessa felt as if she were drifting.

Adrift.

'Mum – would you come down? Now, I mean.' She paused. 'I need you.'

'My darling, of course.' Squirrel was never one to ignore a call to arms. 'I just need to throw some things in a bag and I'll drive right down. I'll be there in time for supper.'

Vanessa put the phone down, shutting her eyes. She felt relief wash over her. She needed someone to take charge, and there was no better person for the job than Squirrel. But she had at least four hours to wait before she arrived. There was nothing for her to do, because the house was immaculate. Mary had changed all the beds. The fridge was still full: Mary had left enough to feed an army. Time spooled in front of her, and she knew there was nothing else to think about now except—

Him. If she shut her eyes she could feel his warmth. He was so much younger yet he'd made her feel safe.

For heaven's sake, she told herself. You were drunk and emotional and, frankly, any port in a storm would have done to make you feel good about yourself.

If he was interested, he would have got in touch by now.

He was probably in the pub with his mates, regaling them with the night's escapade. How the posh bird hadn't wanted to go back to the funeral tea, but had dragged him to the pub, got drunk and snogged him.

Ugh. She was a cougar. A middle-aged woman desperate for affection.

But there had been something, she told herself. A connection. A spark. A spark that had ignited something deep inside her.

That was just lust, she told herself. It had been a long time. After the ectopic, sex had dwindled between her and Spencer. Neither had wanted to indulge, when it reminded them of the elephant in the room. Never mind separate rooms – they'd been in separate houses a lot of the time.

Vanessa sighed. Nathan had been a taste of something. New possibilities. He was a sign that she was still alive. That she still had a heart, and a soul. And other things . . .

Above all else, her evening with him had made her smile. It had been naughty of her, luring him away like that. Making him kiss her. Yet he hadn't minded. He definitely hadn't done it out of a sense of duty. It wasn't in the job description.

She should leave it at that. A little taste of the future and its possibilities. An *amuse-bouche*.

She thought she ought to thank him, though. Good manners were ingrained in Vanessa. She couldn't just ignore his consideration.

At least, that's what she told herself.

She didn't have his number. She'd done a runner before they'd got to the number-swapping stage. She wondered if she could get it off the barman in the Neptune. Or Sam in the café, who'd know him. But she didn't want people talking. She knew what Pennfleet was like. They fell on gossip like a gull on a discarded sandwich: tore it apart, devoured it, regurgitated it.

Then she had a brainwave. She went out of the garden gate and walked down to the harbour. There were quite a few late tourists milling about in the afternoon sun, eating fish and chips. She wove her way through them to a kiosk by the steps that led down to the water. It had piles of leaflets advertising boat trips, fishing trips, kayaking trips. She looked through them until she found the one she was looking for. Pennfleet River Picnics. And there, on the bottom, what was presumably Nathan's number.

She grabbed a leaflet and ran back home.

She sat in the kitchen, staring at it. There was a picture of the *Moonbeam* with Nathan at the helm, and she felt her tummy turn over when she saw it. Now she had his number, she didn't know quite what to do with it. She wanted to acknowledge his kindness of the night before, and the fact that he had jeopardised his job.

Hell, who was she trying to kid? She wanted to hear from him again. She wanted that sweet feeling, the rush, the thrill, the warmth.

She composed and re-composed a text. Fifteen different drafts, before finally settling on something fairly anodyne.

Thank you for looking after me. You are a star. Vanessa x

She thought it wasn't too pushy or gushy. It wasn't over-effusive. Or needy. It was, she hoped, warm and friendly, but wouldn't freak him out, or make him think she was being predatory. He wouldn't show it to his mates, laughing.

She looked at it again, then removed the kiss. The kiss felt over-familiar. A step too far.

She pressed send. They had a signal at the house, because Spencer had fitted a booster. Whether Nathan would have one, wherever he was, was another matter. All she had to do now was wait.

15

'So,' said Sam. 'Are you going to tell me about him?'

It was the lull between lunch and tea, when the café went quiet for about half an hour. Daisy had cleared the tables and was rearranging the cake displays, sweeping up the stray crumbs. Sam thought this was an opportune moment to talk to her. He wanted to do it without Jim earwigging or putting in his two-pence-worth.

Daisy looked a bit wary, but also relieved.

'His name's Oscar. He's in the upper sixth. He's asked me out. That's it, really. We sit next to each other on the bus.'

'And what's he like? What subjects does he do?' It was ridiculous, to use someone's A-level options to pigeonhole them. Sam knew that, but he couldn't help himself. What else was he going to go on?

'I don't know all of them, but I know he does art. He used to do graffiti and stuff, when he was in London. He showed me some pictures. It was awesome.'

'OK. So he's from London too?'

'Yeah – they moved here about two years ago. After his dad went to prison.'

Sam's stomach lurched.

'Prison.' Sam nodded his head slowly. 'Great. For what?'

Daisy frowned and bit her lip.

'Drugs. I think.'

'Wonderful.'

'Hey, don't worry. That's why they moved down here. To get away from it all. And his mum and dad split up ages ago. They don't even speak any more.'

'Oh, Daisy.' Fear squeezed him.

Daisy looked at him with an exasperated smile. She was so young and unformed and naive it terrified him. He knew bad things would probably happen to her, and had to happen to her, to make her grow up and understand how the world worked. Yet he didn't think the need to protect would ever leave him.

'Dad. Don't worry. Oscar is really cool, and not into drugs.'

'He probably wouldn't say if he was. *You* probably wouldn't say if he was.'

Daisy gave him a look. It was pure Louise. It said *For heaven's sake stop worrying about something that isn't a problem.*

'Trust me, Dad,' she said.

'I do trust you. That's the problem. It's other people I don't trust.'

He could already feel his fists bunching in his desperation.

'Dad.' Daisy's tone was a warning. 'Chill. I'm going to his house tonight, and we're going to go and see a band. At the Neptune. If that's OK.'

Sam was silent. This was one of the moments he'd been

dreading. The moment he had to let go; let his precious daughter out into the big bad world.

'Of course.' He could hardly say otherwise. She was seventeen, nearly.

'He wants to check out the opposition. He's started a band. Called The Love Rats.'

'Love Rats?' Sam feigned alarm.

'Just because that's what they're called doesn't mean he is one.' She stood in front of him, hands on her hips, smiling, confident, in control of the situation. 'Just like Brandon Flowers isn't actually a killer?'

The Killers. Louise had loved The Killers. Sam remembered her dancing round the kitchen to 'Mr Brightside'. He really missed her today. Sometimes, it wasn't a dull ache, it was a sharp pain. He would feel it when he woke up, and there was never a particular reason. It was how it was.

'Do I need to have The Talk with you?' asked Sam. 'Because if there's anything you're worried about . . .'

Daisy laughed. 'Dad, we've had The Talk at school a hundred times since I was in Year Seven. I probably know more about it all than you. You don't have to worry.'

He felt odd about it. His little girl, who wasn't a little girl any more but who always would be. To him. And having to deal with it on his own meant he had to accept she was growing up. He couldn't be in denial about it.

He felt her slipping away. He told himself to let go. If he wanted to keep her, he had to let go.

'I'm not going to sleep with him. Not yet, anyway.'

Oh God. Could he handle this? She was actually talking to him about the possibility of sex with this boy. What should he say? What was the right thing to say?

He had to be open-minded, or she wouldn't talk to him anymore.

'Just ... promise me that if there's anything you want to talk about, you will. I know your mum's not here, and that's who you would have talked to. But I'm here for you.'

'Dad. I know. It's cool.'

Was it? Was it cool? It had to be. He had to be. He couldn't lock her up. He nodded. 'Good.'

'So are you OK with tonight?'

'Daze, it's fine. Just keep in touch and be home by midnight. Please?'

She nodded. She came over and gave him a hug. He hugged her back, and told himself he would kill anyone who hurt her, but at the same time reminded himself that they probably wouldn't; if they did it was all part of growing up and she had to go through it.

So many bloody feelings.

Two customers came in through the door. Daisy slipped out of his embrace and went to greet them with a smile, showing them to a vacant table. He watched her chatter away, vivacious, confident. So much of Louise but with a sprinkling of her own Daisyness ...

He hoped this Oscar knew how lucky he was.

16

Nathan was standing at the helm of the *Moonbeam*. In the boat behind him, a thirty-something couple were sharing the anniversary picnic he'd picked up from Sam. A platter of antipasti – salamis and olives and chargrilled artichokes – was laid out on a table between them, together with a chilled bottle of champagne. There were cheeses and salads and fruit tartlets waiting in the hamper.

It was a dazzling and crisp afternoon of the very best kind. They were lucky: it could have been damp and misty and dull. Instead, the river and its banks showed themselves off in the splendour of the golden autumn light. The river itself was dark turquoise and tranquil, drifting with a purposeful somnolence.

Usually, Nathan kept up a running commentary for his passengers, pointing out the landmarks along the river. The rambling house lived in by an infamous artist, the location of many scandalous trysts back in the 1930s. The tiny beach favoured by smugglers who had once rolled in barrels of rum and other contraband onto its shore. The thatched pub owned by a pop star – sometimes he would moor outside and let his passengers enjoy a wine-fuelled lunch here. And then there was the wildlife. Kingfishers and herons. Occasional otters. You needed local knowledge and a sharp eye, both of which Nathan had.

But today he didn't have the energy. He didn't want to engage. The couple seemed quite happy with their own company, so he was left alone with his thoughts. This was always the place where he felt at one with himself. There was never any problem that couldn't be solved by a trip up the river. It emptied his mind and made him realise that as long as he had the *Moonbeam*, that was really all that mattered. He remembered his grandfather bringing her back one afternoon when Nathan was nine. She was almost a total wreck, barely held together, but his grandfather was determined to restore her to her former glory.

Nathan's grandmother had moaned in fond exasperation, for the boat took up far too much of his grandfather's time and pocket for her liking, but her face when Daniel took her out in the boat for the first time more than made up for it. The *Moonbeam* made everyone smile. She was a boat made for romance and adventure.

And they'd dug her out again, all those years later, when Nathan had hit on the idea of the boat trips. It was never going to make him a fortune, but as jobs went it was truly satisfying and heart-lifting.

This summer he'd stepped the service up and done a deal with Sam to supply the picnics, making it a gastronomic adventure. He'd been almost fully booked over the summer, except when the weather was against him. Of course, the winter was a different story, but 'twas ever thus in Pennfleet. He wasn't the only person whose coffers were empty from November to March.

Which was why the driving job with Toogood's had

come in handy. Funerals didn't die off over the winter – on the contrary, arguably there were more. He'd been shocked that Malcolm hadn't listened to the extenuating circumstances. He had thought he would get a warning at most.

And now he'd have to find some other way to supplement his income. He'd got a bit of money stashed away, and his grandad didn't charge him rent, though in return Nathan picked up some of the bills – the electricity and water rates – and paid for a regular delivery of logs for the woodburners, and kept the fridge and larder full. It was an unspoken agreement, but he never wanted to be accused of freeloading.

He'd start putting the feelers out later tonight. He might end up having to go further afield for work, though. The problem smothered him like a cloud, blocking out the beauty surrounding him. The river usually never failed to lift his spirits, but today he didn't see it.

And it overshadowed the memory of the night before. It had brought him up sharp and made him realise the truth. Get real, Nathan, he told himself. You meant nothing to Vanessa Knight. Nothing. It was a drunken kiss, not a gateway to a new life, a new love, no matter how extraordinary it had seemed at the time.

It wasn't as if he hadn't been there before. Been swept away by someone who was better than him. Ruby. Ruby Wallace. Who had picked up his heart and played with it, like a princess with a jewelled bauble, then cast it to one side when something better had come along. And what hurt the most was that something hadn't been a person, but a place. Ruby had thrown him away in her search for the bright lights and excitement and opportunity. She had truly believed the streets of London were paved with gold.

He had loved her. And lost her. And he had never really engaged with another woman since.

He and Ruby had gone out since the age of fourteen. She was the only thing he had liked about school. She was the only reason he got up and managed to get there. Before she arrived, he used to bunk off as much as he could, take his fishing rods and a sandwich and hide himself away for the day. School bored him rigid. He could read and add up. What more did he need?

It wasn't that he wasn't interested in the world and what it had to offer. He could lose himself in a book or a magazine or a television programme and absorb the information: he was well versed in astronomy, the Cuban missile crisis, the life cycle of the kangaroo. But the stuff the teachers droned on about at school seemed so random and irrelevant; their delivery was so dry and dull. And he struggled to compose his thoughts and write them down. Very often he knew the answers or the arguments, but he couldn't pin them down on paper. It made his brain squirm with frustration. They tested him for dyslexia but he wasn't. He decided he was just thick.

So to avoid the humiliation of looking so in front of his fellow pupils, he wagged off as much as he could. Then Ruby arrived and blew his mind.

Her mum and dad had bought a rambling old farmhouse on the outskirts of Pennfleet. Her dad was an architect, and her mum was in charge of renovating the farm.

'It's what they do,' Ruby explained. 'Buy some old dump and tart it up. Dad does the design and then Mum project-manages it and does the inside, then they sell it on and make a fat profit. It's why I've been to seven different schools.'

She radiated something different from the other girls. A glamour and a sparkle, and Nathan felt flattered that she had chosen him above all the other lads to confide in and hang out with. Her parents were very liberal and never seemed to mind where she was or what she was doing or how late she was out. They were inseparable. When Nathan left school at sixteen and moved in with his grandad, and Ruby went to the sixth-form college in Shoredown, they still saw as much of each other as they could.

The trouble began when they went to London for the weekend. Ruby had been dying to go for weeks, and Nathan had finally relented. They headed for Camden, because she wanted to go to the market. It might as well have been Calcutta, it felt so foreign to him. The streets were pulsing with people, shouting, chattering, laughing. Some drunk, falling all over the place. Some . . . well, the acrid scent of weed in the air explained their erratic behaviour.

Ruby darted in and out of the warren of stalls.

'Look at it all,' she said. 'It's wonderful. Look at the stuff!'

Stuff was just stuff, in Nathan's view. He didn't feel the need to clutter his life up with it. But Ruby was a magpie. The more she had, the more she wanted.

By six o'clock in the evening, he just wanted a quiet pint somewhere. Maybe ham, egg and chips. Ruby wanted glitz and glamour and noise. She pulled him into a pub bursting at the seams with boys with eyeliner and peacock hair; girls in deep-red lipstick and fur coats. The music was too loud for anyone to hear themselves, but they shouted at each other nonetheless. The floor was sticky with spilt booze.

Ruby wormed her way to the bar. Nathan tried to follow her, but he got blocked. By the time he got to her she was deep in conversation with a guy in a leather jacket and skinny jeans, his head shaved apart from a top knot. He looked like an idiot.

'This is Gil,' said Ruby.

Gil gave Nathan a smile that said 'Your girlfriend's hot. And she likes me.'

'I'm going out for some air,' said Nathan to Ruby.

Gil's eyes glittered with triumph. Ruby didn't protest.

Nathan walked out into the street, pushing past people in his urge to escape. There, he breathed in the night air to calm himself down. He wondered how far it was to walk to the train station. He wouldn't be able to work out the Tube. Even then, if he got there, would there be a train to Cornwall at this time?

Then he thought he couldn't just leave Ruby. She might act like she could handle herself, but she might get herself into trouble. She might have her drink spiked, get raped, or ... anything could happen. He had to look after her. Even though it seemed she was quite happy to abandon him.

That was how it worked. Boys looked after girls. He pushed his way back in, past the meaty, sweaty bodies.

Ruby was kissing Gil as if her life depended on it.

Nathan gripped Gil's arm. It was puny. If it came to fisticuffs, he'd win hands down.

'Scuse me, mate,' he said politely.

Gil turned and looked at him. 'What?'

'We've got to go.' Nathan was determined not to cause a scene.

'Shame,' smirked Gil.

Ruby looked from one to the other, not sure how to play it. Nathan could see a moment in her eyes when she debated staying with Gil, but she didn't quite have the nerve.

Nathan took Ruby by the elbow and guided her out of the pub and back on to the street.

'He was going to get us some... you know... Es,' she said uncertainly, because she didn't have a clue, not really.

Nathan rolled his eyes. That was the last thing he needed. Ruby off her head on something in the middle of London, causing havoc.

'Let's go and get something to eat.'

'Do you know what?' demanded Ruby, her hands on her skinny hips. 'You're boring.'

'Don't bring me next time,' Nathan replied.

'I won't,' said Ruby. 'I definitely won't.'

It was after that everything started to unravel.

He couldn't satisfy her hunger for something more.

And he couldn't muster up the enthusiasm to share it with her.

'I'm going to go to fashion college,' she told him. 'It'll be amazing. We could get a flat together. In London, Nath.'

'And what would I do?'

'Whatever you want! You can be whatever you want to be.'

'Maybe I'm happy the way I am?'

160

Ruby looked at him as if that wasn't possible. And he felt hurt. He had always thought he was enough as he was.

'I love Pennfleet,' he told her. 'I love everything about it. The way the seasons change. The way everything changes with them. It means it's never boring.'

Ruby's face was screwed up in consternation. 'Can't you try it? Just for a year? Just for me? Pennfleet will still be here.' She was stroking his arm. Wheedling. 'You can't stay here all your life and not try something new. There might be the most amazing thing out there for you and you'll never know about it.'

There was nothing more amazing than taking the boat up the river early in the morning, watching the wildlife in the riverbanks, feeling the breeze in your hair and the sun on your back, gliding along with the current... What could be better than that? How could she not see that?

Ruby wanted something more. Noise. Danger. People. Adventure. Bright lights.

He'd had to let her go.

And he never wanted to have that feeling again. He never wanted to lose his heart to someone whose own heart wasn't in it. He had made do, for Ruby, at the time, before something better came along. He'd been the best option in Pennfleet, but the wider world held more excitement and more choice for her. He didn't want that to happen with Vanessa. He didn't want to be a temporary sticking plaster, to be ripped off when a more realistic option presented itself.

He realised he'd gone further up the river than he should, and the trip was going to be much longer than the allotted two hours, but his passengers didn't seem to mind, and he certainly didn't care; the longer he stayed away from reality the better. He turned the boat round and headed back downriver. The sun was slipping downwards, and the light hit him straight in the eyes, so he pulled the peak of his cap down until they rounded the bend.

As he made his way back into the harbour and moored up to let the passengers off at the steps on the quay, he felt his phone go in his pocket. There was no signal along the river, so he usually had a flurry of texts whenever he got back.

When he saw who it was from, he felt as if he was falling down the slippery steps he was standing on, his heart turning over and over, adrenalin spiking his blood and pooling into his stomach.

Thank you for looking after me. You are a star. Vanessa

He stood for a moment on the steps, staring at it.

He knew if he replied, he would wait in agony for a further response, and then analyse that for some deeper meaning or invitation, and on it would go, the torture. Anyway, what was he supposed to say? 'You're welcome' didn't seem worth the bother. 'My pleasure' sounded a bit . . . pervy. 'No worries' sounded too casual.

If she'd wanted to see him, she would have put a hint, surely. The text was good manners and nothing else. She hadn't even put a kiss, and if she had any feelings for him she would have, surely.

He was already wasting too much time and energy thinking about it.

With a flick of his thumb, Nathan deleted her text.

And with it went her number. He had enough problems without making more of a fool of himself.

17

Kate stood in the middle of the kitchen. She was usually a strategic and orderly sort of person, who started every task with a plan, but today she didn't have a clue where to begin.

She'd put off the job long enough already, by having breakfast out and then going to buy things she didn't really need. She didn't have long. A week was the most she could get away with, to get it ready for whomever she sold it to. It would need to be empty and clean, with all the utility bills paid or suspended – although she would have to keep the electricity on, and the Aga on low over the winter.

She needed someone to keep an eye on it. Maybe Debbie, she thought. She probably wouldn't mind popping in once a week. Freshen the place up if there were viewings. She would pay her, of course. She had no doubt the money would come in handy. All those mouths to feed. Kate couldn't imagine how much it must cost.

She opened a kitchen drawer and immediately her heart sank as she looked at a tangled mess of wooden spoons, corkscrews, knives and chopsticks all tangled up with elastic bands and bottle tops. She had been telling herself that it was going to be an easy job, that her parents weren't hoarders. Nevertheless, they had accumulated. The drawer was bursting, and no doubt there would be more drawers, and cupboards, and shelves, and the shed, and the attic...

She could feel panic set in. She had no idea what to do, or how to establish order.

One room at a time, she told herself. Focus. Kitchen, living room, two bedrooms, bathroom. She would start on her own bedroom. It would be easy for her to make decisions about her own stuff. She was pretty certain there wasn't much she would want to keep. Once she had one room done, and could shut the door and tick it off, she would feel ahead of the game.

One hour later she was sitting on the floor in front of her dressing table. She had only been through three drawers. She had thrown a few items into a black bin liner – old make-up, receipts, broken earrings, an old roll of Sellotape, an empty bottle of talc. Next to her was a pile of letters and cards she was still reading her way through. Each one brought a memory shooting back. Long hidden, the memories were suddenly as clear as if they had happened only yesterday. A forgotten argument, a birthday, an arrangement. There were photos, too, of another Kate, rounder of face, her hair five shades darker, her brows heavy and untouched, floating about in unstructured clothes that put at least half a stone on her, but she hadn't worried in those days.

She didn't want to throw any of it away. It was her history. Fragments and snippets of her life she'd tucked away in a corner of her mind. If she jettisoned it, part of her would go with it. They were aides memoires. And she wanted to remember that other person, the old Kate. Who seemed softer. More rounded. Happier?

Had she been happier?

She hadn't thought so at the time, of course. Teenage torment and the agony of being in your early twenties, when you suddenly realised that your future was up to you, brought their own pressures and stopped you appreciating what you had. Now, looking back, she thought she had been truer to herself in those days. She wasn't so sure she felt like the real Kate Jackson any more. It was only looking at the photos and reading the minutiae of her life that made her realise how far away she was from her true self.

Now, she was a construct. A carefully styled creation who did and said exactly what she ought, at work, in her social life and in her love life – not that she had much time for the latter. When had she lost her own voice? It wasn't that she didn't have opinions; it was that she only had the opinions she needed to have in the circles she moved in. Opinions which were totally irrelevant in Pennfleet. Who here cared about the best new club or restaurant in Manhattan, or who did the best blow dry, or which was the most efficient cab service?

She might be a big noise in her own world, but her clout didn't travel. And there were hundreds of other girls like her in New York: smart, well dressed, well connected, upwardly mobile. They were all after the same jobs, the same men, and the same apartments. They wore the same clothes and had the same hair-dos. Sitting amongst the detritus of her past, Kate realised she had become a clone. Putting that dress on for the funeral had been like slipping back into her own skin.

She shook herself out of her reverie. She was never going to get the job done if she drifted off into self-indulgent navel-gazing. Maybe the personal stuff was holding her up.

In a cupboard, she found piles of her old school books. She steeled herself. They were of no use: ancient drawings of oxbow lakes and pages of quadratic equations. Anyway, they were almost indecipherable, the covers faded orange and red and green. Any knowledge she needed now was either in her head or available on the internet at the touch of a button. She slid them into the bin bag. They landed with a thump at the bottom, more than ten years of education. She felt a sense of achievement when she saw the space on the shelf. She was starting to make progress.

From her wardrobe, she saved a couple of cuddly jumpers, the velvet dress, a red silk skirt shot through with silver thread and her old Paddington duffle coat. The rest she put into the washing machine with a load of fabric conditioner. She would dry it over the Aga and fold it all neatly, to take to the charity shop.

She put all the letters and photos in a box, to sort through at the kitchen table with a glass of wine.

Then she looked at her books, and her heart sank again. How could she get rid of them? Her complete set of Famous Five adventures? Her Daphne du Maurier collection? The Jilly Coopers? She ran her fingers along the spines, and she could feel the words inside, the characters, their escapades – the escapades she had felt a part of.

It would be crazy to have them shipped to New York. There was no room, amidst the few carefully selected *New York Times* bestsellers. These battered and faded volumes would have no place in her magazine-perfect living space.

Yet these books had contributed far more to who she was than anything she read now. They had given her infinite pleasure. She put out a hand and stopped. If she pulled one out she would be lost for the rest of the day.

She would leave the decision for now. Maybe she could cherry pick? But how could you choose between *The Island of Adventure* and *Rebecca*? Or *Frenchman's Creek* and *Riders*? She decided she would go and sort through the kitchen. The paraphernalia in there would be less emotive. She could be hard-nosed about a cheese grater or a can-opener.

Of course, the kitchen wasn't that easy either. It was even more a part of her past than her bedroom, because she had shared everything in it with her parents. Kate found it eviscerating, sifting through all the long-forgotten memories. It wasn't the big things; it was the little ones. Her mother's pie funnel – the shiny blackbird with the yellow beak that had always peeped out from the middle of the pastry. Karen could taste the pastry now, crumbly and buttery against the sharp tang of apple. Although she never baked, she slipped the funnel in her bag to take home. It seemed to represent all the things she wanted to remember from her childhood.

She felt exhausted. It was only five o'clock, but she honestly didn't think she could carry on. What could she do instead? She didn't know anyone to go out for a drink with – Debbie might, she supposed, but she had already taken up enough of her time. She couldn't bear the thought of sitting in the living room on her own, watching television. It was horrible. Half of her wanted to flee. The other half never wanted to leave. She had never felt so conflicted in her life. Maybe she should just go to bed. She could take two pills – sleep round the clock. She'd feel better the next morning. She was alarmed to find the temptation was greater than she would have thought possible. Lovely, lovely dream-free oblivion.

Then she chastised herself. The answer didn't lie in knocking herself out. When had she started thinking that was a solution? Had it become a habit? Her way of running away from things she didn't like? Shocked, she picked up her mother's handbag, where it was hanging on the back of a kitchen chair. She held it in her hands. It was beige, with a long strap, bulging and scuffed. A market purchase, not even leather, bought entirely for its practicality. She'd had it for as long as Kate could remember. One Christmas, she had given her mother one of the bags that had been left over from a launch. Each guest had received one: a suede hobo bag, fluid and soft, in pale grey. It was still in its special linen handbag bag. It wasn't that her mother hadn't appreciated it – she had – but she was terrified of it.

'Just use it, Mum,' insisted Kate. 'It's designed to be used, and thrown around, and filled up with stuff. You don't have to treat it like china.'

Joy had stroked the suede in wonder. 'It's absolutely beautiful, darling. Thank you so much.'

But the bag had never seen the light of day. And Joy had continued to lug around this abomination that offended all Kate's sensibilities. The stitching on the strap was unravelled. The zip had long stuck. If anything was destined for the bin, it was this. Yet Kate knew she wouldn't be able to throw it away. Inside it was Joy's life.

She opened it wide.

Her purse, of course – this had been another present

from Kate, but one Joy had felt she could cope with. It was misshapen and bulging with change. Two ten-pound notes and a fiver. Her debit card – Joy would never have a credit card; she just wouldn't see the point. And a clutch of receipts.

A cellophane packet of Kleenex and a half-eaten tube of Soothers – she must have had a cold recently. A tiny diary, its pages tissue thin: Kate put it to one side to look at later. A see-through rain-hood. A pink plastic comb, several of the tines missing. A lipstick with quarter of an inch of indeterminate pink. Three charity Biros. A mini torch. A packet of peanuts, of the type that hung behind pub bars on a cardboard holder. A spare set of house keys on a knitted frog key ring – she tried to imagine her mother buying it, but she couldn't. Had it been a present? A secret Santa from the nursing staff?

A bottle of perfume. Kate took off the lid and inhaled the spirit of her mother – a dense, powdery scent that made every nerve in her body tingle with nostalgia. It was as if she was in the room with her.

Kate put the bottle down on the kitchen table sharply. She wasn't sure if she could carry on. Memories and hopelessness and grief and love and regret all tumbled about inside her on spin cycle. Her heart felt sick; her stomach felt hollow. She wanted to walk out of the door and walk back in again to find her mother filling the kettle, the wireless on, a packet of Jaffa Cakes on the table, spuds waiting to be peeled in the sink, a casserole bubbling away in the Aga. Her dad ambling through in his overalls, hair wild.

She drew the curtains to shut out the night and turned on the lamp, because the strip light was too bright. Then she dropped everything except the purse, the spare house keys and the diary into the bin. She ran her hand around the lining, just to check there wasn't anything precious hiding in the folds.

Her fingers touched on the edge of a piece of paper. She tugged on it, and it slid out from where it had worked itself inside a hole. It was a piece of notepaper folded into three, the creases almost worn through, so often had it been opened and re-folded. It was pale-blue Basildon Bond, and the writing on it was a slanting script, the hand of someone educated and confident.

Straight away she had the feeling this was something she wasn't supposed to read. Without deciphering a single word, she could tell this was an intensely personal missive: for Joy's eyes only. She should throw it straight in the bin along with everything else. What right had she to delve into her mother's private life now she was dead? There was nothing to be gained.

She held it in the tips of her fingers. She breathed in and out while she thought. People in her world never wrote letters. She didn't think she could remember the last time she had got one. Nowadays, people only really wrote letters when they had something very important to say. Something that could not be spoken. And the fact her mother had kept it, and referred to it over and over again, and carried it around in her handbag meant it must be meaningful. And it wasn't from her father: his writing had been almost illegible, black Biro sliding all over the place with malformed letters, even before his mind had started to go.

She sat at the kitchen table for some time, the letter in front of her. In the end, she decided no harm could come from her reading it. She smoothed it open: the paper was soft through over-handling.

My dear Joy,

Writing this letter is either the most brave or most cowardly thing I have ever done. I will never know. All I do know is that I have no choice if I am to live with myself. Please know that I did not reach this decision lightly. It has taken weeks of deliberation and sleepless nights. I have searched desperately for an answer that did not involve heartache, but it seems that is not an option.

My feelings for you have grown to such a magnitude that I do not feel able to see you any longer. I cannot pretend that you are not all I think about. And as long as P is still alive, this is wrong. I cannot betray her, even though she is no longer the person I married, but a shadow, a ghost.

Today she spoke to me, and it was as if that terrible disease had never happened. She asked me to pass the salt. She gave me a smile and held out her hand for the salt cellar, as she has done so many, many times over the years. My heart leapt into my mouth as my eyes met hers, and they twinkled at me – it was my P back again, and for a moment I had hope.

Then she took the salt and sprinkled it all over her food until the cellar was empty. I sat and watched in hopeless despair. I couldn't bring myself to stop her. In the end, I had to take the plate away before she began to eat, and replaced it with a fresh one.

She is still my wife. I cannot betray her with

another woman. It would not be fair on either of you. It would be a half-relationship, cursed from the beginning, unable to take a natural course or flourish. It would run on guilt, not love.

And so, my Joy, I have to step away. I have valued our time together so much. I have valued your wisdom in helping me find ways to cope with this burden. I value the hope you have given me. Most of all, I value the laughter you have given me: there has been little to laugh about over the last few years, but you made me forget that, just for a moment.

Who knows what the next years will bring? I dread it, but I must bear it. It will be a lonely journey, but it is my duty to care for the woman I love, the woman I married, even if she is no longer really there. I know you understand, because we have spoken about it so many times. And that is why I know you will understand my decision.

I shall think of you often, dear Joy. Please don't think me a coward. I am doing what I hope is the right thing.

With all my love,

R

Kate put the letter down on the kitchen table.

Somewhere, there was a man who loved her mother. A man who, reading between the lines, was married to a woman who suffered the same condition Kate's father had. A man whose loyalty had been tested to its limits.

A man who possibly didn't know her mother was dead.

There was no date on the letter. No address. No accompanying envelope with a helpful postmark. No way of telling how long it had been in her mother's bag – days, weeks, years? And of all the initials for it to be signed with, R must be pretty common. Roger? Richard? Ralph?

She wondered if her mother had ever replied to the letter. It must have meant a lot to her – it had clearly been read a hundred times. Had she sat at this very table and composed an answer? And if so, was it robust and re-assuring? Or crushed and bitter? Kate assumed the former, because her mother had always been such a positive force, yet who knew how she might have felt underneath?

Who was he? Where did he live? And what should she do?

18

Vanessa was stretched out on the sofa in the drawing room. Somehow going back to actual bed felt wrong. A bit sluttish. And she suspected that if she got back under the covers she wouldn't get out again. She was drained from the emotion of the last twenty-four hours and all the tension, not to mention the surfeit of alcohol. So she wrapped herself up in a chenille throw, rested her head on a cushion and fell asleep within moments.

She was awoken by a loud rapping, and realised she had been out cold for three hours. She jumped to her feet and ran to the front door, flinging it open.

There she was. Her mother. Squirrel. In her uniform of jeans, loafers and cashmere cardigan, her ash-blonde hair in a smooth bob, pearls in her ears, her handbag hooked over one arm, a Waitrose carrier bag in the other.

As soon as she saw her, Vanessa knew it was going to be all right. Squirrel would tell her how to feel and what to do. How to manage the rest of her life. She didn't know what to say, though.

'You didn't need to bring anything,' said Vanessa eventually, pointing to the carrier. 'There's heaps to eat here.'

'I didn't fancy eating leftover funeral food.'

Squirrel looked at her daughter, dropped the bag and

put her arms round her. Vanessa breathed in Caleche. The smell of her childhood. The last smell before she went to sleep, after Squirrel had kissed her goodnight.

'Are you OK?'

Vanessa held on to her mother. 'I think so. I don't know. To be honest, I'm not feeling much at all.'

'Come on.' Squirrel scooped up her things and walked inside. 'Tea by the fire. I know it's not that cold yet, but there's nothing that can't be made better by a proper log fire.'

Vanessa put some logs in the grate in the drawing room, along with some kindling, and set them alight, crossing her fingers. Spencer had been military about fire building. No one else had ever been allowed near it. But she had watched him so many times she thought she knew the rudiments, and soon the logs were blazing away. And Squirrel was right. The fire changed the atmosphere in the room completely, melting away the stiff formality of the drawing room and softening its harsh edges. Vanessa drew the curtains against the dusk, and brought in tea and shortbread.

'I am sorry,' Squirrel told her. 'Truly. It must have been an awful shock.'

Vanessa put the tray down on the smoked-glass coffee table that was adept at catching your shins if you weren't careful where you walked.

'I don't think it's really hit me yet. It all happened so quickly. And what with all the funeral arrangements, and people everywhere, it's been a roller coaster. I suppose it will sink in now.'

'You are going to be fine.' Squirrel fixed her with one

of her no-nonsense looks. 'At least, I presume so. How did he leave you?'

Vanessa laughed. Her mother was incorrigible. No doubt she would have been speculating all the way down the motorway. 'You want to know how much I'm worth?'

Squirrel looked affronted. 'Not how much, no. It's none of my business. But I want to know you're secure.'

'I don't know, exactly. I'm seeing the solicitor on Monday. He's coming here.'

Squirrel made a face. 'I hope that doesn't mean bad news. It's never good when solicitors come to you.'

'Mummy, Spencer was difficult, I know that. But I don't think he'd see me starve. I was his wife.'

One eyebrow went up. 'There might be skeletons.'

Vanessa looked at the flames dancing in the fire. She needed to explain. She didn't want her mother to think she was weak. Or useless. Or that Spencer had been a complete villain.

'We didn't have a bad life, you know. You must understand that. In a funny sort of way we rubbed along together. I wasn't unhappy.'

Squirrel pursed her lips.

'I think you could have been happier. Much happier.'

'We'll never know, will we?'

'I'm sorry if I withdrew. It was very painful for me to watch. That's all. Because I wanted better for you...' She cleared her throat. 'I know about living with someone who doesn't bring out the best in you.'

'I know, I know.'

Vanessa hated talking about their rift. It had been painful and unsettling, but she'd been left with little choice. Or so she had felt at the time. It hadn't been possible to

177

have Squirrel and Spencer in her life, because they were both stubborn and strong and uncompromising. Which presumably made her weak.

She felt herself crumpling. She'd held it together over the past few days, but now she felt exhausted. Tears welled up, as if she was six again, but she did nothing to stop them. She needed to cry. She allowed herself to cry. After all, her mother was here to comfort her. She let it all go, in one luxurious burst of emotion, her shoulders shaking as she sobbed. And Squirrel jumped up and rushed over to hold her, pulling her into her embrace.

'You cry,' said Squirrel. 'You cry, my darling.'

Vanessa squeezed her tight, her infuriating, interfering, impossible mother, who understood her better than anyone, and who would be there for her longer than anyone.

'It's OK,' said Squirrel. 'Honestly. It will be OK.'

'I know,' Vanessa sniffled into her mother's décolletage. 'It's just sad, that's all, that we never all worked out how to get along. Honestly, Mum. He was never . . . unkind. I suppose we didn't have much in common, that's all. We never argued. Not like—'

Squirrel winced. Vanessa wiped the tears off her face. She needed to probe her mother. She wanted to know the truth. Now seemed the right time to ask.

'Mum, what happened, exactly? With you and . . .'

She never knew what to call him, the man she never saw. Dad, Daddy. My father. One day he had been there, the next he had gone, and she had never seen him again.

Squirrel seemed to deflate in front of her. Squirrel, who never let anyone get the better of her, and who was scared of nothing.

'Your father was absolutely the love of my life. And if we hadn't had you girls, it would have been perfect. I could have been the woman he needed me to be. He craved attention, you see, and when you two came along I just didn't have enough left for him. I had to make a choice. And I made the one I wanted to make, because you were more precious to me than anything or anyone. You needed me more. I knew he would find somebody else.' Her normally vivacious face was etched with sadness. 'And if he didn't... he always had the drink to keep him company.'

'Oh, Mum...' Vanessa's heart went out to her mother. In that short speech, Vanessa realised just how much Squirrel had sacrificed, and how difficult it must have been. 'He was an alcoholic, wasn't he?'

'Of the most glamorous, disarmingly charming variety. The life and soul of the party, even if he was the only one at it.'

'You poor thing.'

'No. Because I've got you girls. And I had the best of him. Of course it was jolly sad he couldn't carry on being the best he could be, but he was extraordinarily selfish.'

'He doesn't sound very nice.'

'Oh darling – he was *very* nice. Wonderful, in fact. But...'

Squirrel gave a hopeless shrug.

'I always blamed myself when you married Spencer. I convinced myself you were looking for a father figure. Although less like your father he couldn't have been. You found someone who needed nothing from you. Someone who was quite self-sufficient.'

'Mum, that's not really true.'

179

'I can't see what you saw in him.'

'He was dynamic. He was a doer. He had amazing energy. He never took no for an answer. He knew what he wanted and he got it.' Something dawned on Vanessa. 'Like you, Mum. Actually.'

Squirrel glared at her. 'Never compare me to that man.'

'No. No. I know. Sorry. I didn't mean—'

Her mother gave a wave of her hand.

'What a pair we are. Both on our own now. I suspect it's too late for me—'

'Rubbish. Look at you. You're amazing. You could still have anyone you wanted.'

Squirrel played with the rings on her hand, and Vanessa realised she still wore her wedding band, that she'd never taken it off.

'There was only ever one man I wanted,' said Squirrel. 'But this isn't about me. It's about you. And you have all the time in the world to find the right person.' She grinned. 'I'm not going to let you make another mistake.'

Vanessa tutted. 'Mum, Spencer wasn't a mistake. And if I make any more, that's my business.'

'You must be careful. There'll be plenty of gold-diggers out there.'

Vanessa had to get up and walk away.

'I'm going to make more tea.'

She was trying not to laugh again. What on earth would her mother say if she knew about last night? She would be horrified. It was so tempting to tell her. It would distract her from the Spencer issue. Squirrel wouldn't think it was funny, though. She'd probably have Nathan locked up.

At the thought of him, Vanessa felt her stomach dip, as if she was in a plane hitting slight turbulence.

She looked at her phone.

No text.

It had been four hours.

She filled the kettle, frustrated. She knew the signal was bad in Pennfleet, but Nathan was local. He'd know where to get one if he wanted to reply. But then, what would he reply? She'd texted him to say thank you. Maybe he'd think that was that? Maybe he didn't think he needed to respond?

Of course he wouldn't respond. He was probably just getting on with his life. She deleted his number, crumpled up the leaflet and put it in the bin.

19

Kate ended her day with her teeth gritty with dust, her hair matted, her skin grimy. She couldn't remember the last time she had felt so grubby, but the recesses of the kitchen had been thick with grime. She had been in the far corner of cupboards, pulling out ancient tins and jars. Long-forgotten spices that had lost their flavour; packets of rice and pasta way past their best. She had decided to throw every food item away without even referring to its best-before date: there were three bin bags bulging with detritus. She would have to drive to the recycling centre the next day to get rid of it.

And all the time she thought about the letter she had found. In the back of her mind, she wondered if she might find the answer to who had written it elsewhere in the house, but she didn't yet have the strength to investigate. Her mother's handbag had been eviscerating enough. To enter her mother's bedroom was going to take even more courage. That was why she was concentrating her efforts on the kitchen.

At eight, she admitted defeat and ran a bath. Even the bathroom was a crucible of memories. She lay in the water, wondering how many times she had been in this tub as she grew up. She imagined her mum supporting

182

her as a baby, swooshing her up and down in the water. She remembered locking herself in for hours as a teenager, experimenting with hair dye and leg shaving and eyebrow plucking. She remembered the smell of her father's shaving foam lingering in the sink, flecks of his stubble on the porcelain. The Bromley lemon soap in the soap dish that her mother always got for Christmas and which lasted for months, because she only used it on special occasions and no one else touched it. The towels were the same as they had been for as long as she could remember – striped and rough and never quite big enough, in total contrast to the soft white bath-sheets she had in New York.

She climbed out and dried herself and pulled on her nightdress. She felt utterly exhausted, even though by her body clock it was still only mid-afternoon. She went through her bedtime ritual – teeth, face cream – and was about to automatically take her sleeping tablet when she stopped.

Now she was away from her routine, now she was in a different environment, she had the chance to analyse her habit. The words of the doctor came back to her. She had respected Dr Webster for years, and recalled her concern that she'd become dependent.

And of course, it *was* ridiculous. When had she lost the ability to do something as simple as sleep? Her whole lifestyle seemed laughable, but surely not being able to sleep was more than laughable. It was worrying.

It had been Carlos who suggested them, when she revealed she was sleeping badly. He'd recommended his mother's doctor. And it had just been so easy to become reliant. Her life was so hectic and exhausting, and not to have to worry about whether she could get to sleep or not was yet another luxury she could afford.

But here, back in her hometown, that luxury seemed like an affectation. She wasn't a neurotic, or even particularly insomniac under normal circumstances. And her problems weren't real ones. Her stress was manufactured, mostly by Carlos, ironically, who liked to make a drama out of a crisis where possible. It was something he had got from his high-octane family, particularly his mother and sisters, who loved a scene. The tiniest little hitch could become a source of major panic. Kate had witnessed their histrionics unfold with a fascinated horror on more than one occasion: Carlos wasn't one to keep his private life to himself.

She thought of Debbie and Scott, in their tiny house, with their four children, struggling to keep body and soul together in difficult economic circumstances – now *that* was stress. Yet they seemed happy enough with their lot. There hadn't been any hint of complaint. They were stoic, and got on with it, without creating a fuss.

How had she become so detached from reality? She was behaving like a princess. She didn't need bloody sleeping tablets. She tossed the packet in one of the bin liners. If she couldn't get a night's sleep without pharmaceutical assistance, she really had lost the plot. She imagined what her mother would have to say. Joy would prescribe fresh air and a milky drink.

She made herself a cup of cocoa and drank it at the kitchen table, re-reading the letter she had found, mulling over the identity of the man who had written it. The letter was written from the heart, clearly a warm heart. And suddenly, she remembered the phone call of the night before. Had that been him? The mysterious R. His tone had been familiar but tentative. It would certainly explain why he had hung up when she identified herself.

It also meant he had no idea her mother was dead. Kate folded the letter back up. She would start to look for clues as to his identity tomorrow. She was too tired now. She was going to go to bed. Have her first night of sleep without a pill. She was determined she could do it.

She climbed the stairs and came to a halt outside her mother's room. She still hadn't found the courage to go in. She wasn't sure what she was scared of. She didn't really associate her mother with her bedroom. The kitchen had been Joy's domain, the place where Kate always imagined her. But a bedroom was personal, somehow. Possibly the place where a person was most vulnerable; where they allowed their fears and worries in.

And possibly the place she might discover the identity of the letter writer.

Cautious, she opened the door. She slid her hand onto the wall and switched on the light. The light bulb was frustratingly dim, throwing tenebrous shapes into the corners. For a moment she felt afraid, as if something was lurking in those shadows, as if the room might be harbouring a ghost, but Kate wasn't really a fanciful type and her mother certainly wouldn't come back to haunt her.

The bed was neatly made, the green sateen eiderdown smooth and wrinkle-free. There was just one pillow in the centre, and two patchwork cushions neatly placed either side. Kate caught her breath. She had made the cushions at school, one for each parent one Christmas, when she was about eleven. They were hideous, made from mismatched scraps of fabric, with no thought for tone or colour. Yet here they still were, adorning the bed.

In that moment, Kate hated herself. She knew she would never give something like those cushions house room, because they were ugly and badly made and didn't go with anything.

Her parents had loved them, because she had made them, and they had cherished them. Her wonderful mum and dad, who thought the world of her, and her ham-fisted Christmas offering.

She lay on the bed, rested her head on her mother's pillow, and pulled one of the cushions into her, hugging it tightly, remembering her excitement as they had each opened their present, and the genuine pleasure and appreciation on their faces. She was never going to experience that any more – the pleasure of giving to someone you loved and knew well, who would appreciate whatever you gave them no matter how awful it was.

She rolled off the bed, scooped up the cushions, and took them into her own bedroom. She hugged them to her and, within minutes, fell asleep.

She woke at half past one, heart pounding, mouth dry. She was absolutely wide awake. Her mind was racing, a million and one thoughts tearing about like greyhounds let loose on a track. Worry made her guts churn. How was she going to clear out the house in time? How on earth had she been so stupid as to hang up on Carlos? He was an impulsive man. He might well sack her. How could she have thought herself irreplaceable? She couldn't afford to lose her job, not with her lifestyle. How was she going to juggle sorting things out in Pennfleet and placating Carlos? Should she call him now? Apologise? Start sending him through some ideas?

And who was her mother's mysterious letter from? What should she do about it? What did it mean?

Panic rose up in her and she started to hyperventilate. Her palms were sweating. The more she tried to clear her mind, the more cluttered it became. She couldn't focus or reason with herself. She lay for nearly two hours, checking her phone every two minutes. The pillow felt hot; even her hair hurt, her skin itched. She wanted to climb out of her body. It was torture. She tried some breathing exercises she'd been taught in yoga, but they were useless. Anxieties competed with each other in her brain, jostling for pole position. She couldn't work out which was her biggest problem, or how to solve any of them. They accumulated and multiplied, taunting her. *You thought you were so clever*, they seemed to say. *But we're going to get you.*

In the end, she went downstairs, dug about in the bin, found her sleeping pills and, in a state of panic that one wouldn't be enough, took two.

Sweet oblivion.

20

Daisy was meeting Oscar at his house before they went out for the evening. She was nervous, but as soon as she stepped inside she felt OK.

It was funny, she thought, how you could feel at home straight away in some people's houses, but not in others. Some reached out and hugged you and drew you in, and Oscar's was one of them.

There was an energy in it, a joy, that she found comforting. It wasn't even a particularly nice house. It was an ordinary semi on the outskirts of town that looked like nothing from the outside: UPVC windows and pebble-dash, like all the others on the road. But inside, it was a riot of colour and noise and laughter: a swirl of sensory chaos, ruled over by Oscar's mother Alexa.

As Daisy looked further she realised there was order underneath the chaos. There was just so much of everything. Books galore – towering piles of them. Pictures, paintings, postcards, everywhere, in a random display that somehow looked thought-through. Candles, lanterns, ornaments on every shelf and surface. It even smelled wonderful, of bread baking, a citrusy scented candle, wood-smoke from the fire, Alexa's perfume, mysterious and exotic. It was an Aladdin's cave, the walls painted deep coral, the curtains floor-length gold brocade with tasselled tie-backs, the wooden floorboards painted in black and white stripes. It was dramatic and bold and theatrical.

Oscar was half embarrassed, half proud of his home. He had an easy relationship with his younger siblings – three of them, the youngest only six – and was obviously protective of his mum, whom he towered over.

'This is my mum,' he told Daisy. 'Alexa. Mum, this is Daisy.'

'It's lovely to meet you.' Alexa gave her a hug, a proper one, not a polite one. She was a tiny doll, with porcelain skin and a shiny cap of black hair and a button of a mouth painted deep pink. She wore a denim mini-skirt, tights with roses embroidered on them and a pale-blue cardigan with mismatched buttons. She moved with purpose, and the noise and the chaos didn't seem to faze her in the least. Daisy thought she looked about sixteen, but of course she wasn't – she was probably only a bit younger than her own mum had been. 'You'd both better have something to eat before you go out.'

'Mum!' Oscar rolled his eyes. 'She's such a feeder.'

Alexa cut big chunks from a loaf of homemade challah for them to dip into a bowl of baba ghanoush.

'It looks awful but it tastes great,' she assured Daisy. 'And you both need something to line your stomachs.'

'You say that like we're going to go on a bender,' said Oscar.

'I know what that cheap cider's like,' teased Alexa. 'You'll thank me later.'

They devoured the soft, sweet bread, and the aubergine

dip with its kick of cumin and coriander and garlic and lemon.

'Dad makes this,' Daisy told her, 'but it's not as good as yours. Don't ever tell him I said so, though.'

Sam took great pride in his cooking. Not in a horrible competitive way – he just wanted everything to be as good as it could be. When he cooked something, he would grill people about what they thought and how it could be better. They teased him about it incessantly.

'It's only because I care so much!' he would protest.

When it was time to go to the Neptune, Daisy didn't really want to go. She would have much preferred to stay in and watch the telly, snuggled up on the sofa eating the Thai noodles Alexa was cooking for the others. If she was honest, a little bit of her was scared about being alone with Oscar, in case they turned out to have nothing in common. In case he thought she was boring. He seemed to be really easy-going and quite kind, but you didn't end up being that cool, looking that amazing, coming from a family like that, and not have expectations.

Oscar took her hand as they walked from his house down the hill towards the high street, and she felt a bolt of pride zip through her. She felt ten feet tall, walking out with this beautiful boy, and she wished more than anything that her mother could see them.

When her mum had died, she had thought for a long time that life was just to be endured, and not enjoyed. Moving to Pennfleet had been good, because it gave them all something else to think about, and it was easier to live in a house where there were no memories. Not that Daisy wanted to forget her mum, but every time she went into the kitchen in their old house, she couldn't ignore the fact her mum wasn't there. She expected to see her every time. The house in Pennfleet was different, though. Mum's presence didn't linger there – not that she'd been forgotten, of course not. It was just . . . easier. Easier to live without her ghost.

They walked up the high street, which felt so different at night, the lights inside the bars and restaurants twinkling a welcome. It was colder than she'd thought it would be when she'd chosen her outfit: only jeans, and her favourite jumper with the stars on, and a long red scarf her mum had given her wound round her neck. It was a sort of talisman, and it made her feel safe.

'Here – have my jacket,' Oscar said, and even though she protested he shrugged it off. As he slipped it over her shoulders, she felt the weight of the leather, heavy and warm. It smelled of him – coconut shampoo and Oscar – and in that moment she felt something change inside her, a sense that everything was going to be all right.

He smiled down at her. 'If the band's rubbish,' he said, 'we can go back to mine and play backgammon.'

'Backgammon?' That wasn't what Daisy had expected. 'But I don't know how to play.'

'Don't worry. I'll teach you. You can't be in our family and not play backgammon. We're backgammon fiends.'

In our family. He said *in our family*. What a lovely thing to say. And she wanted to be in his family. Not to replace hers, of course not, but because she felt as if she belonged.

They reached the pub. Oscar opened the door for her and they were hit with a rush of heat and noise. He put an arm round her shoulder as they walked in. People looked over at them and she could see admiration in their eyes.

There were people from school, and people she recognised from the café and the yacht club and around the town. Everyone said hello, even people she didn't really know. She felt like a queen. A queen for the night.

At home, Sam was sitting on the sofa flipping through the channels, searching for something that would take his mind off Daisy. Common sense told him she would be absolutely fine. His imagination said otherwise: images of crack dens and people throwing up in gutters and jealous drunk girls throwing punches played out in his mind. He knew he was being ridiculous, but he wished more than anything Louise was next to him, telling him not to worry, that Daisy was nearly a grown-up, that statistically she was far more likely to have a lovely night out than end up in a sex-trafficking ring.

Should he have vetted Oscar before letting her out with him? The fact his father was in prison rang warning bells in his mind, and then he told himself crossly that Oscar shouldn't be tarred with the same brush as his dad. He was probably a perfectly nice boy. He trusted Daisy's judgement. He had to, otherwise he would go mad. And she was only out in Pennfleet, where everything was in walking distance. He didn't like to think how he would be feeling if she had been out in London.

He looked over at Jim, who was engrossed in something on his iPad, frowning as he pored over whatever it was he was reading.

'What's so fascinating?' asked Sam.

'Hot and Horny Housewives,' replied Jim, without missing a beat.

'Wonderful,' said Sam. Damn, he loved his son. His funny, clever, geeky, smart-arse son.

Eventually he settled on watching *True Detective* on Netflix, because he hadn't got round to it yet and everyone said it was great, and before long he was totally absorbed.

Sam was still up, pretending not to be waiting for Daisy when she came in at midnight. He was grateful to her for being on time. And for not being drunk, or reeking of smoke, or worse. She came and sat next to him on the sofa, and rested against him, her legs curled up beneath her.

'Good time?' he asked. Cautious, because you never knew with teenagers, if asking was the right thing to do. Sometimes they just turned on you.

'Dad,' she said, 'I had the most brilliant night. I don't think it could get any better. He gave me his jacket, because I was cold, and he wouldn't let me pay for any drinks, and he walked me home.'

'Quite right too,' said Sam.

Daisy looked at him. 'Really,' she said. 'You have no idea. Most boys are just out for one thing, and don't give you anything in return.'

Sam frowned. 'In return for what?'

Daisy rolled her eyes. 'Don't worry. I don't mean that it was a deal. He was a perfect gentleman.'

What was that code for? Sam couldn't bring himself to ask. But actually, he didn't care what had gone on, because Daisy looked so very happy, and he couldn't ask for more than that. Woe betide Oscar, though, if he ever made his daughter unhappy.

'And his house is amazing,' said Daisy. 'His family are

crazy mad. They play *backgammon*.' She looked at him, mystified.

For some reason this made Sam relax. A family who played backgammon couldn't be all bad.

Daisy lay on her bed later, staring at the ceiling and smiling, reliving every moment of the evening.

She loved her room, tucked up in the eaves. It was painted in turquoise and white, and she had a double bed with a driftwood headboard and a goose-down quilt that hugged her at night. There was a built-in wardrobe and she was doing her best to keep her clothes neatly folded or hung, so she knew where everything was, though sometimes it got a bit messy.

Jim bounded in, wearing his Marvel comic pyjamas and waving his iPad.

'Guess what?' he said in a stage whisper. 'Twenty-seven likes and twelve messages.'

Daisy sat up. 'What?'

'Dad! On the dating site. They're all over him.'

Daisy grabbed the iPad and looked at her father's profile. Her mouth dropped open. 'Oh my God,' she said. 'Dad broke the internet.' She lay back, laughing, waving her legs in the air with glee.

'Come on,' said Jim. 'Let's go through them. Marks out of ten. Anything less than an eight gets binned.'

They sat on the bed, the two of them, scrolling carefully through the profiles.

'Anyone with rubbish grammar – bin,' said Daisy.

'Or too many emoticons.'

'Or women with purple hair and crazy glasses.'

'Where are we on tattoos?'

'Tattoos can go either way. We'll assess them individually.'

'Anyone holding a pint of Carlsberg – bin.'

'Anyone with more than one cat.'

They started to feel disheartened. There was something wrong with each one. Some were too pushy, some just dull and boring. Others came across as so perfect they were clearly lying.

'That photo is so Photoshopped,' said Daisy.

Jim sighed.

'Let's face it. There is no one good enough for Dad. No one who lives up to Mum.'

'Maybe we're missing something. Maybe we need to be less picky.'

'You're kidding? *Less* picky? Dad deserves the best.'

'Let's go through the ones who've just joined.'

Jim clicked through the latest additions. There was still no one. Too geeky, too straight, too wacky, too tarty. It seemed impossible.

And then another profile came up, and Daisy took a breath in, and Jim said, 'She looks nice.'

'Oh my God,' said Daisy. 'It's Oscar's mum. It's Alexa!'

'No way!'

The two of them read her profile. It was sweet and funny and a bit quirky, but very down to earth.

'She sounds really lovely.'

'She *is* really lovely,' said Daisy. 'And get this – her baba ghanoush is better than Dad's.'

'He won't like that.'

'He doesn't need to know.'

'So what do we do now? Message her pretending to be him?'

'I don't know.' Daisy frowned. 'It seems a bit wrong. Especially as I've met her. It's a bit stalky-creepy.'

Jim nodded his agreement. 'I'm starting to think this whole idea was a bit wrong.'

The two of them stared down at the photo. Alexa smiled up at them, her eyes twinkling with warmth.

'So . . . why don't we just set them up? You tell Alexa Dad wants to meet her, and then tell Dad she wants to meet him. In a sort of our-kids-are-going-out-so-let's-get-to-know-each-other way.'

Daisy thought it through. 'Do you think it would work?'

'Yes! You tell her Dad's really protective. And tell him Oscar's mum wants to reassure you he's OK. Parents love that kind of stuff.' Jim was wise for his years.

'OK,' said Daisy. 'They could just go for a drink.'

'And if they work out they've been set up, it doesn't really matter.'

'He'll like her. He will definitely like her. She's cool, but not up herself.'

'And surely she'll like Dad? Everyone likes Dad.'

Daisy thought for a moment. 'What if I split up with Oscar?'

'Never mind that. What if they end up getting married and Oscar ends up as your step-brother?'

'Nooooo!'

The two of them fell about laughing.

Then Daisy sat up.

'I'm going to do it,' said Daisy. 'It could work.'

Jim suddenly looked worried. 'Do you think Mum would think we're betraying her?'

Up to now, it had been a bit of a game to him. He

spent so much of his life online, it hadn't seemed real. But suddenly the idea of his dad with another person was an actual possibility, not just a cyber-experiment.

'No,' said Daisy. 'I really don't. I think she would think it was brilliant. And I think she would like Alexa. So it's all good.'

Jim nodded, trying to look convinced. Daisy's heart went out to him. He could be a nuisance, her little brother. And he tried so hard to be cool and clever and funny, and he was a lot of the time, but he was still a little boy who had lost his mum. So she gave him a giant hug, and for once he didn't wriggle away.

Whatever happened, she thought, they would always have each other.

21

Mary Mac always felt unsettled on Sundays. Now-adays, they were so very far away from what they had once been. When the children were smaller, when Kenny had been in work, Sundays had been a joy. Picnics on the beach in the summer – she had packed up the cool box with hard-boiled eggs and ham sandwiches and squash, and they had spent all day at the little cove that was really only known to locals, because the path was not only well hidden but difficult to navigate. There she would watch the boys sprout freckles and splash in the waves, year after year growing bigger and stronger and more handsome. In the winter there would be walks, and a stop off at the pub, where Kenny treated them all to drinks and crisps. Or they would go into Shoredown, to the cinema. Proper old-fashioned family fun.

That was a distant memory. Now, she cooked lunch for the three of them: herself and Kenny and Ruthie. It was the same every week: beef and Yorkshires, carrots, peas, gravy, crumble, custard. She had stopped making the crumble herself. She bought one from the supermarket, with ready-made custard, because she didn't see the point in bothering. Once, she had loved providing for her family and hadn't considered it slaving over a hot stove one bit. In those days, Kenny had helped – peeling spuds or stringing beans, coring apples and doing the washing up afterwards.

Now, he worked his way silently through it all and Mary had no way of knowing if it was to his satisfaction. She was never left in any doubt that it wasn't to Ruthie's, who chewed, coughed, spat things out and left them ostentatiously on the side of her plate, pushing it away before everything was finished with a look that said 'How can I be expected to eat that?' Mary never rose to the implied criticism. She cleared away without a word and brought in the pudding.

She plucked up the courage to make her suggestion as they finished their crumble. Mary put down her spoon.

'I think we should go for a walk,' she said to Kenny, with a bright smile. 'It's a lovely autumn day. The leaves are starting to turn.'

She was met with a blank stare.

'It's a bit bloody parky,' said Kenny. He was in his old grey jogging bottoms and a yacht club polo shirt, from the days when he and the boys used to sail. He'd long given it up, though.

He'd given everything up.

'No, it's not. Not once you get a pace up. I just thought it would make a nice change. I could do with some fresh air.' She could see Kenny was wavering. 'Come on. We could stop for a cup of tea at that new café on the way back. You should see the cakes in the window.'

Vanessa bought stuff in there at the weekends when Mary wasn't around. Though sometimes she wished she did work weekends. At least they appreciated her at Pennfleet House.

Kenny looked at his watch, as if it might provide him with an excuse. It didn't.

'Maybe.'

'What about me?' demanded Ruthie. 'You can't just bugger off and leave me.'

'Why not? If you don't want to come. And you've got your soap.' Mary kept her tone mild.

'It's not a question of not wanting to, is it? I can't. Not with my legs.'

Kenny looked at his mother.

'The exercise would do you good, Mum. You should get out more. You sit in that chair all day. It can't be healthy.'

Any other day Mary would have cheered at Kenny trying to shift his mother out of her torpor, but today the last thing she wanted was Ruthie tagging along.

'I am disabled,' said Ruthie. Her tone was deadly.

'You're not, though, are you?' said Kenny. 'Not officially. That's just what you've decided. And I think perhaps if you were a bit more positive—'

Mary had no idea where he was getting his courage from, but his timing couldn't be worse.

'You're accusing me of lying.' Ruthie swelled with outrage. 'Your own mother.'

Kenny sighed. 'If you were disabled, you'd be entitled to things. Parking badges. But you're not. And I just think that perhaps if you got some exercise you would feel better.'

Ruthie looked at Kenny, incredulous. 'Tell him, Mary. Would you tell him? I am an *invalid*.'

Mary sighed. There was no point. Yet again, everything was revolving around Ruthie. Her needs, her view of how things should be. And Kenny's intervention was too late. The irony was he should take some of his own advice. He should get out himself. Instead of disappearing into his shed for hours on end, doing goodness knows what. Smoking roll-ups and staring out of the window. She didn't want to nag, because she'd never been a nag, but she hated seeing him disappear into a shadow.

Now, however, she needed to talk to him. She needed her old Kenny back. She needed his support, and his advice, and his strength. She needed the man he had been, not the man he had become. Because she was afraid. Mary had never been afraid before. Even when the boys went to Australia, she took it on the chin.

'Would you come with me, love?' She tried not to sound wheedling.

'I'm not sure I feel like it. Tell you what, you go and I'll do the washing up.'

Mary couldn't protest without making a scene, and she didn't like scenes.

She turned and walked out of the room.

Mary walked out of the back gate, along the road, up the steep steps and onto the footpath that skirted top of the town. It wended its way along the coast, and off it ran smaller paths that led down to the banks of the river and, further along, the seashore. The afternoon was bright and clear, and she could see for miles across the ocean. She breathed in gusts of clean air and felt her hair ruffled by the autumn breeze. She put her head down and marched onwards, setting herself a pace.

She knew Spencer's death had provided her with a distraction. She had told herself that Vanessa needed her, that she didn't have time to deal with her own problems while she was helping with funeral arrangements. It had given her something else to think about. All that catering, all those beds to change, all the running round and looking after the guests. Now it was over, though, she couldn't pretend any more. She had to deal with it.

She had found it while she was in the shower. A lump. What a horrible word that was. Like a thump. The thump of her heart as she'd detected the hardness under her skin, on her right breast. Every day since, she had examined the area and prayed that it had gone away so she didn't have to deal with it. But it was still there. No bigger, she didn't think, but she couldn't be sure. It didn't hurt. It just sat there. Malevolent and smug in its power, knowing that in its two-centimetre diameter it held her future.

She knew she should go to the doctor, but she was too frightened. What if the diagnosis was the worst-case scenario? How would they cope with it? She was the breadwinner, the one who kept the household together. Kenny had already shown he couldn't manage under pressure. As for Ruthie: she couldn't deal with anything that didn't revolve around her. She wouldn't get any support from that corner.

She had to be brave, thought Mary. In any other circumstances, she would have asked Vanessa for advice. But she could hardly heap her problems on her right now. It would be unbelievably selfish. Vanessa needed her more than ever at the moment. So it was up to Mary to find a way through this. She could do it, she thought. She had to. She had no choice.

She would make an appointment, first thing tomorrow.

She knew the worst thing to do would be to ignore it, tempting though it was. She had to be strong.

She felt bleak as she looked out over the open sea. When had life taken a turn and become so difficult, so joyless? She missed her boys more than she could say, and it hurt that they were so far away. She knew they had the chance of a much better life where they were, that there were few opportunities for them in Pennfleet, that raising their families in Australia meant sunshine and solvency. But they'd taken something of her when they left. A little bit of her heart and her soul.

She sighed, stood up, and hunched herself against the wind for the walk home. When she got back the television was on full blast, the table was cleared and the washing up had been done. Ruthie had fallen asleep in her chair, slack-jawed, her breathing stertorous. Kenny was nowhere to be seen. Mary felt weary. All her resolve evaporated, back in the claustrophobic confines. She didn't have the fight.

There was no point in feeling sorry for herself, she decided. She'd have to ask for help. Wasn't that the point of being married?

It was half past ten. Mary switched off her bedside lamp. Kenny was lying in his pyjamas next to her, eyes shut, but she knew full well he wasn't asleep yet. The room was dim with shadow, but she could just make out the shape of him under the bedclothes and see the rise and fall of his chest.

Her heart was pounding, her palms sweating. She could feel the words stuck in her throat. Time and again she tried to push them out, but they wouldn't come. What was she so afraid of? she wondered. Was she scared of Kenny falling apart altogether?

If she didn't speak now she was sentencing herself. Nothing would change. Only she could secure herself her freedom.

'I found a lump.' Her own voice startled her in the darkness.

She could hear Kenny's breathing alter, so she knew he'd heard her. She waited. Eventually he took in a deep breath.

'What sort of lump?'

'Well, I don't know. It's on my . . . you know. My right . . . breast.'

'Oh bloody hell.' He sat up. 'How big is it?'

'Not very.'

There was silence for a moment.

'You need to go to the doctor.'

'I know.' She swallowed. 'But I'm scared.'

Kenny leaned over and snapped on his lamp. He looked terrible. His hair was on end, and the late evening stubble on his chin made his face look grey. They were the same age, but Mary hoped she didn't look as old as he did. She wasn't particularly vain, but it was alarming to think she might look . . . well, haggard. They were both middle-aged, certainly, but Kenny looked like an old man.

'I don't know what to say, love.'

Say something, thought Mary. Or give me a hug. I just need a hug.

'I'll make an appointment,' she managed. 'In the morning.'

'Do you want me to come with you?'

Of course I do, she wanted to scream. Do you think

I want to sit there on my own while the doctor breaks the bad news? Because the chances were it would be. 'It's up to you.'

'Don't you want to be in private?'

'I don't know, really. I don't know what to think.'

She didn't. One minute she could convince herself it was fine; it wouldn't be anything, just a little cyst. And then the next, she had herself dead and buried within three months, riddled with tumours and eaten from the inside out.

Kenny still didn't say much. He turned and touched her on the arm, then took his hand away again, as if whatever she had might be catching. 'You'll be all right,' he said, but he didn't sound at all convincing.

'Yes,' said Mary, thinking she'd have to be. It was her duty to be all right.

Kenny turned off the lamp and lay back down.

'You'll be all right,' he repeated, into the darkness.

Eventually Mary fell asleep, her fears and worries rolling away temporarily.

Kenny stared at the ceiling for hours. He was filled with self-loathing. Self-loathing and fear. He'd been a useless bastard for the past few years. What kind of a man couldn't get a job to keep his wife and family? He was too proud, that was the problem. He'd been a foreman at the boatyard; he'd had responsibility and a good wage. When the yard closed, he couldn't face taking on a lesser job, like a lot of his mates. He'd wanted respect and to be looked up to. Only his stubbornness had backfired and now he was on the scrapheap. He was useless. He was useless and Mary was a saint.

His Mary. His rock. His kind, uncomplaining, patient rock. Only now, he faced the possibility of a future without her. He worried that it was the stress of living with him and having to be the breadwinner that had brought on the lump. He'd read that, sometimes, stress caused cancer. Oh God...

He felt hot with the terror. It was all his fault. He didn't know who to turn to. He couldn't talk to his mum. She'd find some way of turning it on herself. He didn't really have any mates any more, because he'd become a bit of a recluse. He didn't even go to play darts any more on a Thursday, or go fishing. He didn't want to worry the boys, all the way out in Australia – what could they do?

It was up to him. He had to step up. He had to be the man of the house. He had to protect the woman he loved, who had protected him for the last couple of years, even though they never voiced the fact. She was the most selfless person he had ever come across.

Next to him, Mary stirred and gave a little whimper in her sleep. He hoped she wasn't having nightmares. He reached out his hand to find hers. She took it and held it, as tight as tight could be. It was, he realised, the first time they had touched each other for months, and it made his heart heavy with shame. He would hold her hand every night from now on, he vowed.

And he would be the husband she deserved.

22

Kate hoped Dr Webster didn't think she was overly needy when she turned up at the surgery again on Monday morning.

'There's two things,' Kate told her. 'First, I want your advice about coming off the sleeping tablets. What you said really struck a chord. I tried going without one on Saturday night. But it was hopeless. Even though I was exhausted I fell asleep and then I woke up and that was it. I had to take two to get back to sleep.'

Dr Webster looked sympathetic.

'You need to wean yourself off gently. Not just stop. And just now probably isn't the best time to do it, when you're away from home and you've got emotional upset.'

'I can't believe I got so dependent. I didn't realise I couldn't function without them. I'm really not that sort of person. At least, I didn't think I was.'

'It doesn't mean you're any sort of person. It's easily done. That's why I'm not keen on prescribing them for any length of time. I don't want to make any judgements about your doctor . . .'

'Oh, don't worry about judging him. I'm sure he keeps most of Manhattan tranquilised.' Kate thought about his plush waiting room and the groomed women waiting for his attention.

'If I were you I would start cutting the dose gradually. And find other ways to help you relax. Cut out caffeine, definitely. I can give you a link to some helpful articles. It's about breaking the cycle. And it might not be easy. You might like to find a more sympathetic doctor who could help you through it.'

Kate nodded. 'Thank you.' She fiddled with her bag, not sure about the etiquette of her next question. 'There's something else. It's not strictly a medical thing. But I thought you might be able to help.'

She took out the letter she had found.

'I found this amongst my mother's things. I wondered if you might be able to give me a clue who it was from. If he's local, he might be a patient. Or his wife might be...' She passed her the letter. 'It's going to be easier if you read it, rather than me trying to explain.'

Dr Webster read the letter quickly but carefully, her face showing compassion as she came to the end.

'Oh,' she said. 'What a beautiful letter.'

'I know. And I'm worried that whoever he is, he doesn't know about Mum. And I think he should. But I have no idea who he is.'

'I'm so sorry.' Dr Webster looked genuinely apologetic. 'I'm not able to help you. You must know the rules. I can't divulge confidential patient information.'

'I thought that's what you'd say.'

'I'd really love to be able to help. But I can't.'

Kate looked at her. 'Do you mean that you do know who he is, but you can't tell me? Or do you mean that you don't know?'

'I honestly don't know. Though I could probably find out. If I put my mind to it. But it's impossible. I just can't.' She raised her eyebrows as she looked at Kate, as if to say *don't push it.*

Kate leaned back in the chair with a sigh. 'OK,' she said. 'Just tell me this. Do you think I'd be wasting my time looking round here?'

'Without looking into it, I have no idea.'

'I just don't like the thought of him not knowing. Of not being able to say his goodbyes. Pay his respects. Whatever you want to call it.'

'Maybe it's better left? Maybe he's come to terms with not seeing your mum again, and that should be that?'

'Maybe . . . he's living in the hope that one day they can be together?'

'I don't think it's your responsibility.'

'I wish I hadn't read it.'

'Pandora's Box, eh?'

'Exactly.'

There was a pause.

'I'd have read it,' said Dr Webster.

Kate put the incriminating letter back in her bag. 'Thanks anyway. I hope you didn't mind me asking. But I didn't know who else could help.'

'I don't mind at all. Good luck.'

Kate left the surgery feeling as if one problem had been addressed but frustrated by the remaining puzzle. The doctor had been her best lead. She hoped that while she cleared out the house, she might come across another clue. She would have to be vigilant. The letter had touched something in her, and she really wanted to find whoever had written it. For their sake as much as hers.

*

Kenny and Mary sat in the doctor's surgery waiting area. They didn't speak; Kenny offered Mary the newspaper, but she shook her head. Half of her willed the clock to hurry its hands around to the time of her appointment. The other half wanted to stay waiting here for ever. She was glad Kenny was with her. She had no idea how she would react if it was bad news. The receptionist smiled at her as if in sympathy, as if she already knew the diagnosis. She couldn't possibly, could she? Unless Mary was showing some sign without realising it, one that was apparent to everyone else.

Then suddenly her name was called, and her stomach fell down to her shoes, and she wanted to run out of the surgery, but Kenny took her arm.

'Come on, love.'

After a brief conversation and a few questions, Dr Webster settled Mary onto her examining couch. She'd been her doctor for a good twenty years, and they knew each other quite well, and Mary trusted her totally. Her fingers were cool and gentle as she pressed onto the area Mary indicated, feeling round it, lifting up her arm and checking underneath, then going on to examine the other side. It seemed to take for ever. Mary looked at the doctor's face, desperate for signs of concern – a frown, a bite of the lip, an intake of breath. But Dr Webster's face was impassive.

'OK. Do you want to get yourself dressed again and we'll have a chat.'

She left the cubicle. Mary got dressed with shaking hands and a sense of dread. She could hear Dr Webster and Kenny talking – mindless pleasantries about the weather and the time of year. She drew back the curtain and stepped out, then sat herself in the chair next to Kenny.

'Mary, I'm fairly certain that what you have is a breast cyst. It's common enough in a woman of your age. And it's probably benign. But just to make sure, I want to send you to the breast clinic to have the fluid drained off. That should ascertain whether we need to do a biopsy and take the matter further.'

'OK.' Mary wasn't sure how relieved to feel.

'So it's not cancer?' Kenny asked.

'Well, I would be surprised if it was. But I don't want to send you away without double-checking. That would be irresponsible.'

'So it might be?'

'I think it's unlikely. But I can't guarantee it. It's always very difficult with things like that to be one hundred per cent certain. The good thing is I can get you an appointment pretty quickly. I can pull strings.' Here she smiled. 'But I don't want you to worry.'

Kenny blew out his cheeks. 'That's easy to say.'

'Well, of course. I know. And I'm sorry I can't send you away with a definite today.'

'So I'll have to go to the hospital?'

'To the breast clinic. In Shoredown. They'll deal with it quickly, I promise.' Dr Webster began to type into her computer, writing her referral. 'Is there anything else you want to ask?'

'What if it is cancer?' There was an edge to Kenny's voice.

'There will be various things to take into consideration

before we discuss how to proceed. But for the time being, go home and try not to worry.'

Kenny and Mary looked at each other. How could they not worry?

They thanked Dr Webster nevertheless and left the surgery.

In the car park, neither of them was quite sure what to say.

'I'm going to work,' said Mary in the end.

'Work? Can't you give yourself the day off?'

'No. It'll take my mind off it.'

Kenny looked troubled. He looked around the car park, as if there might be some answer lurking.

'Can I have the car, then? I'll drop you off first.'

'Course.'

Mary got into the passenger seat of their car. She felt as if she was in a trance, with Dr Webster's words repeating themselves over and over. She wasn't clear about what to think. She was just disappointed she wasn't any further on. She still had to wait to know her fate. It was the not knowing that was the difficult bit. Certainty she could deal with.

In the meantime, life carried on.

'I'll do us cottage pie for dinner,' she said. 'With the remains of the beef.'

Vanessa lit a fire in the drawing room for the solicitor's visit. She was getting rather adept at it, and found she enjoyed the ritual, even cleaning out the old ashes, sweeping out the fireplace with the special brush. She loved the smell of the logs, and their crackle. The room was so empty and hard and cold otherwise, but the fire softened it somehow.

The meeting took all of half an hour. It hardly seemed worth the solicitor driving all this way. He barely had time to drink the cup of coffee Squirrel made him before he was off again.

'Well,' said Vanessa to her mother once he had gone. 'Now you know.'

'Now we know,' said Squirrel. 'And thank goodness. I wouldn't have put anything past Spencer. A squadron of secret mistresses. A phalanx of long-lost children. I wouldn't even have been surprised to find he had no money at all. Or that he'd left you up to your eyes in debt.'

Vanessa just laughed. She was getting used to her mother's vilification of Spencer.

Spencer's will was a surprise, in that there were no surprises – at least no horrible ones. It was responsible and sensible and fair. There was a fifty grand lump sum to Karina (this made Squirrel spit, but as Vanessa pointed out, it would stop Karina from kicking off), trust funds for Daniella and Aiden, and the rest, including the London flat and Pennfleet House and the residue of his capital and *Poseidon*, was left to Vanessa, as was right and proper.

The only thing no one had predicted was his bequest to Mary Mac.

Twenty thousand pounds, in recognition of her 'making his house a home and a pleasure to come back to'. There was a proviso, and that was that Mary should spend the money on herself, and herself only.

The bequest touched Vanessa.

'What a lovely thing to do,' she said to Squirrel.

'Don't be fooled,' Squirrel shot back. 'It's no skin off his nose, after all. What would have been truly selfless is if he had given her the money when he was alive.'

Vanessa couldn't help laughing yet again. Her mother refused to be moved. Nevertheless, the gesture was kind, and she felt a rush of fondness for Spencer for thinking of Mary, who had indeed worked tirelessly to make Pennfleet House run like clockwork. She couldn't wait for Mary to find out what she'd been left. She deserved every penny.

She knew she should wait for the solicitor to contact Mary himself, but the last thing she wanted was for Mary to open the envelope in front of her husband and mother-in-law. That would severely restrict her choice of what to do with the money. Mary didn't speak about her home life very often, but Vanessa could read between the lines. Her mother-in-law sounded like a tricky customer, and it must be difficult living with a man who had lost his job. Mary had a lot to deal with, but she never complained, and she always had time for other people. She was almost a saint.

So when Mary came in at midday, Vanessa sat her down at the island with a cup of tea.

Mary looked worried.

'It's all right,' she told her. 'It's good news.'

'Oh,' said Mary. 'I thought you were going to let me go.'

'That is the last thing I would ever do. No. I wanted to tell you that Spencer left you some money in his will.'

'Me?'

'Twenty thousand pounds.' As she named the sum, Vanessa felt delighted. It would be a fortune to Mary. She thought of Karina, who would be disgruntled by her fifty grand, even though she didn't deserve it.

Mary just sat there. She looked stunned.

'I can't take that. It's not right.'

'Well, you don't have a choice. It's yours whether you like it or not. And it *is* right. It's Spencer's way of saying thank you for everything.'

'But it was my job.'

'Oh, Mary – you always went above and beyond. You know you did.'

Mary was overwhelmed.

'I can't take it in. Twenty thousand pounds!'

'And you're to spend it on yourself.' Vanessa was going to be strict about that. She wasn't an interfering person – she hadn't inherited that from Squirrel – but she was determined that Mary should indulge in something that would make her life a little better.

'What on earth am I going to spend twenty thousand pounds on?'

'Anything you like. Anything at all. But if I were you, I wouldn't mention it to the others just yet. Not until you've decided what to do with it.'

Mary looked thoughtful. 'I can't not tell them. That would be lying.'

'No, it wouldn't. Anyway, you don't know yet. Officially. I wasn't supposed to tell you. You'll be getting a letter from the solicitor.'

'So it's a secret?'

'If you like.'

Mary thought about it.

'You're right,' she said. 'I'm not going to say a word.'

It was a sign, thought Mary, as she went off to the

utility room to fetch her cleaning materials. Somebody up there, aided and abetted by Spencer, had known what was going to happen to her. The money was there to tide Kenny and Ruthie over, when the worst happened to her. Twenty thousand pounds wouldn't last for ever, but it would certainly help.

All Dr Webster's kindness and reassurance went out of the window. She was for it, thought Mary. She would get to the consultant and he would shake his head sorrowfully. She stood in the middle of the kitchen, a duster in one hand and the polish in the other, and wanted to cry. She couldn't, though, because Vanessa would want to know what the matter was. She had to keep going.

She squirted a dollop of Pledge on to the dresser and began to polish.

Kenny drove as fast as he could from the surgery to Shoredown. He headed for the big retail unit on the outskirts of the town, where the new supermarket had just opened. It stood like a spaceship, all gleaming glass.

He'd seen the advert last week, when he and Mary had come here to do their big monthly shop.

We are proud of our drivers, who help make us the top choice for internet grocery shopping in the area. Help us deliver the goods! If you have a clean licence and are used to dealing with the general public, come and see our recruitment manager now.

At the time he had thought he was too good for the job. Too good to pack up big green boxes of groceries into the back of a van and trundle round the countryside delivering them. Too good to wear the supermarket uniform, with a name badge on, because he'd once been foreman and everyone had known his name and didn't need telling who he was.

Everything had changed. Fear and guilt and remorse and terror all jumbled up inside him. What had made him think he was so special? All that mattered now was that he could make amends.

He strode into the supermarket, his head held high. The sign was still there.

Five minutes later, he was sitting in a blue chair in front of a desk. A thin-faced woman with large glasses ran through a checklist of questions. He was astonished when she seemed delighted by his credentials.

'You're just the sort of person we're looking for,' she told him.

What – a loser?

He thought it but didn't say it.

'I need to do a CRB check, of course, because you'll be in customers' houses. But if all that goes smoothly, we can have you up and driving as soon as.'

She gave him a rabbity smile that made her nose wrinkle.

Bloody hell. It was that easy. Who knew?

Kenny left the supermarket and drove to the other side of the retail park. There were two big electrical places, so he chose the one where they'd bought their washing machine, because it seemed as good a reason as any. He walked over to the computer section and gazed round at the blank staring screens. He had no idea where to start.

His sons had gone mad at him when they moved. How

were they supposed to keep in touch, all the way over in Australia?

'There's an amazing thing called the telephone,' he told them.

'No one uses phones anymore for this kind of thing, Dad. And it's free, over the internet. Over the Wi-Fi.'

'It's not bloody free if you've got to pay five hundred quid for a computer, is it? That's called a false economy.'

He'd stayed stubborn, and Mary didn't push, because she wasn't the pushy type, and once a month they dialled first one son and then the other on a Sunday morning for a ten-minute chat, timed on the egg timer in the kitchen.

Now, however, he walked up to the first assistant he could find.

'I want a computer. Or a laptop. Whatever I need to speak to my sons in Australia. Over the Skype or whatever it is.'

'No problem. What's your price range?'

'I don't care. I just want the easiest.'

He didn't care. All of a sudden the only thing that mattered was Mary. He'd got a few hundred saved up, out of his benefits and what he won on the horses. He didn't know what he'd been saving it for, but it made him feel a bit more secure, knowing there was a nest egg. In case of trouble.

He hadn't expected this sort of trouble. Remembering Mary's face this morning made him shudder.

The assistant was talking to him.

'Have you got Wi-Fi at home?'

'We did have, when the boys were at home. Do I need it?'

'You will do, yes. But if you've had it, you should be able to get it reconnected. Come and look at these.'

The lad showed him a small range of laptops and how they worked. He wrote down on a piece of paper what Kenny would need to do, and who to contact. 'I'll take this one,' he said, not knowing why he had chosen it, but wanting the deal done as quickly as possible. He had other things to accomplish before the close of play.

Jobs and laptops were easy to acquire, it seemed.

Removing his mother was going to be a different story.

He had always known it was going to be difficult. Which was why he had avoided it for so long. He knew he should have nipped it in the bud when she first bowled up. Should have shown her the door after two weeks, when it became obvious that she was far too comfortable. Of course she was, with Mary's cooking and housekeeping, because Mary was kind and selfless and ran round after both of them because she had run round after people all her life.

Yep, thought Kenny, he was a miserable, ungrateful worm who had let his wife run herself ragged, because he was too gutless and lazy to stand up for himself or for her. He'd taken the easy option all the way. Not any more.

'Mum,' he said to Ruthie, who was, surprisingly, not in front of the telly for once, but was sitting at the dining table replacing her false nails. The sight of it made him feel slightly ill. She was surrounded by pieces of white plastic, applying them one by one with glue to her nail-beds.

'Don't disturb me. I need to concentrate.'

'No. This is important. You have to move out.'

Ruthie looked up at him with a benign smile, rolled her eyes in faux fond exasperation and carried on her work.

'I mean it. You've been here long enough. It's time for you to find a place of your own.'

Ruthie gave a sigh of impatience. He was interfering with her concentration.

'You were never supposed to be here for this long.'

She held out her left hand and admired it.

'Don't ignore me, Mum.'

She looked at him with raised eyebrows and started on her right hand.

'What *is* behind all this? Who's rattled your cage?'

'Mary and me, we need our privacy. We were happy to help you out, but . . . you can't stay here for ever.'

'So you're chucking me out? Is that it? Your own mother?'

'No. Of course I'm not chucking you out. We'll help you find somewhere.'

'Me? In my condition?'

'Mum. There is no condition. You're just . . .'

He floundered under her level gaze.

'What? I'm just what, exactly?'

'Well, you need to lose a bit of weight and move about a bit.'

She gave a bark. 'You can talk. And her. She's no Twiggy.'

'At least she gets off her arse.'

'Which is more than you do.'

Kenny flinched. He wasn't going to tell her what he'd done that morning. He didn't want her knowing any of his business. Not at the moment. Not until things were straight.

'There's some flats in Shoredown. We can get you into one. We can sort out your rent – you'll get some help with that from the council.'

'Oh. Do you know, I thought I would get help from my own family. I didn't think I'd have to go begging.'

'It's not begging. You're entitled to it. And you have got some money, Mum. I know you have.'

'Have you been going through my stuff?'

'No. But you have, haven't you?'

Ruthie was shrewd, he knew that. He didn't know how much, but he knew she had cash to dip into. She wouldn't look at him.

He tried a gentler tone.

'I don't want to upset you. But like I said, we need our privacy—'

Ruthie snorted. 'Been reading *Fifty Shades*, has she?'

Kenny felt his heart harden. No one laughed at Mary and got away with it.

'Either you go with my help and my blessing. Or you can bugger off.'

'Well,' said Ruthie. 'That's nice. That's very nice indeed.'

He didn't care what she thought. Everything was different now.

He looked up at the ceiling. It was too much for him. He tried to breathe, but he couldn't.

Even Ruthie, self-absorbed, self-centred Ruthie, could see something was the matter.

'What is it? What's the matter with you?'

He couldn't tell her. Mary wouldn't want her to know.

Mary was very private. Besides, he couldn't imagine her being of any help. He just turned to her.

'Could you, for once in your life, put somebody else first?'

23

On Tuesday, Kate spent the day on what seemed like endless administration, talking to service providers and going into the bank. She realised Rupert was right, that probate was a huge chore. Every time she thought about him she felt agitated, and more than once was tempted to telephone and cancel their dinner. He was only going to make a fool of her again. She remembered he'd offered her the use of his office, and she had to admit it was tempting – he was bound to have Wi-Fi, and a photocopier – but something stopped her. She used the Wi-Fi in Sam's café instead, and the photocopier in the tourist office. It wasn't ideal, but it would do for now.

She looked up the company Rupert ran with his brother. Pennfleet Holiday Cottages. It was a predictably upmarket venture, done in a low-key way, just like the Malahides. They had a signature look for the decor of each cottage – soothing heathers and greys and lavenders. There were picnic hampers on arrival, with tartan rugs; bicycles to borrow; televisions hidden away behind hand-painted doors; piles of board games. All very discreet but well thought out.

Kate recognised Belle Vue would be perfect. It would sleep a family of four very nicely. Rupert could do a refurb over the winter – new kitchen, new bathroom – and have it ready to rent by spring.

She was cross with herself for falling into his trap. But she decided she could play it to her advantage. If she sold to him, she could save agents' fees and not go through the agony of endless negotiating.

She'd had two estate agents value the house the day before, both of whom gave her a price within five thousand of each other. She'd done her research on the internet anyway, and decided roughly what she wanted to ask.

'It's not really the best time of year to go on the market,' said the second, who was full of useful advice. 'You might need to stand your ground. But I think this should sell well. Of course, your other option would be to do it up – you'd get a really good price then.'

'It's difficult, when I'm not here,' said Kate. 'Of course, what I'd really like to do is live here myself and do it up.'

She was surprised when these words came out. It was true, though – as she had cleared the house, she had imagined the tired seventies decor ripped out, a cream Shaker kitchen installed, a modern staircase in glass and steel rising up to the first floor... She could visualise it so clearly, and felt sad that it would fall to someone else, that they would excise any evidence of her and her family and breathe new life into the old stone walls.

'And by the way,' said the agent, 'if it doesn't sell straight away and Pennfleet Holiday Cottages make you an offer, don't have any of it. They drive a hard bargain. Hang out till the spring. You'll definitely get your price then.'

Kate couldn't help laughing. Rupert's reputation went before him. Well, he was in for a shock if he thought he was going to get one up on her.

'Thank you,' she said. 'You've been very helpful. I'll let you know what I decide to do.'

As the agent left, Kate felt rising panic. Carlos was pressing her for a decision on when she was going to get back. She knew she had to have a meeting about the ball as soon as she could. It wouldn't look good to dither. It was the pinnacle of her career. She needed to get the key people on board. She couldn't mess this one up. But she couldn't just walk out of Belle Vue. Or could she? Maybe she should lock it up and leave it, then come back in a month or so, when probate was through.

By the time Debbie came round to help her clear out some cupboards, she was feeling very tetchy.

'Thank God you're here,' she said. 'I'm never going to manage.'

'You just need to be organised,' said Debbie.

'Thank you so much for helping me.'

'It's fine. I'd only be going for a run or going to the supermarket or running errands. It's much more fun to be gossiping with you.'

'Just like the old days, eh?'

'How many times did we sit in this kitchen reading our horoscopes?'

'And drinking that horrible fizzy pink wine that gave you a headache?'

'And trying to finish our sixth-form projects. What a waste of time that was. I did mine on eighties super-models. I mean, really – why?'

Kate laughed. 'I did heraldry. Yawn!'

They set to clearing out the airing cupboard next to the bathroom. It seemed that even old pillowcases and tea towels could bring back memories. Kate hated consigning them to the recycling. She understood the compulsion to hoard, because stuff gave you a sense of identity. But common sense and practicality won the day in the end. And Debbie's insistence that, much as the striped towels reminded her of her childhood, they had no place in her life.

'Keep the good stuff. Just the really special things. Your parents don't want to be remembered through a ratty old towel.'

It was astonishing how long it took to clear out. Kate supposed there was over fifty years of stuff in there – stuff her parents had had since their wedding day.

'This is just the airing cupboard. What about the rest of the house? Oh God . . . I'll never finish.' She looked at her watch. 'And I better go and get ready.'

Debbie looked at her. 'I can't believe you're going out with Rupert Malahide tonight.'

Kate couldn't believe it either. Maybe it was because she hadn't been out for dinner with anyone for months, because work was so busy? Maybe she was flattered? Maybe she wanted to prove something to him?

'After the way he treated you,' Debbie said with indignation. 'What a cock.'

'Oh, you know what? It was just teenage nonsense. It wasn't a big deal.'

Kate tied a knot in the top of the bin bag. She could say that now, but it wasn't how she'd felt at the time.

It was the summer she and Debbie left school, before they went on to sixth-form college in Shoredown – they both wanted to go there rather than stay on at the school, because it seemed more grown-up. They'd spent the months working and playing as hard as they could. The sun shone on Pennfleet every day, and a little rain fell at night from time to time, considerately, to keep any fear of drought at bay and to keep the gardens and allotments plumped up.

It was a summer of sailing, music, laughter and promise. Debbie's dad had done up an old dinghy, which they took up and down the river and round to secret coves in a flotilla with their friends. Kate remembered wearing nothing but a bikini top and shorts day in day out. She remembered the cool water on her skin as she dived off the dinghy into the bright-blue water. Their limbs turned biscuit brown, their hair streaked white-blonde. They were golden girls.

They owned the town. They had no shortage of boys to choose from, both from Pennfleet and summer visitors. They flirted, but that was it. They didn't want to be tied down. They thrived on kisses and flattery, growing ever more confident. Their friendship was strong and it was all they needed. There was no pact; it was just how they operated. Each of them knew that the possibility of someone meaningful was out there, but until he came along, they weren't ready for anything serious. Freedom was paramount.

The yacht club end-of-season disco proved a turning point. Maybe it was the sense that summer was drawing to a close, as the days got shorter and the sun got lower in the sky. Maybe it gave them a sense of urgency, a sense that they needed something more to get them through the long dark winter months. The visitors would be leaving soon and the town would become a ghost of itself, the pubs and bars suddenly empty of noise and laughter.

The Malahide grandchildren were there in force. Their grandmother Irene, chatelaine of Southcliffe, had been a high court judge who'd retired to Pennfleet and was determined to see out the rest of her days giving her extended family holidays to remember. Southcliffe had been the scene of much revelry and high jinks over the years. There were enough Malahides to throw a party without inviting anyone else, but they were sociable and generous and so the young of Pennfleet often found themselves lured up the long winding drive and onto the croquet lawn. Their grandmother was sensible enough not to let the rabble into the actual house, but the garages had a huge empty space over the top of them that converted neatly into a party room. The parties were wild. The Malahides' friends were spoiled, wealthy and high-spirited. The indigenous young of Pennfleet were never quite sure how to treat them. Hearts and noses were broken, aided and abetted by vast quantities of drink.

Tonight, they had come into Pennfleet en masse. They were a yacht club fixture, with a plethora of boats between them. They scooped up all the trophies in the regatta, and no one much cared, because it seemed to have become a given that they would win. It was impossible to know how many of them there actually were, because their ranks swelled and dwindled from weekend to weekend, depending on which of them were down. It seemed that night they were all there. Everywhere you looked, there was a white-blonde head, a vision of good breeding. They had none of the potential faults of English aristocracy: their teeth were perfect; there was no goofiness or underbites or sticky-out ears. They were catalogue perfect, in their faded denim and boat shoes and polo shirts, boys and girls alike.

And it was there Kate found herself pinned down by Rupert's bright, enquiring gaze. Rupert had had a terrible reputation. In another age he would have been called a playboy. He toyed mercilessly with the hearts of the local girls. Rupert, it was said, was his grandmother's favourite and was due to inherit Southcliffe.

That night he was wearing a Breton T-shirt, shorts and espadrilles, with a bandana round his neck. He should have looked ridiculous and effeminate, but as soon as Kate met his gaze she knew there was no question. He made her feel mysterious, alluring, like the girl he had been looking for all his life.

'Come and dance,' he said to her, and it was a command. She had no choice.

They owned the dance floor. They barely touched, but their eyes never left each other as they moved in perfect time to the music, the bass pounding through them. Kate knew everyone was looking, that her friends were exchanging glances. Debbie caught her eye at one point – a warning glance, she thought, a glance that asked whether she knew what she was doing. But she was in too deep by then. She was bewitched.

And then he took her hand and led her away from the dance floor.

Debbie cornered her.

'What are you doing? You know what he's like.'

'I can look after myself.' Vodka had made Kate bold.

'You know what he does! Makes the local girl feel like a princess, gets into her knickers then dumps her.'

Rupert was waiting patiently throughout their whispered exchange. Debbie flashed him a sweet smile then turned back to Kate.

'You're just a plaything. Don't fall for it. You're just his new box of Lego. He'll forget you tomorrow.'

'Debs – I'll be fine.'

That was how his magic worked. He made girls feel invincible. Special.

He led her out onto the deck overlooking the river. The cool night air settled on her skin. The river rippled and shone in the lights from the yacht club. She could hear the water, reassuring, always there, lapping against the bank.

And he kissed her and she thought, *This is it. This is what it's all about.* Everything she'd ever heard about him, she forgot in that moment. Every warning. As he ran his fingers through her hair, and murmured into her ear, his warm lips working their way down her neck to her collarbone, any doubts she'd had melted away. Her blood fizzed as sweet as sherbet inside her.

'Where can we go?' he asked.

And without thinking twice, she led him to the shed where the boats were taken for repair, with its cold cement floor and the smell of diesel, and she fucked him, up against the wall, digging her nails into his back under the rough cloth of his shirt. And they stood, gasping and clinging to each other, and he whispered, 'Oh my God. I didn't know it could be like that,' and she didn't realise he said that to all the girls.

They lay curled up with each other for hours in the darkness, warmed by their lust. Their fingers were linked as they whispered. They rubbed noses, touched foreheads, their breath mingled, their lips grew sore from kissing.

'Come to my brother's twenty-first,' said Rupert. 'Next Saturday. I need you with me. I want you to sit next to me. Promise?'

'Of course.' Kate's heart thudded.

'You'll be the guest of honour.'

'What should I wear?'

'Oh, any old thing.' He grinned. 'Nothing, preferably. Seven thirty for eight.'

He held her tight before she peeled herself away. She had to be home by one. Her parents trusted her and in return she never broke their rules.

'Saturday,' he whispered, and she nodded and walked away, gliding back through the streets and up the hill to home, where she lay in bed, shivering with the cold and the shock, lightheaded and turned completely inside out.

The next Saturday, Debbie helped her get ready for the party. She was quiet, though, whether with disapproval or jealousy Kate wasn't sure. She was too caught up with the evening ahead to worry. She hadn't seen Rupert all week, and she fought her instinct to contact him. She was going to play it cool, and blow his mind when he saw her. She was going to be the belle of the ball.

She wore a black body-con dress, so tight there was no possibility of knickers, and high, high heels. Debbie blow-dried her hair into a sleek sheet of gold, put on false lashes, painted on red lips.

Kate barely recognised herself in the mirror. She looked like a film star, polished and glamorous. She would outshine everyone there, she promised herself. Rupert would be proud to have her by his side.

Her dad, her dear sweet kind proud dad, gave her a lift, for Southcliffe was quite a way out of town. He drove his car halfway up the drive, then she asked him to stop. She was too embarrassed to be seen being dropped off in a battered old Ford. By the time she reached the marquee, her shoes had blistered her feet. But the excitement inside her dulled the pain. She couldn't wait to make an entrance, and see Rupert's face light up.

As soon as she walked into the marquee, she realised her mistake. Everyone inside was in formal dress: black tie or long frocks. And although she got admiring glances from the men, she knew she was all wrong.

'Ooh,' said one man. 'Who ordered a stripper? Brilliant idea.'

'Cracking norks,' goggled another.

And then Rupert saw her, and she saw him mouth 'Oh shit', and the girl he had his arm draped round giggled. And in that moment, she wanted to die.

She could still feel the humiliation, over fifteen years later, but she could laugh about it now. Her naivety. It had taught her a few lessons. And now she was a woman, a grown-up, and she was confident, and because of the circles she moved in, nothing much fazed her. She could handle Rupert Malahide.

She was covered in muck. It was astonishing what the recesses of an airing cupboard could accumulate: cobwebs and dust mice and fluff. She took a long bath, soaking it all away, then blow-dried her hair properly for the first time since she'd been here. She pondered what to wear, thought about the dress she'd brought over for the funeral, but decided that would be way too dressy even for Pennfleet's best restaurant, and she'd made that mistake before, so she settled on jeans and a cream silk shirt. She certainly didn't want Rupert to think she was going to too much effort.

The Townhouse by the Sea was converted from the old custom house on the quay. Kate had expected some soulless identikit boutique hotel decor but was instantly charmed. It was warm, quirky, atmospheric and luxurious. It was dark when she arrived, and the bar and dining area were lit by candles to enhance the subdued lighting.

The manageress, a young girl in her early twenties with a long chestnut bob and laughing eyes, had the knack of making her feel like a longstanding and valued customer. She had a certain polish, but was obviously local, which stopped her sounding too disingenuous.

'You're dining with Rupert, aren't you?' she said. 'I'm Angelica. Come and have a drink while you wait. He's always late, dear of him.'

As Angelica led her to a turquoise velvet sofa, Kate wondered how many of Rupert's dining partners had been led here. If she was one of many. If Angelica was thinking *here goes another one*. If she was, she didn't betray it.

'Can I recommend our autumn cocktail?' said Angelica. 'It's mostly blackberries. And vodka. And ginger wine. It's lethal. But delicious.'

'It sounds amazing,' said Kate

'It's called Bramble On,' Angelica told her. 'I think it's a play on a Led Zeppelin song. We have to humour Luca.' She giggled. 'You'll be meeting him later. He and Rupert are impossible when they get together. If they get carried away, just tell me and I'll sort them out.'

'OK,' said Kate, slightly disconcerted. 'I love the hotel, by the way.'

'We're doing really well.' Angelica was proud. 'Pennfleet is a bit off the beaten track off-season, but we seem to be fully booked all the time these days.'

'I can see why,' said Kate. 'It's charming.'

Over Angelica's shoulder, she could see Rupert arrive. He was in jeans and a grey sweater, so she was pleased she hadn't dressed up.

'Hey. Don't get up. I'm sorry I'm late. I think the cab driver was in another time zone. ' He bent down to kiss Kate, then turned and kissed Angelica. 'I hope you've been looking after my guest, Gel. What are we drinking?'

'Blackberry cocktails,' Kate told him.

'Perfect.' He sat down next to her and picked up a menu. 'Have you looked at the menu yet? Luca is a culinary genius. Honestly. You won't have eaten food like it.'

'I recommend the porchetta,' said Angelica. 'With baked apples. And celeriac puree. And maybe some oysters to start? We've just started serving them again.'

'Does that sound OK to you?' Rupert asked Kate. 'Shall we have that? I totally trust Angelica.'

Kate was a little startled that she hadn't even had time to look at the menu, but somehow Rupert didn't come across as chauvinistic. If any other man had done that, she would have been furious.

'Fabulous,' she said.

Angelica took their menus and glided away. Rupert watched her go.

'I've got my eye on her,' he said.

Kate's heart sank. So he hadn't changed. And how bloody rude. To eye up the staff while he was taking her out. She stiffened.

'Oh God,' said Rupert, with a grin. 'I don't mean in that way. I mean I'm thinking about poaching her for my new project. Though Luca will kill me.'

Kate relaxed a little. 'New project?' she asked.

'I'll tell you about it later,' he replied. 'How are *you*? My grandmother sends her regards, by the way. Have you had an awful few days?'

Kate remembered how, when he focused on you, you felt like the centre of his world.

'Well,' said Kate, 'it hasn't been a bundle of laughs. But I'm coping.' She smiled. 'Though I've been living on cheese toasties and Jaffa Cakes. My personal trainer's going to have a fit.'

What had she said that for? It made her sound like an idiot. Rupert looked at her askance.

'If you're going to start worrying about carbs and fat, you'd better leave now.'

'Oh God,' said Kate. 'I'm sorry. I've been in New York too long. And I've been really looking forward to tonight.'

'I don't really do guilt,' said Rupert. 'About anything. But definitely not about food.'

Kate bit her tongue. She knew as well as anyone he didn't do guilt. He'd never shown a moment's remorse about how he'd treated her. And it was easy not to feel guilty about food when you had a fast metabolism. She imagined he never put on a pound of excess weight. She didn't say anything, though.

Angelica returned with a tray bearing two etched

tumblers, garnished with mint and blackberries. There was a plate of canapés too.

'Onion tartlets with melted Reblochon,' she told them. 'With the compliments of the chef.'

Kate took her drink and picked up a tartlet.

'No guilt,' she told Rupert.

She took a sip of her drink. It tasted of autumn and decadence: warm and syrupy and tart and seductive. She bit into the tartlet: sweet, melting onion combined with the salty tang of creamy cheese.

'Oh my God.' She feigned swooning. 'It's out of this world.'

'I told you. Luca's a genius,' said Rupert, lobbing a whole tartlet into his mouth unceremoniously.

Kate and Rupert's table was right by the French windows at the far end of the dining room. It looked out onto the harbour, where the lights of the town were reflected in the water, flashes of silver and gold on deepest black. There was a snowy-white linen tablecloth, a pewter candelabra stuffed with fuchsia candles, and a silver platter bearing a dozen oysters resting on a bed of ice. Two high-backed chairs covered in grey velvet faced each other. Kate took her seat as Angelica brought over a bottle of Chablis.

'Luca insists you have this with your oysters,' she said. 'He won't take no for an answer.'

'Fine by me,' said Rupert, and Kate smiled her assent. 'Me too.'

Rupert turned out to be a hugely entertaining dining companion. Effusive about the food and wine, he was full of gossip and inside information.

'Luca and Angelica have this fiery on-off relationship,'

he told her. 'He's totally besotted with her, but she leads him a merry dance. I do feel a bit sorry for him. His fiancée left him a couple of years ago – went back to her childhood sweetheart. And he's been mooning round after Angelica ever since. He asks her to marry him about five times a week, but she refuses.'

'So is that why he'd be cross if you poached her?'

'No – he'd be cross because she's so bloody good at her job. He'd never find a replacement. She started off as a chambermaid and now she basically runs the place.'

'So what is this New Project?'

'As soon as it became obvious my grandmother was losing her sight, and there was nothing that could be done about it, we had a family conference. You know what a big part of our lives she's always been. None of us wanted her to have to leave Southcliffe. She *is* Southcliffe.'

He looked at Kate as if asking for confirmation.

'I understand that,' she said.

'It also became obvious that Granny wasn't going to accept help from anyone. She is infuriatingly independ-ent. But you can't live on your own in a big house like that with failing eyesight. So ... as the only grandchild without any real responsibility, or a family, it was up to me to come and live with her.'

'That's very ... dutiful,' said Kate.

Rupert grinned. 'I know the whole town thinks it's because I'm after the house. But that's been put in a trust for all of us ages ago. I do it because I love her, and because she did a better job of looking after us lot than any of our parents did. She was always there for us. If I couldn't repay her for that, what kind of man does that make me? Not that it's exactly a hardship. I love Penn-fleet. I always have.'

'Me too,' agreed Kate. 'You forget the magic, when you're away. But it reels you straight back in.'

Rupert nodded. 'Anyway, we've never been sure what to do with the house long term. We can't just keep it as a holiday home. That's a luxury too far. So, after much debate and number crunching, we're going to hire it out as a party house.'

'A party house,' said Kate. She could see it already in her mind's eye. 'How wonderful.'

'It will be.' Rupert nodded his agreement. 'The idea is to hire it out for birthdays and special occasions. Cashing in on the whole *Upstairs Downstairs, Downton Abbey* obsession that seems to be sweeping the country. If not the whole world. We're going mega-upmarket. Croquet, butlers, maids, tea on the lawn, chauffeur-driven Bentley, billiards... you get the picture.'

'I suppose that's exactly how it was once.'

'Before we got hold of it and lowered the tone. Very probably. Obviously it needs a load of money chucking at it. Our clientele will be people who want only the best. So it's going to be quite an investment. But we hope to be up and running at the end of next year. And we can keep some weeks free for ourselves.'

'What about your grandmother? I thought the whole idea was she wanted to stay at Southcliffe.'

'She and I are going to have an annexe at the back.' He made a face. 'Annexe sounds ghastly but I've made sure it won't be. The architect's got it all planned, specially kitted out for when she does finally lose her sight. I'm the sort of host-cum-manager, so I need to live on site. Though

I'm a bit worried about how I'm going to deal with tricky customers. Tact is not my forte. Which is why I'm after Angelica.'

'How are you going to manage that? I mean, isn't Luca your friend?'

'Ah, well, I'm trying to persuade Luca and his business partner to invest. I want Luca to oversee the menus, and train up my staff. I really want this to be a local project, as far as possible. Pennfleet has changed so much lately – for the better in some ways, but that isn't always good for the people who come from here. I want to use local staff, local suppliers, but I need really good people in place to make sure they are up to the job.'

He was really warming to his subject. Kate could sense his passion and his vision. She was surprised. She had assumed him to be a selfish, out-for-himself kind of person. A user. A charming user, but a user nonetheless. But maybe she'd got him wrong. Or maybe he'd grown up.

'It sounds like a fantastic project,' she said. 'But none of this is why you wanted to have dinner with me, is it?'

Rupert looked at her, startled. 'No,' he admitted, and looked down.

'I'm guessing you want Belle Vue. For your portfolio.'

'Belle Vue?'

He frowned, puzzled, as if he didn't understand. Kate smiled to herself. She would have given him more points if he'd put his hands up.

'My parents' house. I assume you want it for Pennfleet Holiday Cottages?'

He scowled. 'Who told you that?'

239

Kate felt a flicker of triumph. She was one step ahead of him.

'I'll give you first refusal. But I don't want any messing about. I've got a fair price in mind. It would suit me not to have to put it on the open market.'

Rupert sat back in his chair. He took a thoughtful sip from his glass.

'Is that really why you think I asked you for dinner?' he asked.

'Isn't it?'

He stared at her evenly. 'I know you probably don't think a great deal of me, but I'm not that crass.'

Kate felt a flicker of doubt. Maybe she had jumped to conclusions?

'If I wanted Belle Vue, I would contact you through your solicitor and make a formal offer. Not schmooze you like some sleazy wheeler dealer.'

Kate's cheeks started to burn. 'Oh God,' she said. 'I didn't mean to offend you.'

He grinned at her. 'Listen,' he said. 'It's impossible to offend me. If you want to sell your house, we can talk about it. But not now. This is supposed to be taking your mind off things.'

Kate didn't know what to say. She'd thought she was so clever, and she'd got him totally wrong. Unless this was a double bluff, and he was making her feel guilty on purpose. Either way, she shouldn't have mentioned Belle Vue.

'I'm so sorry—' she started, but he put up a hand to cut her off, then refilled her glass.

'Don't worry about it,' he said.

They chatted amicably throughout the rest of the meal,

Kate regaling him with stories of her rather ridiculous lifestyle, and Rupert filling her in with his siblings' escapades. After pudding, which was a sinful damson crème brûlée, Luca the chef came out of the kitchen with a bottle of vintage port to go with the cheeseboard and sat down with them. With his wild dark curls tied back in a bandana, and brooding eyes, he cut a romantic figure.

'I love your cooking,' Kate told him. 'It was like a taste of England for me. It makes me wish I didn't have to go back.'

'It's a great time of year for food,' said Luca. 'I love the autumn. I can be strong and robust again. Get some depth of flavour.'

'Yeah, OK, Luca,' said Rupert. 'We don't need a gastro-lecture.'

Luca punched him on the arm. 'Hey. I'm passionate. Not bloodless, like you.'

'You're preaching to the converted, mate.'

Angelica came to join them as the dining room emptied. Luca forced them into trying different cheeses, and the quince jelly he had made, and his special oat cakes, and the more glasses of port went down, the more they laughed.

Kate smiled to herself. Pennfleet was turning out to be full of surprises. Not what it seemed on the surface at all. She couldn't remember the last time she'd had such a sybaritic evening. Everyone in New York was so in control, and talked about the same old things. Tonight was an eye-opener for her. There was passion and humour and wit and debate in the conversation. She was having the time of her life.

At half eleven, Rupert saw that she was wilting. Recent jet lag, port and bereavement were not happy bedfellows.

'Come on,' he said. 'Much as I would love to sit here till four o'clock in the morning, you wouldn't thank me.'

She was taken aback by his consideration. And charmed when he insisted on paying for dinner. Kate hugged Luca, then Angelica, and neither of them seemed to mind in the least.

'Thank you for the loveliest evening. It's been a tough week, and it's made everything seem brighter. It's been one of the best nights of my life.' She knew she was gushing but she'd had more to drink in one night than she usually drank in a month. And she meant it. Even though she went to more A-list parties than she could count, it had been more fun than she'd had for a long time.

Rupert insisted on seeing her home.

'What's going to happen to me in Pennfleet?' she protested.

'You never know. Some wayward pirate might swoop down and take you off on the high seas.'

'I'll risk it.'

But he wouldn't hear of it.

They walked up the hill together. Every now and then Kate found herself brushing against him. Too much wine, she thought, and steadied herself. And then he took her arm, wordlessly. It was a chivalrous rather than predatory gesture. And it provided her with the balance she needed.

To make sure he didn't think she was reading too much into it, she babbled away.

'I can't believe how much Pennfleet has changed. The whole vibe is totally different from when I was last here.'

'Vibe?' he laughed. 'I don't think we have a *vibe*. Not just yet.'

'Don't take the mickey.'

'You've definitely been in New York too long.'

'*Vibe* is more of a California word.'

'Whatever.' He did a fake American accent.

'You're impossible.' She dug him in the ribs with her elbow.

'I am not,' he told her. 'I'm very very possible indeed.'

She fell quiet. She had no idea what he meant by that.

They came to a halt outside Belle Vue. She looked up the stairs, and suddenly felt dread. It would be so quiet inside. And still. And empty.

She didn't want to go back into the house. She didn't want to face the memories, or the decisions, or the questions. And it was all such a mess inside.

'Are you OK?' asked Rupert.

'No,' she said.

Rupert didn't say a word. He just put his arms around her with no question. She pressed her face against his chest. His jumper was as soft as a kitten. Cashmere, definitely. It smelled of wood-smoke and sandalwood.

'I'm sorry,' she said. 'It just got to me. I had such a lovely time tonight and I'd sort of forgotten. And now I don't want to go in. It's going to be cold and . . .' she gulped. 'Lonely. And it's a total tip. And I ran out of oil. It's freezing.'

'Why don't you come back to Southcliffe?'

She looked up at him in surprise. 'What?'

'Granny won't mind. In fact, she'd be furious if I didn't offer. There's always spare beds made up. You can lie in as long as you want. I can make you breakfast and drop you back tomorrow when you feel up to it. Come on.'

'I can't.'

'You absolutely can.' He grinned. 'And I can show you my ideas. You can tell me what you think. I bet you'll think of a million things I haven't thought of.'

He gave her a gentle push.

'Go on. Go and get your things. We'll walk back down the hill and grab a taxi.'

Kate just stood there, not sure what to do.

'If you don't hurry up, there won't be one. They all turn into pumpkins at midnight round here.'

She needed no second telling.

'Why the hell didn't you tell me before?'

Daniel Fisher stood in the middle of the kitchen, his face dark with rage. He couldn't believe what his grandson had just told him.

Nathan sat with his feet up on the kitchen table, his hands round a cup of tea. 'I was trying to get my head round it.'

'There's nothing to get your bloody head round, lad. Malcolm Toogood thinks just that. That he's too good for everyone else.'

'Grandad – I messed up and that's the truth.'

'Rubbish. His dad would be ashamed of him. Toadying up to the rich incomers like that. He's always been the same, though, Malcolm. Nothing like his father. More interested in money. His dad would have done anything for anyone.'

Nathan looked down into his cup of tea. His nan had always read his leaves for him. He looked at the black specks coating the bottom, and wondered what they held for him.

'You heard from her, then?'

Nathan sighed. 'Who?' Though he knew full well.

'Your fancy woman.'

Nathan sighed. When his grandfather was feeling adversarial, there wasn't much point in having a conversation. He wasn't going to mention the text.

'No.'

'There you are, then. She used you. All part of the service.'

'Grandad, if you're trying to make me feel better about any of this, you're not. You're making me feel worse.'

'It makes me angry, that's all. People today. They don't know how to treat each other. There's no loyalty. No consideration. No bloody manners. It's all me me me.'

'Yeah, well.' Nathan was too tired to argue.

'Just don't turn into one of them, lad. I didn't bring you up to be a user.'

'Don't worry. There's not much danger of that.'

'What you going to do for money, lad? It's a long winter.'

Nathan looked up at his grandfather. His earlier irritation was suddenly replaced by fondness. He cared so much, Daniel. He was old school. He would never understand the world and how it worked nowadays.

'Something'll turn up.'

Nathan wasn't too worried. He was resourceful. He had contacts. He could do some labouring for one of the local builders – there was plenty of that going on.

'I've got people I can talk to,' he said, but Daniel wasn't listening. He was frowning, in another world. In a world where people treated each other with respect and consideration.

'I wish your gran was still here,' he said suddenly, and Nathan stood up to give him a hug. Daniel went to push him away at first, then relented, and let his grandson hold him, just for a second.

'I'll make another cup of tea,' he said, his voice gruff, and he moved away towards the kettle.

Southcliffe was about a mile out of Pennfleet, further down the river. The cab swept in through the stone gates, up the long, sinuous drive and then went clockwise around the circular lawn that lay in front of the house, crunching over the gravel chippings, and came to a halt in front of the entrance. The house was grey stone and heavily Gothic, with an arched front door and pointy mullioned windows. It should have been scary in the moonlight, surrounded by tall trees, the night breeze ruffling their branches, but the lights inside made it surprisingly welcoming.

Rupert led Kate up the steps and opened the door, bounding into the hall, where two hairy lurchers leapt up with glee and came to greet him.

'Jerry! Margo! Basket.' He grinned. 'Named after *The Good Life*. Granny's favourite programme.' The two dogs slunk off, wolf-like. 'Don't worry. They wouldn't hurt a fly.'

Kate watched them settle down again. She had always thought of Rupert as a wolf. A vulpine creature with a hard heart. Or possibly no heart at all. But it seemed the intervening years had made him kindness and consideration itself.

'Granny's in bed, obviously. I'll pop in and tell her you're here so she doesn't get a shock if she finds you in the morning. I'll show you to your room first, though. Unless you want another drink?'

'Gosh, no. I'm going to feel like death tomorrow as it is.'

'No. You were drinking good wine, and I'll give you some water. Come on. You can have the yellow bedroom. It's small, but it's the prettiest room, I think.'

He led her across the black and white marble floor and up the staircase. Kate felt like the heroine in a novel, being led to her fate. She could think of nothing but mad women in the attic, and the portrait of Rebecca that had gazed down on the hapless second Mrs de Winter.

Happily, they reached the appointed bedroom without any interference from unstable first wives. Rupert opened the door and gestured for her to enter.

'Don't worry about what time you get up,' he told her. 'I'll be in my office. Granny will be pottering about. She doesn't get up till nine. Stay in bed till midday if you want. You probably need to catch up.'

'You've been so kind,' murmured Kate, wondering just how dreadful she looked. Her make-up would have all worn off by now.

He lingered for a moment, looking awkward.

'Listen,' he said. 'The reason I asked you for dinner . . . I wanted to apologise. For how I treated you at my brother's party.'

Kate blinked.

'That was years ago.'

'I know. But it was terrible behaviour. The truth is, I didn't think you were going to come. I hadn't heard from

247

you all week. I didn't think you were interested. I thought you'd got better things to do.'

'Seriously?' Kate couldn't help laughing.

'I thought you were amazing. You weren't like any of the girls I knew. You weren't stupid and spoiled. If I'd known you were going to turn up . . .'

He looked mortified.

'Oh.' Kate was nonplussed. This was the last thing she was expecting. She didn't think Rupert had given her a second thought after their night in the boathouse.

He was leaning against the door jamb, looking at the floor. 'That's all I wanted to say, really. Sorry, I mean. For being an arrogant little cock.'

Kate laughed. 'Don't worry. Honestly. I mean, God, it was years ago. I'm kind of over it. I had therapy.'

He looked up, horrified. 'Really?'

She gave him a gentle push. 'No. Of course not. It was teenage-rite-of-passage stuff. I was teasing. But thank you for being sweet. And for dinner. And for this.'

She nodded her head towards the room.

He held her gaze. For a moment, she wasn't sure what was going to happen next. Then he nodded.

'You're welcome.' His voice was gruff. 'Goodnight.'

And he walked off down the corridor.

She watched after him for a moment, then turned and walked into the bedroom.

It was a delight. With walls and silk curtains the colour of daffodils, it was lit by two lamps on either side of the bed. Who had turned these on? Kate wondered. It was almost as if she had been expected. She was too tired to speculate, and still fuzzy from the surfeit of wine. She went to the bathroom, brushed her teeth, slipped into her nightdress and crept into the bed.

It was like climbing onto a cloud. The softest mattress, the warmest duvet, the plumpest pillows. She turned on her side and drew her legs up underneath her. In her somnolence, she felt a hot-water bottle in the middle of the bed, piping hot, but she was too sleepy to wonder who had put it there.

As she drifted off, she thought of her cheek on Rupert's chest earlier. She had felt his heart beating.

It had been beating rather fast.

24

Kate woke up bathed in golden-yellow light, astonished to find that not only had she slept through until quarter past nine without waking once, even though she had forgotten to take her sleeping pill, but also that she had no hangover. She smiled to herself as she jumped in the shower and got dressed. Maybe that was the solution to her sleeplessness – to get plastered every night on expensive wine.

She packed her few things up, tidied the bed and made her way down the staircase into the hall. The house was quiet, but she strained her ears and caught the sound of movement down a corridor. At the end of it she found the kitchen, and Rupert's grandmother, Irene, sitting at the table in jeans and a blue Guernsey, a scarf tucked into the neck. She had her dark glasses on, but didn't seem to need her stick in the confines of her own kitchen.

'Mrs Malahide,' said Kate. 'It's Kate. Joy's daughter.'

Irene stood and greeted Kate with warmth.

'Kate. Rupert told me you might stay the night,' she said, as if it was usual for strange women to find their way into her kitchen of a morning. 'I popped a bottle in the bed but I do hope you weren't cold?'

'No, I was just right. Thank you. I slept like a top. But let me help.'

'No. It's fine. It's a nuisance, this eyesight thing, but it's surprising what I can still manage. Rupert makes a terrible fuss. Of course I can't drive or anything, and it will get worse, but otherwise . . . I just have to do things more slowly. Sit down.'

Kate took a seat at a long table covered in a red oil-cloth. She imagined all the Malahides crowded round it in their youth, Irene distributing rations. The kitchen was so out of date it was almost fashionable again. She watched as Irene put the kettle on the Aga – three times the size of the one in Belle Vue – and pulled a saucepan out of the cupboard.

'You're to sit there and talk to me while I boil you an egg. Now tell me – how are you, my dear? I'm so sorry about your mother. I was very fond of her. We were on the flower rota together and we used to spend the whole time laughing. Neither of us were natural flower arrangers.'

'I'm fine, really. Obviously it's been hard. But everyone's been so kind.'

'Well, yes. Joy attracted kindness. Because she was so very kind herself.'

'People keep saying.'

'We need more Joys in this world. One of those people who gives, but who isn't a sickly saint. I wish I could be more like her but I don't have the patience for other people that she had.'

Kate could imagine that Irene didn't brook any non-sense. Joy had been endlessly patient and sympathetic

251

with people, but it was only now that Kate was starting to realise how unusual that made her.

'When you're growing up you don't realise that your parents are special in any way, do you?' she said. 'Quite often you don't see it until it's too late.'

'There's no need to feel bad about it. It's the same for all of us. As parents you don't expect to be appreciated. Funnily enough, one's grandchildren can be more appreciative. It's a much more satisfactory relationship.'

'You and Rupert are very close, aren't you?'

Irene gave a mischievous smile.

'Yes. I've got the measure of him and I've worked out how to get the best out of him. He could have come to a sticky end. He's what in the olden days would have been called a bounder. Or he was.'

Kate found herself completely under Irene's spell. She watched as she moved about the kitchen, filling the teapot, dropping a brace of brown eggs into the saucepan, slicing a fresh loaf of bread. And as she watched, she wondered if perhaps Irene might be able to shed some light on her mystery. She'd lived in Pennfleet a long time. She was a pillar of the community and knew lots of people. Who knows, maybe Joy had even confided in her at some point?

'Can I ask your advice about something?'

'Of course.' Irene brought over the teapot and placed it in front of her.

Kate took the letter from her handbag.

'I found a letter in Mum's handbag. I wondered if you might know who it was from.'

'You'll have to read it to me.'

Kate unfolded it and read it aloud, the words affecting her as much as they had the first time.

'Oh,' said Irene as Kate finished. 'Oh. How terribly sad.'

'It's awful, isn't it? I had no idea. And I don't know how to find out who he is. "R" isn't exactly helpful.' She laughed. 'I'm assuming it's not Rupert.'

'I think I know who it is. Robin Jessop. He lives about two miles away, upriver, in Elverscott.' She shook her head in sorrow. 'He and his wife retired down here about ten years ago. Then she gradually started "losing it", as they say. Now he's a full-time carer for her.'

'Like Mum was for Dad.'

'I imagine they met at the dementia support group in Shoredown.'

Kate nodded. 'I know Mum used to take Dad there.'

'And Robin takes Nancy. It's a bit of respite, I suppose. A chance to meet other people in your position.' Irene sighed. 'Oh dear. Other people's lives. Sometimes we just have no idea, do we?'

'I know,' said Kate. 'What do you think I should do? I think he phoned the house the other night while I was there. As soon as he realised it was me, he hung up. I don't think he knows about Mum.'

'Possibly not. Elverscott's quite isolated, and I don't suppose he gets out all that much.'

'Do you think I should go and see him?'

Kate felt grateful that she could take advice from someone like Irene, who was both wise and analytical.

'I do, actually,' Irene said eventually. 'I think it will be difficult and awkward, but I think to fly back home without letting him know would be . . . cruel.'

'That's what I thought.'

Irene put her head to one side, thoughtful. 'Would you like me to come with you? For moral support? I don't know him terribly well, but it might help him. To have a familiar face.'

It was tempting to have Irene to lean on, but Kate thought it was the coward's way out.

'That's sweet, but thank you. I think it's something I need to do on my own.'

'I have his address.' Irene pulled an ancient address book covered in Liberty fabric from the side in the kitchen. 'He's a very lovely man. Very gentle and thoughtful. He'll appreciate you going to see him. He won't think you're interfering.'

Kate was filled with dread at what she had to do, but she felt she had no choice. She had been struck by the depth of feeling in Robin's letter, and his courage, and his regret. She needed to meet him. She copied the address down.

'By the way, is Rupert here? Or is he out and about?'

'In his office, further down the corridor. But have your breakfast first. Your eggs are just about done.'

Kate found Rupert in his office, which was utter chaos. He had paperwork piled up around his ears, empty cups, Margo and Jerry at his feet and Classic FM blaring out Elgar. He looked up as she came in.

'You obviously slept well. Some of us have done half a day's work already.'

She smiled, perfectly happy to be teased. She handed him a mug of coffee Irene had given her.

'I just wanted to catch up with you before I left. To say thank you for a fantastic evening.'

'My absolute pleasure. It was good to have someone to go out with. It can be a bit isolated here once the summer is over.' He moved some papers around on his desk. 'And if you do want to sell Belle Vue, of course we'd be interested in having a look. If you sell direct to us, there'd be no agent's fee.'

Kate narrowed her eyes. She wasn't sure if she trusted him. Had he just been buttering her up? Feigned a lack of interest to make her feel bad?

'I'll let you know the asking price,' she told him.

He stood up. 'Let me walk you round the grounds before you go. Tell you my plans. I'd love your take on it.'

Kate hesitated. She had a lot to do, but it was tempting. She was curious indeed. 'That would be lovely.'

She borrowed a pair of Irene's gum boots, and a wax jacket, and they made their way outside. There was a lacy mist hanging over the grounds, so they couldn't see the sea in the distance. Silver dew clung to the lawn, and the air was sharp and fresh, the scent of ozone underlying the woodier smell of dying leaves underfoot.

They walked over the lawns at the back of the house, towards the cliff that towered over the sea and gave the house its name.

'I know we've got the beach at our disposal, but we're going to have to build a pool, because people expect it. So we're putting it here. An infinity pool, so it feels as if you might fall over the cliff edge and into the sea.'

'It'll be spectacular.'

'I hope so. I want it to blend in with the surroundings

and be as natural as possible. There'll be changing rooms and a bar, all in wood. All very mellow.'

The mist was starting to clear and, gradually, before their eyes, the ocean appeared. Kate wondered how many hours she had spent out there. The playground of her youth.

'Come on,' said Rupert.

He led her back over the lawns and round to the walled garden.

'We've let this run to seed, because Granny can't keep it up. But I've found a wonderful girl from the agricultural college. She's going to restore it to its former glory. We're going to supply all the fruit and vegetables for the house. And there's going to be a cutting garden, for flowers. And we're going to keep chickens. For eggs.' He laughed. 'Obviously.'

Kate felt a twinge of envy. 'It's a fantastic project. You're very lucky. And I think it'll be really successful. It's exactly what people want – wealthy people who live in cities. A breath of sea air, luxury, a bit of history . . .'

'Do you think so?' Rupert looked anxious. It was the first time Kate had ever seen him less than confident. 'To be honest, I haven't a clue what I'm doing.'

'You just need to keep an eye on your spending. Do things in phases, rather than trying to get everything up and running all at once.'

'But I want it to be perfect. Now!' He laughed at himself. 'If you think of anything I've overlooked. Or have any brainwaves . . .'

'Sure. But you seem to have it covered.' She looked at her watch. 'Listen, I better go. I've got a million things to do before I fly back. My boss is champing at the bit.

But thank you – for a lovely night. And I'll let you know about the house—'

She felt the warmth of him through his jumper as he leaned in to give her a hug. They both stood still for a moment. Kate felt awkward, and knew damn well that was exactly how she was supposed to feel. Rupert smiled and raised his eyebrows. God, he was a player, even now. A leopard never changes its spots, she reminded herself.

She raised a hand to say goodbye, turned and walked away as quickly as she could, feeling as if somebody had tipped a tub of glitter into her stomach.

Then realised she had no way of getting back to Penn-fleet.

She turned. He was standing with his arms crossed, smiling at her.

'I'm guessing you'd like a lift?' he said. 'Cos it's a long walk.'

25

'Darling,' said Squirrel to her daughter, 'there's something we need to discuss.'

Vanessa's heart sank. What now? 'Is there?'

'This house,' said Squirrel. 'It's like a bloody mausoleum. Please tell me you're going to redecorate.'

Squirrel had long thought whoever had been given the contract for the interior design of Pennfleet House should have been taken out and shot. It was more like a tacky Mayfair hotel than a seaside retreat: all marble and high-gloss wood and shiny chandeliers. The drawing room was perfectly suited to a gaggle of hookers, with its L-shaped leather sofas and the smoked-glass coffee table that lay in wait ready to bark your shins. There were hideous paintings of scantily clad women wrapped around wild cats.

Who on earth had looked at a beautiful house like this and decided to rip the heart and soul out of it? Someone who had only seen Spencer's cheque book; someone who couldn't be bothered to teach him that less is more.

'Let's rip it all out,' she said to Vanessa. 'Rip it all out and start again. It will be therapeutic for you.'

'But it cost a fortune,' Vanessa protested. 'Do you know how much that marble is a square metre?'

'No,' said Squirrel. 'Nor do I care. Someone will take it off our hands. I'll phone round.' Squirrel had a magical phone book containing the numbers of people who could provide anything, do anything, and take anything away – sometimes all three at once. 'Gibbo will take it all out and put down some oak floorboards. He'll get rid of this lot on some tasteless oligarch.'

It upset her that Vanessa, with her wonderful eye and her artistic touch, had had to live in such a monstrosity for so long.

Vanessa looked at her mother and began to laugh. Only Squirrel, she thought.

Squirrel was on a mission. She threw her arms out.

'It needs wood and chalky paint and linen and velvet. Softness. Pale blues and creams. And Christ – that ghastly artwork. Get a dealer down. Get rid of it.'

'I can't just wipe all evidence of Spencer out, Mum. I can't just pretend he didn't exist.'

'Why not? Come on, darling. It'll be a project. Something to take your mind off things.' She looked around the kitchen. 'I don't understand why anyone would put high gloss and stainless steel in a seaside house. You need pale-grey tongue and groove and soft white marble.'

Vanessa could see what Squirrel was trying to do. Distract her. She appreciated her efforts, but looking at a few paint charts wasn't going to do the trick.

Although maybe it would? From the first day Spencer had brought her to Pennfleet House, she had fantasised about restoring it to its former glory. All the period detail was still there, under the glitz. Spencer had been so proud of what he had made it, almost childlike in the pleasure he took, that she had never had the strength to work on him. So she had concentrated all her efforts on making the shop as beautiful as she could. Adrift was where her energy and spirit lay.

Now, though, there was nothing stopping her bringing that spirit into her own home.

And it might, just might, stop her looking at her phone every two minutes. He hadn't contacted her. Of course not. She'd been a drunken Friday-night distraction. An anecdote. The comfort she had taken from him had been an illusion.

'Maybe you're right,' she told Squirrel. 'It could be fun.' Yep, thought Vanessa. It was time to stop fantasising and join the real world. 'Anyway, I'm going into the shop this morning. I haven't been in for nearly a fortnight. I need to catch up with the girls and get back on track. And I've got a meeting with an artist later. Will you be OK?'

Squirrel held up a Farrow and Ball paint chart. Vanessa laughed.

'I'll see you later,' she said.

Squirrel watched her daughter go. She had such mixed feelings. It was wrong to be glad that Spencer wasn't in her life any more – she wouldn't wish anyone dead – but she was pleased that Vanessa had a chance for a new beginning. It was horrible, as a mother, to know your daughter deserved better. She knew she and Spencer hadn't seen eye to eye, and there had been a clash of personality, but he definitely hadn't been the person who was going to make Vanessa fulfil her potential, even though he had spared no expense on her. Their life had revolved around him, for the most part. Yes, Vanessa had her shop, but even that had been controlled by Spencer, quietly, in the background.

She hoped her daughter would blossom and flourish. It was all you could wish for, really, at her age, that your children were happy. She prayed Vanessa would find someone else, eventually, and not end up like she had. Still in love with the man she had married. Even though she couldn't live with him, and had had to let him go. No one had even come close to David, so she had never bothered. Who wanted a pale imitation? Not Squirrel.

She wondered how he was doing. Whether he had someone else. Lots of someone elses, probably, in the intervening years. David was profoundly attractive, and a ladies' man, even though she was fairly sure he had never been unfaithful. Drunk, most of the time, yes. And irresponsible. But not unfaithful.

They had loved each other. But he had loved the bottle just that little bit more. And that didn't sit easily with Squirrel, who took parenthood very seriously. Even now, at over sixty. People could call her bossy and controlling if they liked, but it was done out of love.

She sat at the island. The house was quiet, but for Frank Cooper's jackhammer purr. She looked at Vanessa's Mac, on the side. And something drove her towards it. She'd had endless opportunity to Google him before, but something had always stopped her. A sense that the time wasn't right.

But somehow, with Vanessa free, Squirrel felt released. As if she could revisit the past. She slid the mouse until the screen came up, clicked on the browser and typed in his name.

David Brown. Antique dealer. There he was, living in a tiny village in south-west France.

*

The girls who ran the shop were delighted to see Vanessa. She was the perfect boss. She left them to get on with things and trusted them to use their initiative, but injected a burst of infectious enthusiasm whenever she came in, full of praise and ideas.

The three of them spent an hour going over what had sold in the past week or so, debating samples that had been left, making appointments with new artists they were interested in, and deciding on a new theme for the shop windows. The silver and blues of summer seemed too bright now.

'Anything golden or copper or bronze,' suggested Vanessa. 'We need to mellow it down. Give it an autumnal feel. Maybe use the bronze hare sculptures as a centrepiece?'

The door opened and a woman walked in, carrying a large canvas swathed in bubble wrap. She was dainty, about Vanessa's age, with a black bob and smiling eyes, in a red military jacket, jeans and boots.

'I've come to see Vanessa,' she said.

Vanessa came forward.

'You must be Alexa,' she said, and they shook hands. 'It's lovely to meet you. Come into the back – I'll make you a coffee.'

They went into the back room. Alexa had sent her some jpegs of her artwork a few weeks previously, and Vanessa had been interested, but needed to see the work in the flesh. Alexa laid the canvas on the table.

'Let's have a look,' Vanessa said, and Alexa undid the bubble wrap.

Vanessa took in a deep breath.

It was recognisably Pennfleet harbour. A very loose

impression of the river and the boats and the houses and the sea beyond, it was painted over in a wash of the brightest and most vibrant colours imaginable – turquoise and orange and fuchsia and yellow. It was bold, yet subtle.

Vanessa felt a flutter in her gut, the one that told her she had found something really special. She was untrained, but she had a good eye, a good instinct. This was one of those paintings that, every time you looked at it, you saw something new. It drew you back in, time and again.

'I absolutely love it,' she told Alexa.

'Oh!' said Alexa, looking rather overwhelmed.

'Is this the sort of thing you always do?'

'No. I've just started doing this since I moved here. At the risk of sounding horribly, horribly pretentious, I've tried to put my urban influence over a more traditional maritime theme. I hope it works.'

'I think these would fly.' Vanessa held up the canvas to inspect the technical detail. It was flawless. 'I'd really like to do an exhibition.'

She never usually offered an exhibition on the basis of one painting. She liked to put things in the shop first to see if they sold. But something told her to snap Alexa up. Take ownership of her.

'You're kidding?' Alexa went pink. 'An exhibition?'

'I'd need about a dozen pieces. For spring?'

Alexa looked floored. 'Well, of course, yes. I mean, that's amazing. Though I don't know how I'm going to manage it. It's not so much time, as space. I've got four kids. I have to clear off the dining-room table every morning when they go to school, then clear away my artwork when they come home.'

Vanessa bit her lip. 'I can see the problem. These pictures must take – how long?'

'Well, a couple of weeks each, at least. Which would leave me enough time. It will be difficult. But I'll find a way round it.' She smiled, and her face lit up. 'I can't miss this opportunity. It's way more than I hoped for.'

'I think you've got something really special. I'd love to work with you. And let me know if there's anything I can do to help. I don't want you to bite off more than you can chew.'

'No! The last thing I want to do is mess up.'

Vanessa held out her hand and the two women shook on it.

'We're going to put you on the map,' said Vanessa. 'Would you leave this with me? So I can think about how we curate the exhibition?'

'Of course,' said Alexa, who would, quite frankly, have left her right leg with Vanessa if she'd asked for it.

Alexa walked back home in a daze. She was part delighted, part terrified. Spending weeks on a painting to get it just right was very different from producing twelve pieces to order. But she was going to do it if it killed her.

She'd taken a big risk, moving down here with the kids, after her stupid husband had gone and let her down. She'd been terrified that Oscar would go off the rails and start getting into trouble, and that the others would follow suit, inheriting their dad's irresponsible, rebellious streak. She'd gambled there would be less trouble to get into in Pennfleet and so far she had been proved right. But money was tight. She was on benefits, up to her eyes in them, and that didn't make her proud. Her art had been her only way out that she could see. With four children it was difficult to go out to work. The minute the smallest had gone to school, she had thrown herself into her painting, which had been on hold for so many years. But it came back to her, the magic.

And now someone else had seen that magic. She couldn't believe it. She had no idea how much she would make. An exhibition was only the first step. People still had to buy the paintings. And she would have to invest a lot of money in canvases and paints up front. She didn't know how she was going to fund that, just yet.

But it was the most wonderful opportunity. Alexa decided to celebrate and went into the café on the hill to buy the biggest, squidgiest brownie they had.

'And a skinny soy latte.'

The man behind the counter smiled at her.

'That's a bit of a contradiction.'

'I wouldn't usually do the brownie. But I'm celebrating.'

'Won the lottery?'

'Not in so many words. But almost. In fact, better.' Alexa took the brownie from him, wrapped in a brown paper bag. She'd sit out in her tiny garden and eat it when she got home.

She waited while he made her coffee. Her eyes fell on an advert on the wall. Puppies, she thought, and her heart contracted at the thought of the kids' faces if she brought one home. She'd been thinking lately that they needed a dog, something to get them all out.

A hundred quid would buy an awful lot of paint. But what was paint in comparison to dog joy? She put the contact number into her phone, then took the coffee that was being held out to her.

'I'm tempted too,' said the man.

'Aren't they cute?' said Alexa. 'But what's a bitzer?'

The man grinned. 'Bitzer this, bitzer that. A Heinz fifty-seven, in other words.'

Alexa laughed, and handed him her money.

She left, and Sam watched after her. She'd lit up the café in the few moments she'd been in there. He wondered who she was. Then his next customer arrived, and in a moment she was forgotten.

Vanessa was going through her price lists, deciding what to mark down over the winter months to make space for new work, when the door tinged and an elderly man walked in. He was typical Pennfleet, with a weather-beaten face and bright-blue eyes and a shock of white hair, wearing blue overalls. Not a typical customer.

'Can I help you?'

He pointed a finger at her.

'I want a word with you,' he said, 'if you're Vanessa Knight.'

Vanessa frowned. What had she done? Parked somewhere she shouldn't? Parking was a constant problem round here, and there were often altercations.

'I am.'

His voice was tight with anger.

'You can't just go trampling over people. You in your big house, with your big boat. I don't care if you just buried your husband.'

Vanessa's mouth fell open. 'I'm sorry? I don't know what you're talking about.'

'My grandson lost his job on your account. Not that you're bothered. You just take what you need and leave him on the scrapheap.' He looked round the shop. 'Look at you, with your bloody overpriced paintings. Where's he supposed to get work from now, eh? In case you don't know, jobs are like hen's teeth round here in winter. But I don't suppose you're bothered.'

'I'm sorry,' said Vanessa again, 'but I don't know who your grandson is.'

Though she had a horrible feeling she might be able to guess.

'Nathan Fisher. Although I don't suppose you even bothered to ask his name.'

His face was red with fury, and he was trembling. Vanessa thought she could see tears in his eyes. But before she could mollify him, the man turned and stormed out of the shop.

The two girls looked at Vanessa. She was bright red with embarrassment. And horror. She'd had no idea Nathan had lost his job. She was mortified.

She went to the back of the shop and got her handbag.

'I'll be back later,' she told the girls, who nodded, round-eyed. In all the time they had known her, Vanessa had never caused any scandal.

She drove as fast as she could, to the industrial estate where the undertaker's office was. She remembered coming here to sort out the funeral arrangements. It seemed like a lifetime ago. She parked, jumped out of the car, and pushed open the door.

Malcolm Toogood was at his desk. He stood as she walked in.

'Mrs Knight – how nice to see you.' He was good with names and faces. You had to be, in his business.

She didn't bother with niceties.

'I need to talk to you. About Nathan Fisher.'

Malcolm Toogood blanched visibly and launched into a grovelling apology.

'Mrs Knight, I am so sorry. He's been disciplined. I can assure you. It's absolutely not the sort of behaviour we expect at Toogood's.'

Vanessa cut him short.

'I'm not here to complain. Quite the reverse. I put him under rather a lot of pressure and I don't want him to get into any trouble.'

'Well, I'm afraid it's too late. He was in breach of all our rules. We have a reputation to upkeep. I can't have my staff running amok all over town.'

'Please. Overlook it just this once. He took very good care of me. Very good care.'

For a moment she wanted to laugh as she remembered.

Mr Toogood breathed in through his nose.

'I'm afraid Nathan has already been dismissed, so there's nothing I can do.'

She could sense his disapproval not just of Nathan but of her. Sanctimonious fool.

Vanessa had learned a few tricks from her time with Spencer. She was going to employ one of them now.

She cleared her throat. 'Mr Toogood, I think given your considerable bill, which I and my solicitor haven't yet been through, the least you could do is turn a blind eye. I'm sure Nathan is usually an exemplary employee. Everyone is allowed one mistake.'

She was behaving in a way she had heard Spencer

behave so many times, and she hated doing it. But it seemed to work.

'Is that a threat, Mrs Knight?'

She paused for a moment. 'Yes. I think it probably is.'

There was a long silence as she waited for his reaction. She could see him turning over the options in his mind. Eventually he nodded.

'Very well. I'll call him. And reinstate him. Assuming he hasn't found employment elsewhere.'

'Thank you,' she said, smiling sweetly. 'And thank you again for a lovely funeral. I'll be sure to recommend you to everyone I know.'

26

Elverscott was a couple of miles up the river from Pennfleet, the quaintest of fishing villages, no doubt also peopled by second-homers and incomers. There was a popular walk from Pennfleet to Elverscott along the river, which for most people culminated in lunch at the excellent thatched pub rumoured to be getting a Michelin star.

Kate drove around until she found the Jessops' house, a handsome whitewashed cottage with a stunning view of the river that probably doubled its value.

She parked her car on the road outside and tapped her fingers on the steering wheel. There had been no guidebook to consult on how to approach your mother's possible paramour to tell him she had passed away. But she still felt that to keep it from Robin was wrong, although he may well stumble across the news at some point. She felt it was her duty to her mother to tell him herself. Would he be hostile, or welcoming?

She walked up the path to the front door. The garden was pretty and rambling, and she could imagine it in summertime, all honeysuckle and roses, smelling sweet, buzzing with fat bumblebees. It was, she told herself, the garden of a good person – it had clearly been cared for.

She told herself she wasn't going to hesitate, although her stomach was in a tight knot. Before she could think about it too much, she knocked. Moments later, she heard footsteps and someone inside undoing a chain. It was too late to run off, but she wanted to.

The door opened.

Robin Jessop – presumably – was tall, slightly stooped, with kindly eyes and a full grey beard. He wore a fleece, and walker's trousers with lots of zips and pockets.

'Oh,' he said. 'I was expecting the postman.'

'Mr Jessop?' asked Kate, not feeling she could call him Robin.

'Depends who is asking.' He was teasing her. 'You're not from HMRC?'

'No.'

'Thank goodness.' He looked at her, eyes bright with curiosity. 'So who are you?'

'Kate,' said Kate. 'Jackson.' She cleared her throat. 'Joy's daughter.'

He paused for a moment, digested the information, then gave a sharp breath. 'Of course you are. I can see it now. Your mother has shown me lots of photos.'

'Can I come in?'

He stood to one side. 'Of course.'

Kate walked past him, straight into the main room, which was large but cosy, with low beams and walls lined with books. By a far window, she could see a chair with a figure in it. A woman.

Robin came into the room behind her. She spoke in a low voice.

'I'm so sorry to be the one to have to tell you. And I

wasn't sure whether I should. But I found your letter to Mum ... in her handbag.'

Robin flinched. His face seemed to have fallen in on itself. 'I take it this isn't going to be good news.'

'I'm afraid ... my mother passed away. The funeral was on Friday. I'm sorry I didn't know about you sooner. I didn't find the letter until afterwards. I would have told you otherwise.'

'What happened? Was she ill? Oh dear God ...' He put his hands up, as if he didn't quite know what to do with them, clenching and unclenching his fists.

Kate told him, as sparing of the details as she could be. There was no way to break the news of a death in an uplifting fashion. Robin listened, and nodded, then put his hand on her shoulder. He seemed quite calm, once the news had been broken.

'You poor girl. You must be devastated. I know how close you were. She spoke about you all the time.' He was trying so hard, but as he spoke his voice broke. 'I'm sorry ...'

'This is such a strange situation. And I don't know what to do to help. And I don't know what to say.'

A voice came from the chair in the corner. 'What's going on?' It was a querulous, commanding tone.

'It's all right, darling. Just a neighbour.' Robin smiled at Kate, then spoke in an undertone. 'My wife, Nancy. You understand, of course? She suffers ...'

'Dementia. Yes, I understand. Like my father. I guess that's how you met?'

'The dementia centre.' He gave a wry smile. 'Not the most glamorous of rendezvous. Not exactly the Ritz.'

Kate saw that underneath his efforts to remain calm, Robin was shaking.

'Listen,' she said. 'If you want to spend a few minutes alone, I can sit with your wife.'

Robin considered her reply.

'That would be extraordinarily kind.' He was struggling with the effort of putting on a brave face. 'I'll go and walk in the garden for a few moments.'

He hurried away, and Kate realised how upset he must be, and how awkward he felt. No one wanted to share fresh grief with a total stranger. She walked across the room and sat in the chair opposite Nancy, who was dressed smartly in a corduroy skirt and striped blouse, and still wore her jewellery and make-up. Kate would have had no idea there was anything wrong.

'If you're from the library,' said Nancy, 'that last one was atrocious.'

'Well,' said Kate. 'We'll have to see if we can do better for you next time.'

She knew there was no point in denying she had anything to do with the library. She could remember that from her father. Once they fixated on something, they would not be deterred. And maybe being from the library was safer than the truth.

'What do you think you'd like to read next?'

Outside, she could see Robin walking down to the bottom of the garden; he stood with his hands behind his back and his head bowed. She could see his shoulders shake.

'Not Jane Austen. Bloody tedious,' said Nancy.

'Yes,' said Kate. 'I quite agree.'

The whole scenario was completely surreal. She

wondered what her mother would think if she knew what she had done. It was the sort of situation Joy would have handled with great aplomb. Nothing rattled Joy: it was why she was so good at her job. So Kate owed it to her to manage it with grace and kindness.

'Would you like me to read to you?' she asked Nancy, who just stared at her blankly. So she picked up a copy of the *Radio Times*, and read an interview with James Nesbitt, complete with Northern Irish accent, which seemed to rivet her no end. So much so that at the end, Nancy clapped, just as Robin came back in. He looked a little pink around the eyes, but otherwise composed.

'Thank you so much,' Robin told Kate. 'And before you go, I do just want to tell you how very proud your mother was of you.'

'I feel so terrible that I wasn't here to help her with Dad. This has brought it all back, what she must have had to go through.'

'Ours is a very particular kind of purgatory. And there can only be one way for it to end. Which is, frankly, no great comfort.' He managed a wry smile. 'But you mustn't feel guilty. Joy would have hated that.'

'I know. Mum was one of the most selfless people on the planet. Which kind of makes it worse.'

'She was wonderful.' Robin's face started to crumple. 'Oh dear. I had hoped . . .'

He couldn't really voice what he had hoped. He pulled out a large white handkerchief and blew his nose. But Kate knew what he meant. She waited quietly while he gathered himself together, wiping his eyes and folding the hanky up.

'I feel very privileged to have known her,' he said. 'And

I am so very grateful to you for coming to see me. It went beyond the call of duty.'

'It was a very beautiful letter that you wrote.'

Pain flickered across his face. 'I didn't write it lightly. But I'm sure you understand. Nancy's still my wife and there are – occasional – moments of lucidity. It didn't feel right. It wasn't fair on Joy. She needed someone unencumbered, who could give her the attention she deserved.'

Kate could think of nothing to say. All he needed was a hug. So she hugged him, and he cried a little bit more, while Nancy poked at him with the walking stick she kept beside her.

'Don't think I can't see what you're up to,' she shouted.

Robin and Kate looked at each other. There was nothing to do but laugh.

'You have to laugh,' he said. 'Or else...'

'I'm going back to New York at the end of the week. But I'd very much like to keep in touch.' She gave him her card. 'Please. If you ever want to talk, just get in touch.'

He took it, and slipped it into the pocket of his shirt. He looked at her.

'You are very like her, you know. You've left me with the same warm feeling.'

Kate caught her breath. It was such a wonderful thing to say.

'I can never live up to her,' she told him. 'But I'm going to try.'

27

Nathan was lying in bed, toying with the idea of getting up – although he couldn't quite see a reason for it, except the puppies would need sorting out – when his phone rang. He ignored it for a moment. There wasn't anyone he could think of he wanted to speak to.

Curiosity got the better of him. He picked up his phone and saw it was Malcolm Toogood.

'Hello?' he said, cautious.

'Nathan. It's Malcolm.'

'Yes.'

'Look, I've had a chance to reflect on things.' Malcolm liked to use words like 'reflect'. Why couldn't he just say 'think'? 'I was a bit harsh on you. I possibly overreacted. So, if you haven't found any other gainful employment...'

Course he hadn't. Where was he going to find gainful employment at this time of year?

'... I'd like to offer you your position back. You've been exemplary over the years, apart from this one aberration. I'd be a fool to let you go because you've made one mistake.'

Part of Nathan wanted to tell Malcolm to stuff his job, because he had been hurt to be sacked so unceremoniously. But he didn't, because it wasn't in his nature, and because he wanted the job back. There was bugger all at the Job Centre. And he liked driving for Toogood's. He liked the ceremony, and feeling he had been part of helping people through the ordeal of a funeral. It was strangely satisfying.

'Oh,' he said. 'That's cool. Great. Thank you.'

'Actually, you don't have me to thank,' replied Malcolm. 'Thank Mrs Knight. She insisted I reinstate you. She was very anxious you shouldn't get into any trouble.'

'Really?'

'Widows. They're dangerous things.' Malcolm gave a long-suffering sigh, as if he spent his life batting them away. 'There's a funeral tomorrow afternoon. In Shore-down. If you're free.'

'I'll be there,' said Nathan.

He got himself up, showered, got dressed and sorted the dogs, then went down to see Sam and grab a coffee.

'How's tricks?' asked Sam.

'Complicated,' replied Nathan. 'But I've just got my job back.'

'That's good. Isn't it?'

'Turns out Vanessa had a word with the gaffer.'

Sam looked impressed.

'Do you think I should thank her?' asked Nathan. 'Or just let it go?'

Sam thought for a moment.

'Would you spend the rest of your life wondering what might have happened if you didn't? Would you spend sleepless nights, torturing yourself? Would you wander round, pale and listless, a shadow of your former self?'

Nathan laughed. 'All of the above.'

'Then yes. Go and see her. What's the worst that can

happen? What have you got to lose? And let's be honest, everyone likes to be thanked. People don't do enough of it.'

Nathan nodded. 'That's a point. It would be rude not to, right?'

'*Very* rude.'

Sam handed Nathan his latte.

'Listen, mate, have you still got those puppies?'

'I've got two left,' Nathan told him. 'I had a woman come and reserve one yesterday. I'm keeping one for myself. Do you want one?'

Sam paused for a moment. 'I must be mad,' he said. 'But yeah – I think I do.'

'Come up and have a look tonight.'

'I can't tonight,' said Sam. 'I'm meeting my daughter's boyfriend's mother for a drink.'

'Sounds complicated.'

'She wants to introduce herself because the kids are going out together. It'll make a change, I suppose.'

'Any idea what she's like?'

'Well, Daisy seems to like her.'

'Is she single?'

'Ex-husband in prison.' Sam made a face.

Nathan grimaced. 'Dodgy. Come and see them on the way home if you want. It'll give you an excuse to get out of it.'

'I might take you up on that,' said Sam. He wished he could find a way of getting out of it. The last thing he wanted was to make polite conversation with Oscar's mother. He imagined some gangland moll, like something out of Lynda La Plante, all cleavage and Cockney

278

rhyming slang. Wasn't that what he'd come all the way here to get away from?

After leaving Sam's, Nathan went up to the florist. Not the one that Malcolm used for funerals, which churned out hideously garish arrangements, but the trendy one at the top end of town that had opened earlier in the year. He spent a long time examining each bloom, breathing in their scent and stroking the glossy leaves. In the end, he decided on twenty cream roses, their petals tinged at the edge with bright green, mixed in with burnt-orange freesias.

The florist arranged them all in a loose bouquet tied in a cream organza ribbon edged with old gold.

'She's very lucky, whoever she is,' she told him. 'Do you want to write something to go with it?'

'I suppose so, yes.'

She handed him a square card with a matching envelope, and a pen.

He chewed the end of the pen while he thought. The scent from the blooms was making him giddy, and he didn't have a clue what to say. He wasn't used to writing down his feelings. Eventually he managed a short message.

Thank you. You've saved my life! Thinking of you. Nathan.

He hoped it wasn't too invasive or stalky. Just thoughtful. And open-ended. It was true, though. He had done nothing but think of her. It was strange how, up till now, he hadn't really been aware of her, except as a vague presence who lived nearby, someone who people occasionally referenced. Now, she was all he could think of. Her eyes, her smile, her laugh, her scent, her touch, her mouth. Vanessa Knight. Her name was on repeat in his brain.

'That'll be sixty-four pounds.' The florist interrupted his thoughts.

Nathan paled, then pulled out his wallet. He wasn't going to argue. He'd never bought a bunch of flowers before, after all, so he had no idea if this was normal.

'You have chosen the most expensive flowers,' said the florist kindly. 'But there's no way she won't love them. And they'll smell wonderful for days.'

He held the bouquet carefully in his arms and walked back down the high street, hoping he wouldn't bump into any of his mates. They wouldn't stop until they found out who the flowers were for, and they would tease him endlessly.

He curved around the edge of the harbour and along the road to the entrance of Pennfleet House. He pushed open the gate, walked over the immaculate granite sett driveway and up to the front door. The knocker was in the shape of a dolphin. He used it to rap hard, three times. It sounded businesslike and assertive.

He could hardly breathe as he waited. He'd decided not to rehearse what he was going to say. He felt sure that the words would come easily, as soon as she saw him. It would be natural. It would be instinctive.

He could hear someone coming towards the door. His heart was juddering, like a car engine that was missing. He wasn't sure whether to smile. It would seem hostile not to, but he didn't want to look like a creepy stalker. The door opened just as he settled on a slightly sheepish grin.

There was a woman standing there. Slight, blonde, sixty-something.

'Oh, how lovely,' she said. 'Those are beautiful.'

'They're for Vanessa,' he said.

'How kind. Shall I say who sent them?'

'Um . . . Nathan.' He cleared his throat awkwardly. 'Nathan from . . . after the funeral.'

'Nathan from after the funeral.' As she smiled at him she gave him an expert look up and down. She must be Vanessa's mother, he thought. There was something in the voice. And the eyes. Although her smile didn't quite reach hers, the way Vanessa's did. 'You're very sweet, Nathan. She will love them. Thank you.'

He was just about to pluck up the courage to ask if Vanessa was in. But before he could, the woman stretched out her arms, whisked the bouquet from him and shut the door.

'Nathan from after the funeral?' asked Squirrel meaningfully, holding out the bouquet to Vanessa, who was stirring some soup for their lunch.

Vanessa tried to look casual, but there was a definite pinkness to her cheeks as she read the card.

'Oh, how gorgeous. Yes, um – he was very kind to me after the funeral. There was a bit of a misunderstanding with his boss, which I sorted out. I guess this is his way of saying thank you.'

She breathed in the scent, shutting her eyes.

'He was very attractive,' ventured Squirrel.

Vanessa nodded. 'I know . . .'

She opened her eyes again, put the flowers down on the island and opened the cupboard to find a vase.

'When you say kind ...?' Squirrel wasn't going to stop until she found out the details.

Vanessa put the vase next to the flowers then began to unwrap the brown paper they were wrapped in.

'We had a bit of a ... skirmish. Nothing too outrageous. Just a ...' Vanessa started snipping the ends with a pair of scissors. There was a smile playing on her lips. 'I kissed him.'

'Vanessa!' Squirrel was scandalised.

'I know. It was really naughty. But I needed to do it. And he didn't mind.'

Squirrel's mouth was open in horrified delight.

'That's outrageous.'

'I know!' Vanessa filled the vase with water. 'But please don't have a go at me. I can't take it at the moment.'

'Have a go at you?' asked Squirrel. 'I applaud you.'

'What?'

Vanessa looked at her mother in amazement. This wasn't the reaction she was expecting.

'But he's almost half my age.'

'So?' shrugged Squirrel. 'You were half Spencer's. So what's the problem?'

'It's different, isn't it?'

'I don't see why it should be. If he makes you happy.'

'Mum, it was nothing. It was just a ... bit of a ...'

'Your eyes are sparkling. I haven't seen you look like that ...' Squirrel thought about it. 'Well, since before you were married.'

'It's not appropriate, though, is it? I'm old enough to be his mother, almost.'

'So?' said Squirrel. 'You're both grown-ups. And he's

282

definitely keen. His face fell like the guillotine when I answered the door.'

'You don't seriously think I should take it further?'

'Why not? Darling, if he wasn't hoping for something more, he wouldn't have brought you these. They must have cost a fortune.'

'Bless him,' said Vanessa, looking at her handiwork. 'I don't suppose he could afford them.'

'He's keen.'

'So what am I supposed to do?'

'Thank him for the flowers. Ask him out.'

Vanessa shook her head.

'Vanessa, you deserve some fun. You've been locked up here like Rapunzel. Let your hair down!'

Vanessa ruffled her hair and looked down at the floor, smiling.

'I don't think I'm ready for it.'

Squirrel tutted. 'You're mad. Go for it.'

Vanessa looked up. 'You never did. After Dad.'

Squirrel, in her control-freak way, began to tweak Vanessa's arrangement.

'No. Well. That's different. Anyway. That might change.'

'What do you mean?'

'I'm going to go and find him.'

Vanessa put her hands on her hips. 'My dad?'

'Yes. I think it's time. I've waited long enough.' She pulled out a freesia and reinserted it towards the back of the arrangement.

'But what if . . . he's got someone else?'

'Do you know, I don't think there is. I've just got a feeling. And if there is, well, it's not meant to be.'

Vanessa was alarmed. Squirrel was off on some fantasy mission. She couldn't help feeling she was idealising her father's memory. Couldn't she remember the constant drama?

'Mum. Don't get hurt.'

'Oh. Don't you worry. I can look after myself. I'm going to drive back up to London tonight, sort out some things, then get the ferry tomorrow.'

Squirrel gave Vanessa a smile, and Vanessa thought she would like just one ounce of Squirrel's bravery and confidence. Just one ounce.

28

The thing with October, which people always forgot when it was being bright and sunny and vivacious, was that it could be moody. There could be a sudden swing, and there you were, with pendulous clouds and choppy seas and a nasty swell and a wind that could not be misconstrued as an autumn breeze, but a force in itself, ruthless and relentless.

Which was exactly what happened that afternoon, at about three o'clock.

'We need to get that boat in,' said Nathan's grandad, eyeing the sky and the water with concern. 'I don't like the look of that sky. We'll be in trouble at high tide if the rain starts.'

Nathan looked up at the sky. He was used to judging the conditions, but his grandfather knew the weather better than anyone; better than any barometer or forecaster. If he said the boat needed to come in, then it did. After all, they hadn't spent all that time restoring her only to let her be damaged in a storm. And it did look ominous. Tinged with green, which was never good.

'Let's take the trailer down the harbour then,' he agreed. 'It's about time I took her out the water.' The *Moonbeam* would go into one of their sheds for safekeeping over the winter, until the picnics started up again in springtime. She wasn't really built for winter expeditions.

The two of them went out into the yard and hooked up the trailer to Daniel's ancient Land Rover Defender just as the rain began. They rattled down the track from the cottage to the main road and along the high street to the slipway.

'Ah, it's going to be wet rain, this is,' said Daniel, and by the time they got to the slipway they couldn't see out of the window.

Nathan jumped out and ran along the pontoon to their mooring. By now the rain had started in earnest. It wasn't taking any prisoners – and with it was a gale and a half that was whipping up the waves.

By the time he started up the engine of the *Moonbeam*, he could barely see across the water. The sky seemed to meet the sea in one big watery blur the colour of slurry. The town disappeared behind the deluge. He steered his way between the other boats that were swaying up and down, the waves slapping their sides. The *Moonbeam* wasn't made for choppy waters, and it was all he could do to keep her on course as the wind suddenly changed and came from the south.

With it came a flash of lightning, and a tremendous crash of thunder. The storm was right overhead. He could see the waves throwing themselves right over the pontoon, and over the walls of the decks that backed the buildings along the harbour. Anyone having a crafty cigarette outside would find themselves with wet shoes, he thought.

He could see his grandad waiting at the foot of the slipway. He steered towards him, and as he did, he looked to the left, to Pennfleet House. He could see Vanessa outside on the terrace that overlooked the water. She was looking for something – he thought he could hear her cry out through the wind and the rain, but he couldn't be sure.

He made it to the slipway, and jumped into the shallows where his grandad was waiting with ropes to pull the boat out of the water and onto the trailer. It was tough work for two people, made worse by poor visibility and the fact they could barely hear each other. But eventually the *Moonbeam* was made safe.

'Let's get her back, then,' said Daniel.

Nathan looked back to Pennfleet House. He could still see Vanessa. She must be soaked to the skin. What was the matter? What was she looking for?

Daniel saw him looking.

'Go on then,' he said. 'Go and see what's going off. But don't come crying to me when it all goes pear-shaped.'

Nathan touched his grandad on the shoulder in appreciation. Behind him he heard the throaty grumble of the Land Rover start up as he ran down alongside Pennfleet House and jumped up over the wall onto the terrace.

Vanessa was standing looking out over the water, her hands protecting her face from the rain, shouting. Her blonde hair was plastered to her head, and her clothes were drenched.

He came up behind and touched her arm. She whipped round and he could see the distress on her face. He couldn't tell if she was crying because she was so wet.

'What is it?'

'My cat. Frank Cooper. He was on the wall. There was a big wave.' She couldn't tell him any more. She was too upset.

'Did he go in?'

She nodded. He took her hand and they stood looking together into the mighty swell of the waves, a churning soup of grey-green that was hurling itself indiscriminately around the harbour.

Vanessa put her face in her hands. Poor Frank Cooper. She couldn't bear it.

Nathan held her. 'I'm so sorry,' he said. 'I'm so so sorry.'

'It's OK.' She wasn't going to cry in front of him. 'It's my fault. I should have got him in ages ago, before the rain started. But I didn't realise.'

'How could you have? Don't blame yourself.'

The rain was lashing down on them. Another wave came over the wall, and he pulled her out of the way.

'You should go inside,' he said.

They stood staring at each other as the rain poured down on them, buckets and buckets of it. There was another huge flash of lightning, and it lit up their faces. Then the thunder.

'You're going to catch your death,' Nathan said eventually.

'Come in and get dry,' she said.

They hadn't taken their eyes off each other. Nathan tried to wipe the water from his eyes.

'You know what'll happen if I come in?' he said.

'Yes.' She bit her lip.

'What about your mother?'

'She's gone back up to London.'

'So she's not here?'

Vanessa smiled. 'No.'

Nathan nodded. 'That's good, then.'

*

288

She gave him the guest bathroom, and a pile of fluffy white towels.

She had the hottest shower she could stand in her own room, then pulled on a big jumper and leggings and went to the kitchen to make hot chocolate. She stood at the back door to see if Frank Cooper had by some miracle appeared, but he hadn't. She couldn't think about him, his dear little ginger body being tossed about on the waves.

The milk came to the boil. She was pouring it carefully into two mugs when Nathan came into the kitchen with a towel wrapped around his waist. She put the pan down with a bang.

'Hot chocolate?' she asked, but her voice came out as a whisper. She handed him a mug.

They sipped slowly, standing by the island.

'Doesn't look like the rain's going to stop,' she said.

'No,' he said, and he was staring at her, and he put his cup down, still holding his towel in place, then put his spare hand behind her head and pulled her to him, and she tasted chocolate and promise and moments later his towel fell to the floor.

Alexa was tempted to cancel her drink with Daisy's dad when she saw the rain. It was what her mum would have called stair-rods, and she would be wet through in seconds. But she told herself not to be such a wuss. This would be the first time she'd been out on her own since they got to Pennfleet. And Oscar insisted.

'It would be really rude to cancel, Mum.'

He was looking after the little ones for her. He was a good boy, Oscar. So Alexa dug out the giant cagoule she had bought when they moved here, and put it on over the black dress with the white collar she had chosen to wear. She had been going to wear ballet flats but they wouldn't last two minutes, so she put on her trusty biker boots. Then she found an umbrella.

The wind nearly blew her all the way to the Townhouse by the Sea, where they were supposed to meet. She dried herself off as best she could in the ladies', and reapplied her eyeliner. She wanted to look as respectable as she could. Oscar was smitten with Daisy, and she didn't want any trouble. She'd had enough of that in her life.

She settled herself into a window seat, and watched the rain lash the window. There was something very comforting about being tucked up inside while the elements did their thing outside. And when the waitress came to take her order, she asked for a glass of Prosecco. She hadn't had time to celebrate her commission yet. It was the first chance she'd had to really think about it.

She was just toasting herself with the bubbles when the man she assumed was Daisy's dad walked in and looked around. She raised a tentative hand to identify herself, and as he took off his hat, she recognised him straight away.

And he her.

'Skinny soy latte, chocolate brownie,' he grinned, pointing at her.

She laughed, and stood up.

'This is mad. Daisy said you had a café,' she told him, 'but I didn't realise it was yours. I'm Alexa.'

'Sam.'

For some reason, it felt right to kiss him on the cheek, even though they had only just met.

'I got myself a glass of Prosecco,' said Alexa.

'Sounds like a great idea,' replied Sam, who liked the fact she'd just gone ahead and got what she wanted. He ordered one for himself from the waitress, and sat down in the window seat next to her.

'So Oscar said you wanted to meet me? I know you're probably worried, because you've heard things. About my ex. But the thing is . . .' she was gabbling, because it was always embarrassing talking about it, 'yes, he's in prison, but it was a sort of fraud thing to do with out-of-date drugs he was selling on. Not that that excuses it, of course, but I didn't want you to think that he was some sort of crack baron and that Oscar came from a dodgy family—'

'Hey hey hey hey shush a minute,' said Sam. 'What did you say?'

'Um – which bit?'

'About Oscar saying you wanted to meet me?'

'Yes. That's what he said. And he told me to meet you here.'

'But that's what Daisy said.'

'Sorry?' Alexa looked puzzled.

'Daisy said you wanted to meet me.'

'No.' She shook her head. 'I mean, not that it isn't lovely to meet you, of course. But—'

Sam started to laugh. 'Little buggers.'

'What?' She still hadn't cottoned on.

'I think we've been set up. By our kids.'

She thought about it for a moment, and then smiled. 'Oh my God.' She tucked her hair behind her ears. 'This is so embarrassing.'

'What the hell,' said Sam. 'We might as well enjoy ourselves.'

The waitress brought him his Prosecco. He raised his glass to hers.

'It's very nice to meet you.'

'It's very nice to meet you, too.'

And she smiled again, and he noticed the gap between her front teeth, which was kind of cute. And he thought about Louise, and he thought she would probably be laughing her head off too, at the scenario, and might very well be cheering him on. He hoped so.

'So, skinny soy latte,' he said to her, 'what is it you actually do?'

Two hours later, they hadn't stopped talking. They discovered so many things they had in common – music, favourite recipes, artists, books. Places they wanted to go.

The rain was still lashing down.

'Listen,' said Sam. 'We'll get soaked again if we go home now. Shall I see if they've got a table? Shall we have supper?'

Alexa panicked for a moment, because a meal here wasn't going to be cheap, but then she remembered her commission and decided that she deserved dinner out with a lovely man.

'That,' she said, 'is a totally brilliant idea.'

Nathan was still there when Vanessa woke in the morning.

The first thing she saw was his lean, toned back with the mermaid tattoo on the right shoulder. She put out a finger and traced the ink. His skin was warm and like velvet. She swallowed. She couldn't even begin to think about the night before.

'That tickles,' he told her, and she could hear laughter in his voice.

'I'll stop then,' she said.

'No, don't.'

Then she thought, shit, I need to make myself look presentable before he turns round and sees the horrible truth. 'I'm going to make us tea,' she whispered in his ear, and scampered into the bathroom.

In the mirror, she held up her hands and gave a silent scream of joy, then did a little dance, then set to making herself look as if she had just woken up looking utterly ravishing. Teeth, moisturiser, comb through hair then ruffle, a smidge of mascara, a slick of lip-gloss. A squirt of perfume.

She looked in the mirror. And was surprised to realise she looked about ten years younger.

In the kitchen, she looked outside to see if Frank Cooper had reappeared, but he hadn't. The harbour was as calm as anything, the day bright with just a light breeze. It was as if the storm had never happened.

She took up a tray with two mugs of tea into the bedroom. Nathan was lying on his back, his arms hooked around his head, smiling at her.

'We should talk,' she said, sitting on the bed next to him.

'Oh, really?' he said. 'Must we?'

She handed him a mug of tea, and he sat up.

'Look, I think you're totally amazing. But I've just lost my husband. I'm kind of all over the place. And I'm old enough to be your mother. Almost. You belong with someone your own age. If we got together, one of us would get hurt. Probably both of us. It would be... awkward. It's a lovely idea. In theory. But on balance...'

She trailed off. Nathan was staring at her. 'On balance

what?' he asked, putting his tea down on the bedside table. Then he gave her the laziest, sexiest smile, put out a finger and touched the hollow at the base of her neck, by her collarbone. She shivered. Swallowed.

'On balance?' he repeated, drawing a tiny circle with the tip of his finger.

She couldn't speak.

'On balance?'

'Oh fuck it,' she said, reaching out an arm. She hooked it round his neck and pulled him towards her. 'If it all ends in tears, don't come crying to me.'

That's just what his grandad had said. But he didn't think there would be any.

'We're going to have a lot of fun before the tears start.'

He was kissing her neck. Vanessa was squirming with the thrill of it.

He put his other hand up and held her head in his hands. Stared into her eyes. 'You're beautiful.'

She could feel herself blushing. 'I bet you say that to all the cougars.'

'Will you be quiet? I don't care how old you are.'

They stared at each other for a moment, smiling, in that *I can't believe this is really happening* way. Like they had the first night. The magic was still there.

29

In the end, Mary didn't have to wait as long as she thought for her results, because Dr Webster knew the consultant, and he phoned her as soon as he knew, and she asked him if she could tell Mary herself.

'You're all right, Mary,' she told her. 'We'll need to keep an eye on it, but that's good practice anyway. I'm so pleased. I know it's a horrible scare.'

Mary could think of nothing to say but thank you. When she'd taken in the good news, she'd go up to the surgery and take Dr Webster a little something to show her appreciation. Not everyone would get that treatment, she suspected, and she was grateful.

She went to find Kenny. He was in his shed, but instead of sitting and staring into space with a roll-up he was sorting out his fishing gear, which had lain in a tangle for months. She couldn't believe the change in him, even though they were living under the strain of not knowing.

But now they did.

'I'm OK,' she told him. She wasn't one for effusiveness, Mary. Nor was Kenny, much, but the embrace they gave each other said everything they needed to know. Sometimes you didn't need words.

'Come into town with me. Now.'

Kenny looked puzzled. 'What for, love? I got the shopping. We've got tea.'

'There's something I want to do.'

He could hardly refuse her request. He grabbed his coat, and she got hers, and they walked down the hill into Pennfleet. The high street was fresh and lively after the storm. It was almost as if it hadn't happened.

Kenny followed Mary up the street into the travel agents, where they sat down in front of a young girl who smiled and asked them where they wanted to go.

'Australia,' said Mary, and Kenny looked at her as if she was mad.

'I've been given a chance,' she told him. 'I want to breathe the same air that my boys are breathing. I want to put my grandchildren to bed in their own bed. I want to get a taste of their life so I can imagine them when I'm back in Pennfleet.'

'I totally understand that, but how are we going to pay? I mean, I know I'm working but—'

And she told him about Spencer's bequest. And how she'd kept it quiet until she knew she was all right, because they might have needed the money to tide them over.

They sat for a moment while the travel agent tapped away at the keyboard. Mary reached out and took Kenny's hand. She was so proud of him, for getting his job, and standing up to Ruthie, who had agreed to find her own place and had already made arrangements to go and see a couple of flats. Quite good-naturedly, it seemed. It was funny, she thought, how out of bad could come good, sometimes. How people proved their mettle.

'OK – so, two tickets from Heathrow to Sydney. Fifteenth of December. Returning in four weeks.'

'First class,' said Mary.

'It's very dear,' said the agent.

'I don't care,' said Mary, and smiled.

Thank you, Spencer, wherever you are.

On Kate's last night in Pennfleet, she felt shattered. But Debbie had called round to say goodbye, so she couldn't just flop. The two of them shared a bottle of wine Debbie had brought round. Kate had to rummage in one of the boxes she had packed up to get out two glasses. Everything was ready to go first thing in the morning, either shipped over to her in New York, or off to Recycling, or the charity shop.

'So when's it going on the market?'

Kate realised she'd been so busy she hadn't filled her friend in on what had happened. She hadn't told her about spending the night at Southcliffe, either. She didn't want a post-mortem on what it meant, or what it might mean. Because it meant nothing.

'I might have a buyer for the cottage already. Rupert Malahide.'

Debbie was staring at her. She looked strained. 'Oh. So that's why he asked you out for dinner.'

'I guess so. But it would save me a fortune in agents' fees. He's supposed to be making me a formal offer.'

'How much?' Debbie's voice sounded strangled.

Kate wasn't sure she wanted to tell her. 'Well, we haven't quite agreed on the price.'

Debbie leaned forward. 'Roughly how much? More than three hundred?'

'Well . . .' Kate felt awkward. 'Just over.'

Debbie sat back again and digested the information.

'Oh.'

'What's the matter?'

Debbie looked away.

'Scott and I would have liked your cottage.'

'Really?.'

'We worked out we could just afford it. If we sold ours and got an interest-only mortgage. I'd probably have to get another job but now Leanne's at nursery . . .'

'Isn't it far too small?'

'We were thinking about a loft conversion.' Debbie's voice was small. 'But there's no way we could afford over three hundred. We're just local scum, you see. We don't get a look in when it comes to buying the pretty houses.'

Kate was shocked at the venom in her voice.

'Debbie—'

'We get left up the arse end of town where we belong.'

'I'm so sorry.'

'Don't you worry. No one else does. The likes of Rupert Malahide certainly don't. He won't be happy till he's bought up the whole town and stuffed it full of toffs like him.'

Debbie gulped at her wine, then put her glass back down.

'Debs – you should have said. You should have told me. We could have worked something out, maybe.'

'No. It was just a stupid dream. Who was I trying to kid?'

Her voice broke.

'Sorry. It's just hard. Four kids. Keeping body and soul together. We've got so many plans but we never seem to get anywhere. I didn't mean to have a go at you. It's tough, you know. Trying to scratch a living. Picking up the crumbs left by the rich people.'

'I get it,' said Kate, putting her hand over hers.

'I know you haven't got any choice. Rupert would buy your place anyway. And I'm just jealous, I suppose. My life doesn't change from day to day and yours seems so . . . glamorous. We seem so different. But we were the same once.'

'Don't be jealous,' said Kate. 'I envy you, too. Your lovely husband and your amazing kids.'

'You're joking.' Debbie looked surprised.

'My life's ridiculous. It might seem glamorous, but it's superficial. It has no meaning. Not really.'

'I wouldn't mind doing a swap. You can come and look after my lot for a week.'

Kate laughed. 'I can tell you. I have my fair share of tantrums to deal with.'

Her heart sank slightly as she thought of Carlos. It had been good to be away from him. She'd found time to breathe. But even from here, she could sense his neediness. Her inbox was crammed with agendas, dates for meetings, possible menus, prices, venues to visit. She was going to have to hit the ground running.

'Come here.' She wrapped Debbie in a hug. She thought about how many times they'd done this. Not least after the debacle at Rupert's brother's twenty-first, when Debbie had hugged away her humiliation.

She didn't have friends like this in New York. She'd have to get some, she decided. It would be the first thing she worked on when she got back.

After Debbie left, after a lot of hugs and a few tears and some slightly tipsy *I love you*s, Kate sat in the silence of the kitchen. The silence of the emptiness was deafening:

even the radio had been packed up to go to the recycling centre in Shoredown.

Part of her wished she could stay to see the sale go through, but there was no point. Her life had to go on. And Robin's life, and Nancy's life, and Debbie's life, would carry on without her. They didn't need her

Bed, she thought. Just a few ends to tie up tomorrow, and then the drive up to Heathrow. If she stayed up any later, she would get maudlin. Think about all the ghosts in the house. She'd take her last tablet. And boy was she going to need it. All she wanted to do was sleep.

'I think you children should know,' said Sam, 'that you can't go round messing with people's lives. It was a terrible thing to do. You lied, for a start. I didn't bring you up to tell fibs.'

He was doing his very best to keep a straight face. Daisy and Jim were looking mortified. They hated getting into trouble with their dad, because he rarely told them off.

'But I thought you got on?' said Daisy. 'Oscar said his mum thought you were lovely.'

'That's not the point,' said Sam. 'And you need to understand the implications of what you've done.'

Daisy and Jim looked at each other.

'Wait there,' said Sam, and walked out of the room.

'He's really mad,' said Daisy.

'I don't understand,' said Jim. 'It's just not like him.'

'Maybe he's embarrassed. Or feels bad about Mum.' Daisy sighed. 'We should have left it alone.'

'We did it for the best reasons.'

'And I thought something was going to come of it. I really did.'

Sam walked back into the kitchen with a box.

'This,' he said, 'is your punishment.'

He put the box on the island.

Jim and Daisy opened the lid and peered inside.

'Oh my God,' breathed Daisy. 'A puppy. An actual puppy.'

Jim put his hands in and pulled the little dog out. He was beaming from ear to ear.

'I love her already,' he said.

'So you were joking,' said Daisy to her dad, who was laughing his socks off. 'You didn't mind? About the set-up?'

'No,' said Sam. 'I didn't mind.'

'Hang on. Oscar just got a puppy that looks a bit like this.' Daisy frowned. 'Is this his sister?'

'Do you think?' said Sam, looking innocent.

When Alexa had told him she was getting one of Nathan's puppies, it was the encouragement he'd needed. He was already imagining a walk along the coast path with the puppies, a stop off in a pub by a roaring log fire...

'They've called him Andy,' said Daisy. 'After Andy Warhol. So we should call her Edie. After Edie Sedgwick.'

'Who?' said Jim.

'Let's just watch her over the next couple of days,' said Sam. 'And get to know her. Then we can decide on a name.'

And he sat back and watched his two children take the puppy onto the floor, and fuss over her, laughing with delight, and he felt warm inside and the ache-that-never-left-him seemed to fade, just a little bit.

At Pennfleet House, Vanessa and Nathan were sharing a bottle of wine while she cooked spaghetti bolognese. She was coming to terms with the fact that Frank Cooper had gone and was never coming back.

'He was such a good companion,' she told Nathan. 'He kept me company when Spencer wasn't here.'

Nathan put his glass down and took her hand.

'I want to take you to see something.'

'What?'

'I'm not telling. You might like it; you might not. But if you do, you can have it.'

Vanessa frowned. 'What is it?' she demanded.

'Turn off the pasta. Follow me.'

She did as she was told. She followed him up the high street to his grandfather's house, and into his yard.

'Just don't look round you,' said Nathan. 'It's pretty grim. There's been no woman's touch here for over ten years.'

Vanessa just laughed. There was a certain charm to the ramshackle yard. You got the feeling you might find all sorts of treasures. And as Nathan opened the door of a shed and ushered her inside, there was treasure indeed.

There was just one left. A little girl. The smallest, bundled next to her mum.

'Oh my goodness.' Vanessa scooped the puppy into her arms and nuzzled her. 'She is beautiful. What is she?'

'Well, Monkey's a border terrier. But no one has a clue about the dad. So she could be anything. She could end up a giant, or not get much bigger than she is now. It's a risk.'

'She's got giant paws.'

'Yes. Bigger than her mum's at that age.'

Vanessa held her up and looked at her in delight.

'I've never had a dog.'

'Dogs are easy,' Nathan assured her. 'And I know she's no replacement for Frank Cooper . . .'

'No one would ever replace Frank.' Yet Vanessa held the puppy even tighter. 'Can I really have her?'

'I'd love it if you did.'

'Poor Monkey, though.' Vanessa looked down at Monkey.

'No. She'll be fine. She's got me. She can't wait to have me all to herself.'

Vanessa stroked the puppy's head. It shut its eyes in appreciation.

'It's the nicest present I've ever had.'

'What are you going to call her?'

Vanessa thought of the moon that had hung overhead, that first night, in the Neptune garden.

'Luna,' she said, and tucked the little dog inside her coat, where it snuggled up and, moments later, fell asleep against the warmth of her new mistress.

30

If Squirrel had stopped to think about it, if she had tried to plan, or phone ahead, she would never have done it.

She slept like a top on the ferry, woken by the curious strumming of a harp that was the ferry company's signature wake-up call and always made her feel as if she was being summonsed to heaven.

She was very much still alive, though. She showered and dressed as quickly as she could. She wouldn't bother with breakfast yet – she would stop for coffee and croissants after she had done a couple of hours' driving. She had a long journey ahead of her.

She rolled off the ferry, reminded herself to keep on the right, and set off, her AA map of France open on the front seat beside her. The route was pretty simple. She just had to keep going south. She estimated it would take her six hours, as long as she didn't stop too often. She would be there before nightfall.

She didn't mind driving. Her car was small but powerful, and she was an excellent driver. And she had plenty to think about on the journey. What this might mean. What she would say. How she might feel.

Just after three o'clock she drove into the little town that was nearest to her destination. It was typical: the square, the mairie, the church, the bars. And a hotel. Large and square, the windows painted dark burgundy, the Lion d'Or looked welcoming. She parked in the square nearby and made her way to the entrance.

Inside the reception was dustily opulent – stone floors, ochre walls, gilt and velvet chairs and strikingly modern paintings. As was so often the way in France, it was a little more chic than its exterior suggested.

Squirrel made a booking for that night in her rusty schoolgirl French.

'*Une nuit,*' she said, with more firmness than she felt.

Tomorrow she would leave, perhaps drive south to Montpellier or Carcassonne, where there might still be some sun.

The receptionist appraised her with chilly eyes. Was she a threat to anyone in this town? She was too aloof to question Squirrel on her reasons for being here, but that she was dying to know was apparent.

Squirrel decided to tease her by asking directions to where she was heading. The receptionist drew a sketchy map on a piece of hotel notepaper, complete with arrows and landmarks.

Squirrel went to her room – surprisingly chic, with black and white striped wallpaper and a grey satin bed-cover. She took a shower to wash away the residue of travel and wake herself up, then dressed in fresh jeans, a pink silk shirt and pink pumps.

She swept out through Reception, her caramel suede jacket over one shoulder, because the sun meant it was still warm but by dusk she would need it.

She followed the directions, driving down tiny narrow lanes flanked by flat fields, passing crumbling farm buildings and cottages that made her mouth water. She smiled to herself. No middle-class English woman worth her salt was immune to the appeal of a little gîte in the French countryside.

Eventually she turned down a track that wasn't even Tarmaced. The car bounced over the rough ground until she stopped in a little clearing next to an ancient Peugeot. There, nestled in the shade of a walnut tree, was a tiny pigeonnier with a wriggly tin roof. It was what an estate agent would call unspoiled, and what anyone with common sense would call tumbledown. It was charming, glowing the colour of gingerbread in the late afternoon sun.

She saw him. He looked no different, except the slightly too-long hair with the sweeping side fringe was now streaked with grey, and he was thinner. Dressed in jeans and a navy linen shirt and big boots, he was picking walnuts off the floor and hurling them into a wicker basket.

She felt as if she had come home, although she had never been here before. The familiarity was overwhelming. She could, if she breathed in, smell his warmth, the faint trace of citrus on his skin from his cologne. She could imagine the touch of his long, slender fingers.

How had she lived without him all these years?

She supposed it was all too easy to forget the frustration, the humiliation, the anger and the sadness of living with him. The days when she had no idea where he was, and the worse ones when she did. His inability to handle any responsibility. The overwhelming excitement of his euphoria, followed by the inevitable dark days when he wouldn't get up, or wash, or eat.

Of course, she knew now, because every time she read an article about it, or saw a documentary on the television, she recognised the symptoms. But back in the day, people just said, 'Oh, that's just David.' 'Just David' enabled him to behave exactly as he wished, with no concern for anyone else on the planet.

Had she known it was a sickness, an illness, could she have done anything to help him?

More importantly, had he discovered the truth in the meantime, or was he still subject to the terrifying swings in temperament? Had he shared his life with anyone else, and had they been able to manage?

All these questions and many more flittered through her mind. And then he looked up and saw her. He didn't miss a beat.

'Blasted walnuts come crashing down on the roof. Make a hell of a din.'

His voice had always been a little too big for him, gravelly and deep. She could have listened to him recite anything: a shopping list, the shipping forecast, because he imbued every word with nuance and promise. Even with just those few words of introduction, he had told her so much more.

She walked over to him and they looked at each other. Up close, she could see his face was lined, but he wore it well.

'I was just passing,' she told him, with an impish grin.

'Excellent,' he replied, lifting up the basket. 'Come on in. You're just in time for an aperitif.'

She followed him, thinking how it only felt like yesterday since she'd seen him. They would snap back together, like two pieces of Lego. When it was good, she thought, it had been so very good. She watched him sling the basket onto the stone paving outside the front door. He seemed more physical, easier with his body. She was intrigued. He had been such a city person, his life made up of bars and taxis and pavements and night-time.

Inside, the house was cosy, the downstairs an open living area with a wooden staircase rising up. The stone floor was warmed with rugs. At one end there was a long wooden table with mismatched stools. Around it the walls were hung with shelves. On them were bowls made of pottery, enamelware and wood containing deep-red onions, lemons, speckled apples, garlic, loose change, walnuts. There were jars filled with spices, pulses, rice, pasta next to copper saucepans and empty tins stuffed with wooden spoons and implements Squirrel couldn't identify. There was an ancient sink and an even more ancient cooker, on top of which was perched a metal espresso maker. It was as unfitted a kitchen as you could get. She loved it.

David took down two dumpy glasses from a shelf and sloshed two inches of white wine into each. No change there then. Yet he was still alive and looking in rude health, so she wasn't going to comment.

'Just the local plonk,' he told her. 'I'll get out something more special for tonight. Assuming you're staying... for supper?'

'I'll be driving.'

He nodded. 'I'll make it something very special. You can have one glass.'

She couldn't quite look him in the eye. She took the glass from him and sipped. It was surprisingly good.

Actually, that wasn't a surprise. David took his wine very seriously. If only he hadn't drunk quite so much of it.

He filled a bowl with some fat glistening olives, flecked with fresh herbs. The smell was intoxicating. Squirrel realised that her morning croissant had been a long time ago.

'So when you say just passing...' He put his head to one side and smiled at her, his eyes laughing.

'Actually, I wasn't just passing. I wanted to see you. Don't ask me why.'

Squirrel didn't see any point in dissembling. He wouldn't fall for it, anyway.

'I'm really pleased. It's good to see you. You look... as wonderful as ever.'

Squirrel shrugged, a little embarrassed. She knew she looked good for her age, but she felt awkward under his scrutiny, because suddenly it really mattered what he thought and she hated herself for that.

He leaned forward. 'How are the girls? Tell me everything.'

She stared at him for a moment. How could she not want to berate this man for walking out on them all those years ago? Surely she should rip him to shreds now she had his attention? Tell him just how hard it had been, being a single mother. The exhaustion, the worry, the loneliness.

Yet she knew he had done the right thing. That worse would have happened had he not left them. He'd had enough self-awareness to know that. She felt desperately sad that it hadn't been in her power to redress the problem. And now, she felt no anger.

'They are wonderful,' she told him. 'You would be so proud.'

She told him about their older daughter – her jobs, her marriage, her various offspring, her home in Seattle.

'And Vanessa . . .' She paused for a moment. 'She's had a difficult time, but I think she's going to turn the corner. She's got a few things to work out, but I have faith.'

Knowing Vanessa was on her way to being settled was one of the reasons she had felt able to make this journey. It had taken all this time, but now it was her moment. To lay the ghosts.

'How about you?' she asked. 'What are you up to?'

'I do a bit of English coaching. Help out on some of the local farms. And I pick things up at the local brocante. My mate comes over with a van once a month and sells it all at his shop in Bath. We split the profit.'

He grinned, and Squirrel grinned, imagining him picking up bits of French tat that the good people of Bath would coo over, and pay over the odds for. He had a good eye, did David.

'You look amazing,' he told her. 'You look the same as the day I left.'

Squirrel winced. She tried not to think about that day, or the dark days afterwards.

She remembered the first Christmas after he had left, when a solemn-eyed Vanessa had asked if 'her Father Christmas' was going to come.

'My daddy, I mean. My Father Christmas.'

It had nearly finished Squirrel, that question.

She'd wept alone in her room that night, then pulled herself together and stuffed their stockings and thought that, if he were still with her, he wouldn't be there to help with the presents, he would be in some Soho watering hole having made a promise to fetch things from

Selfridges, which he would forget. It was hard to convince yourself you were better off without someone when you missed them so very much.

Yet again, she wondered if Vanessa had gone for Spencer because she was looking for the father she had never had. Spencer, for all his faults, had been the polar opposite of David. In control. He never missed a beat, or an opportunity. Had Squirrel forced Vanessa into Spencer's arms, by driving David away?

She told herself to stop punishing herself. You couldn't be responsible for people's choices, in the end.

He put out a wooden board with salami, which he hacked up with a Laguiole knife, and tiny cornichons. And while she nibbled on those, and sipped her golden-white wine, he made a cassoulet. The kitchen was soon filled with the rich scent of garlic and tomatoes.

'This is my quick version,' he told her. 'Made with ready-made confit. It's cheating, really. I'll make you a proper one one day.'

'When did you turn into Raymond Blanc?' she laughed.

He gave a mock Gallic shrug.

'When in Rome.' He chopped up garlic, lemon and flat-leaf parsley and mixed them in with some bread-crumbs.

'This is the man who couldn't boil an egg.' She watched in admiration as he scattered the mixture on top of the cassoulet and slid it into the oven.

'Yes, but you know I'm an obsessive.'

Yes. It was just a pity he wasn't obsessive about his family. Squirrel took another sip of wine and reminded herself not to slip back into bitterness. That wasn't what this trip was about.

He went to fill her glass, an automatic gesture, but she put her hand over it. 'I mustn't. I'm driving.'

'You can stay. With pleasure.'

She thought of the comfort of the hotel room at the Lion d'Or. And imagined the masculine asceticism of his bedroom. Wooden floors. A brass bed. No clutter.

She didn't have to make an excuse to anyone for sleeping with him. She was, after all, still his wife. She still bore his name. They had never bothered to divorce.

She took her hand away and let him pour more wine that fell golden from the bottle. He filled his own glass, then clinked it gently against hers.

'It's wonderful to see you,' he told her.

As she looked at him in the candlelight, the shadows flickering across the angles of his face, she remembered why she'd never bothered with anyone else. She knew she might well get hurt, she knew that within days she would want to kill him, she knew he would not have changed, not really. But she wanted to feel her skin on his once more.

31

Terminal Five was brightly lit and full of distractions, so Kate didn't have time to think much about the trip ahead. She bought some chewing gum and a magazine, then realised that at this rate she wouldn't even have time to peruse the duty-free perfume before boarding. She strode towards the check-in as her phone rang.

It was Carlos. She would answer, if only to placate him and stop him bombarding her.

'I'm just about to check in.'

'Oh, honey, that's great. We'll have a car come get you tomorrow.'

'Actually, I was hoping to have Friday off. And come in on Monday.'

Carlos's voice changed.

'Kate, I'm not paying you good money to work part time. You've already had more time off than you asked for.'

Carlos always became evil when he was stressed. He said stuff he didn't mean. Made demands that he knew were unreasonable. And there were usually flowers or champagne to make up for it afterwards. But Kate didn't have time for it any more.

'Carlos, forget it. I'll have jet lag. I'll be in no fit state.'

Sometimes she had to play the crisp English bitch. Carlos loved it. It was one of the reasons he employed her. He thought it added class. He and his clients all thought she lived in a house like Downton Abbey. She had never disabused him or them.

'You get in here tomorrow or you won't have a job. I need your input. I'm surrounded by morons.'

Kate stood still as people milled past her to get to the check-in desk. She knew she was standing in an inconvenient place, but she was rooted to the spot. Who did Carlos think he was, calling her in like that?

All she could hear was Carlos repeating 'Kate? Kate?' He sounded like a crow cawing.

Eventually she found her voice.

'Carlos, my flight's about to be called. I have to go.'

She heard him protesting as she hung up. She stuffed her phone back in her bag, walked over to the check-in desk and held out her passport and paperwork. She felt as if she were sleepwalking

The girl behind the desk was about to flip her passport open when Kate grabbed it.

'Sorry. Could I have that back?'

'You don't want to check in?'

So many things were running through Kate's mind. She didn't have long.

'Miss? There are people waiting.'

Kate put her passport back in her bag, turned and walked away.

She didn't want to go back to New York. She didn't want to go back to her superficial, orchestrated lifestyle, where, it seemed, somebody else owned your ass, and if you didn't jump, you could go and hang.

She wanted to live in a place where people really cared about people. Where the air was clean and the sun was bright. Where she could walk out of the door in no make-up and no one would mind. Where people had known her mother and her father. Where people knew who she was.

She pushed back through the tide of people and out to the taxi rank.

'Could you take me to Pennfleet?' she asked the driver.

He frowned. 'Where's that then, love?'

'Cornwall.'

'You're having a laugh.'

'No.'

'That's going to take what – five hours?'

'Yep.'

'It's going to cost you a few hundred quid.'

'I don't care.' She pulled open the door.

He started up the engine with a shrug. 'M4, M5?'

'Yeah.'

'I'll have to stop for a pee at some point.'

'Of course. No problem.'

She settled into her seat. The cab pulled away and snaked through the rest of the cabs. Behind the terminal she could see planes taking off. She wondered if one of them was hers.

In minutes, they were on the motorway. A large blue sign said 'South West' and her heart lifted. She could see a snake of red tail-lights in front of her. Leading the way.

'Wake me up when we get to the end of the motorway,' she said to the driver. 'I'll direct you from there.'

She didn't care if it was rude not to talk to him. She was paying. She probably wouldn't sleep, but she had a

315

lot to think about. She folded her pashmina into a small square and rested her head on it. Faces glided in and out of her mind as she relived the past week: Debbie, Sam, Dr Webster, Robin ... They were all going to be part of her new life. She started to make plans. She would join the church flower rota, in honour of her mother. She'd take Debbie with her when she went to pack up her New York apartment – she'd buy her a ticket on her air miles. They could go out like they had when they were teenagers. She would sit for Nancy so that Robin could have a break every now and then. Again, in memory of her mother. What she would do for money she had no idea yet, but she wasn't daunted.

When the driver woke her, she guided him through the twisty lanes – the back route known only to locals. It was pitch black, the high banks on either side of the road creating a tunnel. The only light was the stars peppering the sky.

'Jesus,' said the cab driver. 'This is the arse end of nowhere.'

She couldn't be bothered to contradict him. Eventually they reached the roundabout and turned off into the road that led down to Pennfleet. Street lights and houses loomed either side as they made their way towards the centre of town. How many times had she made this journey? she wondered. Even in the dead of night it lifted her heart. She opened the window to breathe in the sea, and a gust of wind blew in.

'Bloody hell,' said the driver. 'It's a force ten gale out there. Shut the window, love.'

Soon, they were embraced by the cottages of Captain's Hill. She felt as if they were closing in to hug her.

'I'll never get the cab down here.'

'Yes, you will. You can get a coach down here, no problem.'

She could name each house as she passed it. She knew every window box, every hanging basket. This was where she belonged. Not some swanky Manhattan apartment block, where nobody knew her name.

'Just here, on the left,' she directed. 'The blue one. Belle Vue.'

Not that he could see it was blue, in the dark. But he drew up outside the cottage, and she felt her heart swell. It was a curious mixture of pride and fondness and relief. More than anything, she felt safe. Safe and secure. She didn't think it was cowardly to want that. She'd tried other things, after all. New York had been exciting and exhilarating and glamorous, but she didn't want that for ever.

She paid the driver with her credit card, and gave him a substantial tip. He didn't seem grateful but then he didn't seem the type to be grateful for anything. She watched him do a three-point turn that turned into an eight-point turn because of the narrowness of the road, then drive off up the hill.

She turned and looked up at the house. The night breeze ruffled her hair, a gentle caress of welcome that was like a kiss on her skin.

She was home at last.

32

It was the last weekend in October. The weekend the clocks went back, and Pennfleet was ready to celebrate. Banners proclaiming *Turn Back Time* were stretched across the streets, together with glittering lights and luminous clock faces that spun in the breeze. People from miles around were coming to Pennfleet to join in the fun. There was live music, and fire-eaters, and a fairground, and the shops were all going to be open late, and most of the restaurants had done special menus.

Vanessa was briefing the girls on how much discount they could give if people wanted to buy anything. She looked at her watch. She just had time to change before Nathan came down to pick her up.

'I think I can manage to get to the quay by myself,' she'd joked, but he insisted. He was old-fashioned in so many ways, and Vanessa realised she was properly looked after and protected. Yet respected, too. He was chivalrous, but not chauvinistic.

She hurried back down the street and into her house. She was only going to swap one pair of jeans for another, but her make-up could do with a touch-up, and she wanted a decent silk scarf to tuck into her jacket.

She went back down to the kitchen to check on Luna,

and took her outside for a final wee. She was going to leave her here – the town's antics might be too much for a tiny puppy. She stood on the terrace while Luna pottered about, looking over at the harbour and the lights of the town. She could hear the music from the funfair in the carpark.

And then she heard another noise. She froze. Listened harder, but it was definitely there. A faint miaow. She turned around to see if she could find the source of the noise. Her mouth fell open.

'Frank Cooper!' she cried.

For there, looking considerably thinner, his coat staring somewhat, was Frank Cooper, nose to nose with Luna, sniffing at her as if to say 'What are you doing on my patch?' Vanessa flew across the terrace and scooped him up.

She felt filled with joy. It was the one thing that had been marring her happiness, for every morning she looked for him. Every morning she missed his four paws landing on her chest as he woke her. But he was back, and it was all going to be perfect.

If some people looked at her relationship with Nathan in disapproval, whether because of the age difference, or because it had been a rather short time since Spencer's death, she didn't much care. It was her life. Their life. And they certainly weren't doing anyone any harm. Even his grandfather had taken a grudging shine to her.

'She's all right, boy,' he'd told Nathan, which was positively effusive for Daniel.

When Nathan turned up, she was still bubbling with the excitement.

'He must have got swept down the river and took his

time finding his way back,' said Nathan, rubbing the marmalade cat between the ears.

Vanessa was amazed when Frank Cooper settled down happily with Luna on the big rug on the kitchen floor.

'I think it's love,' said Nathan.

'Yes,' said Vanessa. 'I think it probably is.'

She and Nathan walked hand in hand up to the quay, where long trestle tables had been set up. Over the top of them were a series of arched trellises interlaced with fairy lights and garlands made of autumn leaves, berries and acorns. Peeping out from amongst them were woodland creatures whose eyes lit up – squirrels and mice and foxes. It was like a woodland grotto, spooky yet magical.

'You're crazy,' Sam told Alexa when she put on the finishing touches.

'You should see the inside of my head.'

'I can only imagine.'

Sam, who was on the festival committee, had persuaded Alexa to help out with the decorations, not realising quite how fertile her imagination was. She had thrown her heart and soul into it, and loved doing something that was part of the community. She had held back from mixing in for so long, self-conscious about what people might think of her, worried that they might gossip about her past and speculate. She was thrilled to find they didn't much care at all, as long as she mucked in.

Sam, meanwhile, was in charge of food.

Along the length of the trestles was an edible centre-piece: plaited sourdough rolls, deep-fried sage, parsnip crisps and chunks of pork crackling. To go with it, Sam served brown paper cups full of soup: creamy pumpkin, parsnip and apple and a deep-red borscht. A huge spit-roast hog was turning, ready to be cut up and served in thick slices with chunky homemade apple sauce and bowls of crunchy Thai coleslaw with a hefty kick. Afterwards, there was sticky parkin, and plum and orange cake.

'Do you think we should go back and check on the puppies?' asked Sam, thinking how beautiful Alexa looked, in a red coat with a white fur hat like a halo around her head.

'I think they'll be all right for a while,' she told him. 'They've got each other.'

Andy and Edie were snuggled up in a pen in Sam's living room, brother and sister, snoozing away, quite oblivious to the celebrations.

The townspeople milled around, their breath visible in the cold night air, their hands clasped around the soup cups. Screams from the fairground could be heard, along with the thumping of the bass. There were stalls set up leading down to the harbour, selling clutter and nonsense. Children rushed about clutching their pocket money, buying sparklers and glow lights and plastic swords and pirate hats.

At eight o'clock, Oscar and his band The Love Rats played on a temporary stage set up by the quay. They were supporting the main act due on later, but it looked as if they were in danger of upstaging them entirely, as they played a blinder. Oscar was dressed in skinny jeans and a silk paisley shirt, a scarf round his head, black eyeliner under his eyes. Somehow his shyness disappeared when he was on stage, and he became cocky and charismatic, showing off to the crowd, the consummate rock star. A crowd of girls quickly gathered, gazing up at him.

'Impressive,' Jim had to admit to Daisy. It took a lot to impress Jim.

Daisy felt a bubble of happiness. Not just because of the kudos of going out with the coolest kid in town, but because of the way things had turned out. Sam had talked to her and Jim not long after their blind date.

'I think Alexa and I are going to . . . go on a date,' he told them. 'A proper date. We're going to take it slowly, of course. We're not going to rush into anything. And I know you like her, but there might be times you find it a bit weird. It might take you by surprise, and that's OK. But I want you to be able to talk to me about it if you want.' He looked sheepish. 'It's weird for me too, you know.'

Daisy and Jim looked at each other.

'Mum would love her,' Daisy told him. 'I know she would.'

'Yeah,' agreed Jim. 'She'd think she was cool.'

Sam looked a bit glassy-eyed.

'I'm so proud of you both,' he told them, and turned away.

Behind him, Daisy could see the portrait of Louise, and she was smiling, and telling them it was going to be OK.

And Sam and Alexa had been almost inseparable since. Not in an icky way, with embarrassing displays of affection, but in a way that benefitted both their families. They cooked big meals, and went on walks with the puppies, or took trips out to riverside pubs, and any of their combined children could tag along too. They amalgamated almost seamlessly, yet it didn't feel forced.

Daisy in particular liked having Alexa in her life. She really did.

Earlier, Alexa had painted her an intricate face mask in black and silver, painstakingly applying it with a thin brush so it looked like a lace veil. Daisy had loved being in her kitchen, the crazy Brazilian music on the CD player, the kids running in and out, the exotic scent of a pomegranate candle filling the air. She loved the female companionship: the companionship of a woman older and wiser than her. She'd missed that in her house of boys. And Alexa seemed to know just how to be with her: kind and gentle but not too familiar. She wasn't her mum, and never would be: maybe more like an older sister. She was irreverent and funny and made rude jokes too, and her laugh was infectiously raucous.

Jim took a little longer to bond, but he'd put himself in charge of the puppies and their training, and spent hours with them doing recall and teaching them to sit. It was the perfect challenge, and got him away from the iPad.

Sam stood to one side as Oscar came off the stage and went straight to find Daisy, not paying any attention to the entourage clamouring for his attention.

'What,' Alexa asked Sam, her eyes shining with mischief, 'do you fancy doing with the extra hour tomorrow?'

Sam pondered for a moment. 'The crossword?' he suggested with a grin.

'Excellent idea,' she nodded, and bit into her toffee apple. It shattered into shards, and Sam reached out to catch the broken bits as they fell from her mouth.

Sam gazed at her as she laughed, and thought how lucky he was, to have had two such amazing women in his life. Not to mention his children. He could see Daisy and Oscar with Jim and the little ones, lighting up sparklers and waving them round, still kids at heart even though they seemed to have grown up so fast this year.

He'd made the right decision, he thought. He put his arm round Alexa and looked around the harbour, at the people he'd made friends with, at his café up the road.

Pennfleet, he realised, was his home.

Kate took a sip of the hot buttered cider. It was buttery-sugary-cinnamony nectar, with a kick of rum that warmed her stomach. It was just what she needed after a tough week. She had woken up the day after she had deliberately missed her flight feeling panic-stricken but determined in equal measures.

Carlos had been incandescent when she broke the news to him. There had been talk of lawsuits. Kate hadn't fallen for any of his hot air. What could he do, from that far away? She didn't feel guilty about letting him down. She was pretty sure that by this time next week he would be in love with her replacement – and there would be plenty of girls queuing up for the job. And she had left him with a brilliant legacy. She would read about the ball in a few months' time in the gossip columns, and feel, no doubt, a prickle of regret that she wasn't there.

Only a tiny one, though.

The question now was what she was going to do with her life. There weren't really many career options for A-list party planners in Pennfleet. But Kate didn't want to do anything like that this time round. She wanted to do something with a bit of meaning, though she wasn't trained for anything much else. She had some savings, and her mother had left a small amount of money, which would tide her over while she made a plan of action: maybe she would go back to college and retrain. In the meantime, she had the cottage to do up. Now it was empty, she could see its potential, and she felt excited about breathing new life into it.

Debbie had been thrilled when she'd banged on her door and told her she was staying.

'That's awesome!' she said. 'It'll be great to have someone to hang out with.'

She was here now, with Scott and the kids, their breath sweet and fingers sticky with candy floss. Scott was going to take the kids back in a bit, so Debbie and Kate could watch the main band on at nine. It really was almost as if time had been turned back: they had gone to the festival since they were teenagers. Here they were, in their jeans and their scarves and bobble hats, clutching their cider, as if they were still sixteen.

Kate felt Debbie give her a sharp nudge in the ribs. 'Look out,' she told her. 'It's matey.'

Kate looked through the crowds to where Debbie was pointing and saw Rupert. He'd seen her, and was walking towards her, looking puzzled. He was in jeans and a tobacco suede jacket with the collar turned up.

'What are you doing here?' he asked.

'Nice to see you, too,' replied Kate.

'I thought you were going back to New York?'

'Yes, well,' said Kate. 'I couldn't face it. I just couldn't bear the thought of selling the cottage, of letting go, of never coming back to Pennfleet.'

'So you're staying?'

Kate took a sip of her buttered cider. Then she nodded. 'I guess so.'

She looked down at the ground for a minute. Her heart was pitter-pattering, and she realised that Debbie had melted away into the crowds.

Rupert was frowning. 'You might have told me.'

She realised he was cross.

'I was going to phone you,' she said. 'I'm so sorry. I know you wanted to put in an offer—'

'Never mind the bloody cottage.'

Kate stared at him. 'What, then?'

Was there something else she didn't know about? Had they discussed something she had forgotten?

'You!' said Rupert. 'I really wanted to kiss you that night, after we went to the Townhouse. But I thought you were going back to America, and I didn't want a one-night stand. So I didn't.'

'Oh,' said Kate, rather nonplussed. 'Well, that was very restrained of you.'

'I know. It was probably the first time in my life I've been such a gentleman.'

He looked so indignant she burst out laughing.

'I don't know what's so funny,' he said.

She stepped closer to him.

'What about now?' she asked.

'What about now?' He was still cross.

'Do you want to kiss me now?' She looked at him from under her eyelashes, knowing she was being coquettish. Knowing she was teasing and testing him.

He stared at her, straight-faced, not replying. She held

his gaze until her nerve broke, and she looked away. She'd guessed him wrong. How embarrassing.

Then *he* burst out laughing, and grabbed her, pulling her in and looking down on her. 'What do you think?'

His expression was intense. He stared right into her eyes. She didn't think this was a game.

How did life do this? How did life whirl you from being a Manhattan party planner in head-to-toe Prada to standing in the arms of your childhood crush, in jeans and a jumper and a woolly hat, three thousand miles away?

Of course, the catalyst had been the death of her mother. Had Joy not died, Kate would be in some meeting or limo or bar, making someone else's dreams come true. She would, of course, give anything for that not to have happened. Yet it was only by discovering the true nature of her mother that she'd had the courage to turn her back on her old life and step into a new one.

Rupert hadn't been part of her decision to stay. At least, she hadn't thought he was. Although now he was here, staring down at her, maybe he was, subconsciously? Of course, they might only last a few weeks before drifting apart. Or maybe they belonged together. Who knew?

There was really only one way to find out.

Just before midnight, Nathan and his grandfather rowed over to the opposite bank and set off the fireworks they had planted out earlier. As the clock struck midnight, a shower of silver and gold shot across the night sky over Pennfleet, lighting up the upturned faces down below. Faces filled with joy and wonderment, happiness and hope. And the clock turned back, and the little town enjoyed a secret hour, a secret hour in which to cement friendships and explore new love and to make plans for the future – a future as bright as the stars above.

THE END
OR INDEED, THE BEGINNING